Where the Wind Carries Us

Stories of Grief, Hope, and the Roads Between

Brett C. Persson

Where the Wind Carries Us:
Stories of Grief, Hope, and the Roads Between

@BrettCPersson

www.brettcpersson.com

Nudous Publishing, LLC

www.nudouspublishing.com

info@nudouspublishing.com

Digital ISBN: 978-1-964793-93-1

Paperback ISBN: 978-1-964793-92-4

Note from the Author

Stories often come to us at just the right time. Some arrive quietly from old memories, and others show up all at once, pushing us to pay attention. The stories in this book were written from moments like these, times when life can change in a small but important way.

Each character you'll meet carries something difficult: sadness, guilt, or questions they don't know how to answer. But they also carry strength, even when they don't feel it. I wanted to show not only the hard parts of life, but also the moments when people choose to keep going, try again, or finally let something go.

If you see yourself in any of these pages, I hope it reminds you that you are not alone. We are all shaped by the things we've been through and the people we've loved. And no matter how tough things get, there is always something, hope, kindness, or even a small change, that helps us move forward.

Thank you for reading these stories. I hope they stay with you long after you finish the book.

-Brett C. Persson

Content Note:

This collection includes stories that explore themes of grief, loss, addiction, past trauma, incarceration, emotional distress, and spiritual struggle. While none of the content is graphic, some readers may find these topics emotionally challenging. Please read with care.

Table of Contents

When the Streetlight Flickered..1

What Remains of Me Without Her...51

Familiar Faces 61

The Edge of the City 103

Where the Light Didn't Reach 121

The Wind Takes All Things 131

When the Sea Calls: A Journey Beyond the Shore 167

The Things We Try to Outrun 193

The Roadside Angel.. 231

When the Stranger Comes Along... 275

The Girl Who Refused to Break... 327

Bench 42 379

Embers Before the Storm... 405

Between the Knock and the Silence 435

When the Streetlight Flickered

Chapter 1

Evan stood on the same street corner as he always did. The cracked sidewalk, the flickering streetlight, and the cold wind rolling in from the coast never changed. It didn't matter if it was Saturday night or any other night; this corner stayed the same, and so did he.

People walked past him in small groups, laughing or heading somewhere with purpose. Cars rolled by with music turned up too loud. Everyone seemed to be going somewhere that mattered, everyone except Evan.

He stuffed his hands into the pockets of his worn jacket and looked down on the empty road. Most people in town ignored him now. A few nodded out of habit, but their eyes slid away fast. Evan didn't blame them. He didn't really want to talk anyway.

The corner had become his hiding place. It was the one spot where no one asked questions. He didn't have to pretend he was doing okay. He could just stand there and let the night swallow him a little at a time.

A gust of wind brushed against his face, carrying the smell of the ocean mixed with car exhaust and old rain. He tried to imagine this place when he was younger, when the town felt bigger, and dreams felt real. He used to believe that if he worked hard, he could leave and never look back. But now the corner felt like a magnet pulling him back, no matter how far he tried to go.

He told himself he was "waiting for a friend," even though he knew that wasn't true. No one was coming. He wasn't waiting for anyone. He was waiting for *nothing*, and that scared him more than anything else in his life.

Across the street, a group of high school kids rushed by, wrapped in bright jackets and loud voices. They didn't even glance his way. He remembered being like that, full of plans and energy, thinking the world was wide open. But life had a way of closing in fast. One bad year, one tragedy, one mistake, and suddenly the world wasn't open anymore. It was a narrow hallway you couldn't escape.

The streetlight above him flickered again. It flashed bright for half a second, then faded to its usual dull glow. The brief light showed Evan's reflection in a store window across the street, tired eyes, messy hair, and a face that looked older than twenty-one. When the light dimmed again, the reflection disappeared.

Evan sighed and leaned back against the cold brick wall behind him. He didn't know why he kept coming to this corner. Maybe it was a habit. Perhaps it was guilt, or maybe it was the only place where he didn't feel judged. Or perhaps it was the hope that *something* might change if he stood here long enough.

But nothing changed.

A car turned the corner and sped past, its headlights sweeping over him. For a moment, he thought about stepping away, heading home, or just wandering until morning. But his feet stayed planted. The corner held him there, like a memory he couldn't shake.

He pulled his jacket tighter as the wind picked up again, whispering against the empty buildings like it knew something he didn't. Evan closed his eyes for a moment and breathed in the cold air.

Another Saturday night.

Another hour on the corner.

Another reminder that he was stuck, waiting for a life that never arrived, and he wasn't sure how much longer he could keep standing there.

Chapter 2

Evan didn't stay on the corner long after midnight. The wind grew colder, and the town got quiet in that heavy way that always made him feel small. He finally pushed himself away from the brick wall and began the slow walk home.

The streets were mostly empty now. A few porch lights glowed behind closed curtains, and a dog barked somewhere in the distance. Everything felt still, like the whole town was holding its breath.

When he reached his house, he paused at the front steps. The porch light was on, just like his mom always left it. It made the house look warm from the outside, but Evan knew better. Warm wasn't the right word. Quiet was. Heavy was. Lost was.

He slipped inside and closed the door gently, not wanting to wake anyone, even though he knew his mother rarely slept anymore.

The house felt frozen in time. The same pictures hung on the hallway walls. The same carpet covered the floor. The same lemon-cleaning-spray smell drifted from the kitchen. His mother cleaned constantly now, as if wiping down surfaces could erase what had happened.

Evan took off his shoes and tried to move quietly, but the floor creaked under him anyway. It always did. This house knew how to speak, even when the people inside didn't.

As he walked toward the kitchen, he noticed the lamp was still on. His mother sat at the table in her robe, staring into a half-empty cup of coffee. Her short brown hair looked messy, and her eyes were red, like she had been crying again. She tried to hide it when she heard him, straightening in her seat.

"Oh, you're home," she said softly, forcing a smile that didn't reach her eyes. "I was just…thinking."

"You're always thinking," Evan said before he could stop himself. His tone came out sharper than he meant.

Her smile tightened. "I worry about you, that's all."

"I'm fine."

"You don't look fine."

He opened the fridge, pretending to be busy. "It's late. You should get some sleep."

"So should you," she replied. "You're out there every night. It scares me."

Evan shut the fridge a little too hard. "Mom, I'm just walking. Standing around. I'm not doing anything."

"That's exactly what scares me."

The words hit like a slap. She didn't say it to be cruel; she was just tired, worn down by months of holding everything together. But it still hurt because it was true.

Evan wasn't doing anything. Not anymore.

He sat at the table, across from her. For a moment, they both said nothing. The clock ticked louder than usual. It felt like the whole house was listening in.

Finally, she spoke. "Your father would have wanted, "

"Don't," Evan cut in quickly. "Please."

Silence dropped over them again. Heavy. Thick.

His mother looked down at her coffee, her hands trembling slightly. "I'm sorry," she whispered. "I don't know what to say to you anymore."

Evan looked away. He didn't know what to say either. They were two people trapped in the same grief, but instead of reaching toward each other, they kept drifting apart.

After a long moment, he stood up. "I'm going to bed."

Before he reached the hallway, his mother called after him. "Evan?"

He didn't turn fully, just looked back over his shoulder.

"Your room is clean," she said quietly. "I…made your bed earlier."

He nodded, unsure how to feel about that. Part of him was grateful. The other part felt like he was still a child, stuck in the same room he grew up in, while life passed him by.

"Thanks," he murmured.

He climbed the stairs and entered his room. Everything looked neat and perfect, like a museum display of who he used to be. His childhood trophies lined the shelf. Old posters hung on the walls. His desk was spotless.

He sat on the bed and rubbed his face with both hands. Being in this room made his chest feel tight. This wasn't home anymore. It was a memory someone else was trying to keep alive.

He lay back and stared at the ceiling. He wished he could say something to his mother that would make things easier, something that would ease the heaviness in the house. But the words wouldn't come.

The house creaked again, like it was sighing.

Evan closed his eyes. He didn't know how to fix anything. He didn't know where his life was going. He only knew that tomorrow night, he'd end up on that same corner again. Because the corner, for all its emptiness, made more sense than this house full of ghosts.

Chapter 3

The next evening, Evan left the house before sunset. He didn't want another quiet argument with his mother. He didn't want to sit at the kitchen table pretending everything was fine. He needed air, fresh or not, real or not. Anything felt better than the house.

He walked toward the bus stop, where the old route still ran into the "village" part of town. It wasn't really a village at all, just a few blocks of older shops, narrow streets, and people who didn't seem to fit anywhere else. Some called it the "arts district," others called it "the place parents warned their kids about."

To Evan, it was neither good nor bad. It was simply different. And different was enough.

The bus rattled down the road, shaking slightly with every bump. A few passengers sat scattered around, an older woman holding grocery bags, a man in a faded army jacket, two teenagers laughing too loudly at their phones. Nobody looked at each other for more than a second. Everyone kept to themselves, as if sharing the same space didn't mean they had anything in common.

When the bus stopped near the village, Evan stepped off and felt a shift in the atmosphere right away. The air smelled like a mix of incense, cigarette smoke, cheap food, and the heavy scent of rain on old pavement. Music echoed from somewhere, a guitar being poorly played, a drumbeat from a basement bar, someone singing off-key.

Here, people weren't quiet. They weren't polished. They weren't trying to look perfect.

That was why Evan came.

Evan walked past a thrift store with mannequins dressed in tie-dye shirts and mismatched boots. A man with long hair sat cross-legged on the sidewalk, drawing pictures in chalk even though the colors washed away a little more with each passing car. Across the street, a group of teens leaned against a brick wall, their eyes half-closed as they smoked something that wasn't a regular cigarette.

Further down, Evan saw two drag queens standing beneath a neon sign, laughing as they fixed each other's makeup. Their bright wigs and glitter outfits didn't match anything around them, but somehow, they fit better here than they did anywhere.

He kept walking, absorbing everything. The colors, the sounds, the people, it was messy and loud, but it felt honest. The village had no clean edges, no forced smiles, no small-town lies. Everyone was broken in some way, and no one pretended otherwise.

Evan liked that more than he wanted to admit.

He turned a corner and saw a narrow alley with murals painted along the walls. Some were beautiful, some were strange, and some looked like they had been created by someone who never finished what they started. A girl with purple hair sat at the end of the alley, playing a soft tune on a small keyboard. Her voice drifted through the air, warm and raw:

"You got everything, but nothing's cool…"

Evan paused, surprised. The words hit him right in the chest. He wondered how many people in this village felt the same way.

As he moved closer to the main street again, he noticed the people more clearly. The junkies with sunken eyes. The artists who looked like they lived off coffee and hope. The lonely wanderers and the ignored dreamers. None of them looked like they belonged in the neat, quiet neighborhoods Evan came from.

But they didn't look lost either. They looked…free.

And he couldn't tell if that was comforting or terrifying.

He shoved his hands in his pockets and kept walking. He didn't know exactly what he was looking for. Maybe he wasn't looking for anything at all. Perhaps he just wanted to feel something for the first time in a long time.

As he reached the end of the block, a man leaning against a lamp post glanced at him, just a quick look, nothing more. But there was something sharp in his eyes. Something that made Evan pause.

It was the first moment in hours that anyone had actually seen him. The man gave a faint smile, almost like a secret greeting. Evan wasn't sure why, but a shiver ran down his spine.

He shook it off and stepped back toward the bus stop, the village lights glowing behind him like a strange, welcoming fire. He didn't know it yet, but tonight was the night everything would start to change.

Chapter 4

Evan didn't plan on going back to the village the next night, but his feet took him there anyway. Maybe he just wanted a distraction. Perhaps he wanted noise instead of the silence waiting at home. Or maybe the village felt like the only place where he didn't feel completely invisible.

The sun had already set by the time he stepped off the bus. Neon signs flickered on, glowing pink, blue, and green. The street was busy tonight, music drifting from open doors, cars rumbling by, people talking in groups as they huddled in doorways or leaned against buildings.

Evan walked slowly, letting the sounds wash over him. He blended into the background here, but it didn't bother him. At least nobody expected him to smile.

As he reached the end of the block, he saw the man again, the one who had looked at him the night before. He was leaning against the same lamp post as if he hadn't moved at all. The dim light above him made his face hard to read. Not young, not old. Strong but not threatening. Sharp eyes, like he noticed everything and forgot nothing.

The man wasn't dressed like the other people in the town. No bright colors, no ripped jeans, no loud accessories. Just a dark jacket, clean shoes, and a calmness that felt out of place here.

This time, the man's eyes followed Evan as he approached. Not in a creepy way, more like he was studying him. Evan tried to look away, but the man spoke before he could.

"You're back," the man said, his voice low and smooth.

Evan blinked. "Do I know you?"

"Not yet."

Something in his tone made Evan pause. The man stepped forward one slow, easy movement at a time.

"People usually wander through here once," he said, "just to look around. But you...you're different. You came back."

Evan didn't know how to answer. "I'm just walking."

The man smiled a little, like he didn't believe that for a second. "Everybody's walking. Not everyone is searching."

Evan crossed his arms. "Who says I'm searching?"

"I do," the man said. "You carry that look. The one people get when they don't know where they belong. When they're stuck between going home and running away."

Evan felt a flash of irritation. "You don't know anything about me."

"Maybe not," the man replied. "But I know the village. And I know the people who end up here."

He reached into his pocket and pulled out a small metal lighter, not a cigarette, not a joint, just the lighter. He flipped it open and closed, the metallic click echoing in the air.

"You want something," he said. "Maybe you don't know what it is. Maybe you're afraid to say it. But you want it."

Evan swallowed hard. The man's words were too close to the truth. He didn't know how this stranger saw so much with just one glance.

"What's your name?" Evan asked.

The man gave a faint, amused smile. "Around here?" He paused for effect. "People call me Captain Jack."

The name rolled off his tongue like a secret title. Evan had heard it passing, murmured by kids at school, whispered by people who stayed out late, painted once in graffiti on the old bridge. Captain Jack. The man who could "get you high tonight." The man who helped people escape.

Evan didn't believe half the stories. But looking at him now, he wasn't sure what to think.

Jack slid his lighter back into his pocket. "Don't look so nervous. I'm not here to drag you into anything."

"I'm not nervous," Evan said quickly.

Jack chuckled. "Sure, you're not." Then he stepped back against the lamp post, blending into the shadows as he belonged there. "You'll know when you're ready to talk. I don't rush people."

Evan hesitated. He didn't want to walk away, but he didn't want to stay either. Something about Captain Jack pulled at him, a strange mix of curiosity and fear.

Finally, Evan took a slow breath. "I didn't come here for…whatever you think."

Jack nodded. "Of course you didn't. Nobody ever does. But they always end up finding something anyway."

Evan frowned. "What's that supposed to mean?"

Jack tilted his head. "It means you're standing on the edge of something. And next time you come back, you'll know exactly what you're looking for."

"Who said I'm coming back?"

Jack smiled again, quiet, confident. "You did."

Evan didn't argue. He just turned and walked away, feeling Jack's eyes on him until he reached the end of the street.

He didn't look back. But deep down, he knew Jack was right.

He would be back.

Chapter 5

Evan left the village later than he meant to. The bus ride home felt longer this time, as if each stop dragged on forever. His mind kept replaying the moment he met Captain Jack: the calm voice, the sharp eyes, the way he seemed to understand Evan without asking a single question.

Evan didn't know if that scared him or comforted him.

When he stepped into the house, the living room light was still on. His mother had fallen asleep on the couch again, curled up under a thin blanket with the TV playing some late-night talk show she wasn't really watching. Evan stood there for a moment, staring at her tired face. She looked older than she had last year. Sadder, too.

He turned off the TV and gently placed the blanket higher on her shoulders. She didn't wake up.

The quiet pressed down on him as he climbed the stairs. It was the kind of quiet that wasn't peaceful; it was the kind that made you feel like a ghost in your own home.

His room wasn't the same as when he left it. His mother must have cleaned again. His blanket was neatly folded, his clothes were stacked on his chair, and the floor was spotless. It was almost too perfect, like she was trying to hold onto a version of him that didn't exist anymore.

Evan sat on the edge of his bed and looked around. Everything felt trapped in the past. Trophies from middle school soccer. A stack of old comic books. A poster of his favorite band from freshman year. None of it matched the storm he felt inside.

He leaned back and rubbed his eyes. He wanted to sleep, but his mind wouldn't quiet down. Instead, memories crept in, memories he never asked for.

He saw the backyard pool, blue and calm under the morning sun. He saw the ambulance's flashing lights. He saw the way the neighbors whispered behind their hands. He heard someone say, "He didn't suffer long," even though no one really knew.

Evan's chest tightened.

He remembered the night before it happened. The muffled argument. His father's anger. His mother's tears. Evan shut his door, pretending not to hear anything. Pretending he didn't feel the family falling apart.

And then the next morning…the silence.

People told him the death was an accident, that sometimes, bad things happen, and that no one was at fault. But Evan didn't believe that. Not fully. Not deep down. There were parts of the story no one talked about, pieces that didn't fit. Things he was too afraid to ask.

He ran a hand across his face.

Life had stopped the moment his father died, and Evan didn't know how to start it again.

School had been the first thing to fall apart. Classes became too hard to focus on. He stopped turning in assignments. He withdrew from friends and skipped days until it felt pointless even to try. Eventually, he dropped out, telling everyone he "needed time."

Time for what? He didn't know. He still didn't.

He reached for the small music player on his nightstand and pressed play. A soft song filled the room, one he used to love. But now it only made him feel heavier. He shut it off quickly.

"I'm going nowhere," he whispered into the quiet.

It didn't feel dramatic. It felt true.

He wanted something, anything, to push him forward. A plan. A dream. A new beginning. But all he had was the same corner, the same house, the same heavy emptiness.

And now, Captain Jack's voice echoing in his mind:

"People come back when they're searching."

Evan hated how much that stuck with him. He didn't want to be someone who needed help. He didn't want to be someone Captain Jack noticed. But he was.

He could feel it.

The next day passed slowly. He tried to read. He tried to watch TV. He tried to help his mother in the kitchen. None of it worked. His thoughts kept drifting back to the village, to the lights and noise, to the people who didn't fit but somehow seemed more alive than he did.

By the time night came, Evan already knew what he was going to do. He didn't fight it.

He grabbed his jacket, left the house quietly, and walked toward the bus stop again.

Because home felt like a memory… and the village felt like a place where something, anything, might happen.

Chapter 6

By the time Evan reached the village again, the sky was already dark. The neon signs glowed brighter than usual, and the street noise seemed louder. People moved like blurry shapes in the night, drifting in and out of shops, bars, and shadowed alleys.

Evan kept his hands deep in his jacket pockets as he walked. He didn't know what he was looking for, maybe a distraction, perhaps an escape, or maybe just someone who noticed he existed. The village felt alive in a strange way, and for a few minutes, that made him feel alive too.

He wandered past the thrift store and the alley with the murals. He passed the girl with purple hair, who was singing again, her voice floating softly above the noise. But even the music couldn't settle him tonight. Something felt wrong, like the air was heavier than usual, thick with pressure he couldn't explain.

As he turned down a quieter street, his phone buzzed in his pocket. When he pulled it out, the screen flashed with a message from the college he had tried to forget about.

FINAL NOTICE:
Withdrawal Processed
Student Status: Removed

Evan stopped walking.

He stared at the screen, waiting for the words to change, but they didn't. The message was short, cold, and final. There was no apology, no "reach out if you need help," no second chance. Just confirmation that he wasn't going back, that the door had closed.

Evan sank onto a bench near a bus stop and lowered his head into his hands. He already knew he wasn't going back, but seeing it written out made everything feel sharper. It was like the last piece of his future had snapped clean in half. School had been the one thing people expected him to fix, the thing everyone believed he could return to when he was "ready."

But now it was gone, officially gone.

A lump formed in his throat, and he struggled to breathe for a moment. He wasn't angry. He was empty. Completely empty.

A group of teens walked by, laughing loudly. Their voices hit him like static. He didn't look up. He didn't move. He didn't know how.

After a long moment, he let out a shaky breath and leaned back against the bench. His chest felt tight. His hands were trembling, though he wasn't cold. He felt a small tear slip down his cheek before he could stop it.

"Pull yourself together," he whispered. But the whisper didn't help.

He didn't want to go home. Not like this. Not with this new weight sitting on his shoulders. He didn't want to see his mother's worried face or hear her soft voice ask if he was okay when they both knew he wasn't.

He didn't even want to be in the village anymore. Everything felt too loud and too bright. He wiped his eyes with the back of his sleeve and stood up. His legs felt weak, but he forced himself to move. He didn't know where he was walking; he just needed to do something, anything, besides sitting there.

His steps led him back toward the street corner where Captain Jack had stood the night before. Evan hadn't planned on seeing him again, but the memory of Jack's calm voice floated back to him:

"People come back when they're searching."

Evan was searching, and he had been searching for a long time, and he didn't want to admit it.

He reached the corner and waited, staring at the lamp post. The light buzzed quietly, flickering every few seconds like it was unsure whether to stay on or go out.

Minutes passed. People walked by. Cars rolled past. Nothing happened. Then, just when Evan began to step away, a familiar voice came from behind him.

"Rough night?"

Evan turned and saw Captain Jack standing a few feet away, hands in his jacket pockets, looking the same as before, calm, still, almost like he had been expecting him.

Evan swallowed hard. "How did you… "

Jack raised an eyebrow. "This corner isn't crowded. It's easy to see when someone's falling apart."

Evan tried to glare, but it didn't come out right. His face felt too tired for anger.

Jack stepped closer, not too close, but close enough. "You look like a kid who lost something important."

Evan let out a bitter laugh. "You could say that."

"You ready to talk this time?" Jack asked.

Evan hesitated. He thought about saying no. He thought about walking away. But something inside him cracked, just a little, just enough.

"I don't know," he admitted quietly.

Jack nodded slowly, as if he respected that answer. "That's honest," he said. "Most people pretend they've got it all figured out. You don't. That's why you're here."

Evan didn't respond. He couldn't.

Jack gave a faint smile. "Come on. Let's walk."

Evan wasn't sure why he followed. Maybe it was because he didn't want to be alone. Maybe it was because Jack made him feel seen in a way no one else had in months. Maybe it was because everything inside him felt heavy and broken.

Or maybe it was simply because he had nothing left to lose.

Chapter 7

Evan followed Captain Jack without asking where they were going. The village noise faded behind them, slowly replaced by the soft hum of streetlights and the whistle of wind pushing between buildings. Evan kept his eyes on the ground, hands deep in his jacket pockets, while Jack walked a few steps ahead, calm, steady, almost like a guide.

They didn't talk for a while. Evan wasn't sure if Jack expected him to say something or if he was giving him space. Maybe both. The road sloped upward as they reached the edge of town, where old houses sat far apart, and the streetlights grew dimmer.

"Where are we going?" Evan finally asked.

Jack glanced back. "Somewhere quiet."

Evan almost stopped walking. "I don't want to go home."

"It's not home," Jack said. "But it's connected."

Evan frowned, confused, but he kept following. The road turned into a narrow dirt path that wound up a hillside. Weeds brushed against their legs, and stones shifted under their shoes. The wind grew stronger as they climbed, tugging at Evan's jacket and stinging his eyes.

When they reached the top, Evan recognized the place instantly.

The hillside overlooked his neighborhood, the same one he had ridden bikes through as a kid, the same one he ran through after school, the same one he hated now because it held too many memories. From there, he could even see the roof of his house and the faint glow of the backyard light his mother always kept on.

He swallowed hard.

"This is where you used to come with your dad, right?" Jack asked softly.

Evan felt the words hit him like a punch. "How do you know that?"

Jack didn't answer. He didn't need to.

Evan remembered the memories before the darkness, his dad showing him how to skip rocks down the dusty hill, pointing out constellations, telling him stories about when he was young. This hillside had once felt huge and magical, like a place where anything was possible.

But then life changed. His father changed. The fights started. The silence grew. And eventually, the hillside became just a hill, abandoned and forgotten, like a piece of his life he didn't want to touch.

Evan lowered himself onto a flat rock at the top and wrapped his arms around his knees. "Why here?"

Jack sat beside him, leaving a respectable space between them. "Because this is where it began. Before the noise. Before the pressure. Before you got stuck."

Evan didn't say anything. He stared at the lights below, tiny and distant, like sparks floating in darkness.

"I lost school," he said quietly. "I know it doesn't matter now, but...it was something. And now it's gone."

Jack nodded slowly. "And your father?"

Evan's breath caught. He didn't know whether to answer or walk away. Jack didn't push. He waited.

After a long moment, Evan whispered, "I don't understand anything anymore. I don't understand why he changed…why things got so bad…why he ended up," His voice cracked. He stopped.

The wind howled across the hillside, filling the silence.

"You're carrying too much," Jack said. "More than someone your age should."

Evan felt the pressure in his chest rising again, tight, sharp, impossible to control. "I don't know what to do."

Jack leaned forward, resting his elbows on his knees. "You're trying to move forward while dragging everything behind you. But it's too heavy. Anyone would fall."

Evan looked at him through blurry eyes. "Then what do I do?"

Jack took a slow breath. "You don't have to let go of everything. Just enough so you can breathe."

Evan shook his head. "It's not that easy."

Jack sighed, "It never is."

They sat in silence again, watching the small-town flicker far below. For the first time in months, Evan didn't feel angry. He didn't feel numb. He just felt…tired. Deep-down tired. The kind that settles into your bones.

"You know," Jack said gently, "you're allowed to be lost."

Evan wiped his eyes with the back of his sleeve. "I don't want to be."

"You won't be forever," Jack assured.

Evan wasn't sure if he believed that. But sitting here, with the wind pulling at his hair, the town glowing below, and the past and present mixing, he felt something he hadn't felt in a long time.

A tiny spark of hope. Small. Unsteady. But real.

Jack stood and nodded toward the path. "Come on. Let's get you home."

Evan followed him back down the hillside, the wind pushing at his back as if urging him forward.

For the first time in a long time, he didn't fight it.

Chapter 8

The next morning, Evan woke earlier than he expected. Sunlight slipped through the blinds in thin stripes, painting the room in soft gold. For the first time in a long while, he didn't feel crushed under the weight of waking up.

The night on the hillside stayed with him. Not the pain, not the memories, but the feeling of letting something go, even if only a little. It was like he had finally let a breath out he didn't know he'd been holding.

He sat up slowly, rubbing sleep from his eyes. The house was quiet, but not the suffocating kind. More like the world was giving him space.

He got dressed and stepped outside, feeling the cool morning air brush his face. The street looked identical, neighborhood houses standing in their usual places, birds hopping across the dew-covered lawns, but something in him felt different.

He walked without a plan, without trying to escape anything. His feet carried him toward the edge of town, near the open road that led toward the hills. The wind picked up as he walked, pushing against him in soft, steady waves. It felt almost familiar, like a voice he hadn't heard in a long time.

When he reached the top of the hill again, the view opened wide beneath him. The town looked small and fragile in the morning light. The breeze swept across the grass, bending it in long ripples. Evan stood there quietly, letting the air move over him.

He wasn't surprised when someone stepped up beside him, but it wasn't Captain Jack this time.

It was Lena, the girl with the purple hair, who sang in the alley. She held a small backpack and a notebook covered in stickers.

"I saw you walking up here," she said softly. "Didn't think anyone came to this spot anymore."

Evan gave a small smile. "I didn't either."

Lena sat on the nearby rock and looked out at the view. "This place is special," she said. "It's where I come when I want to remember things. Or forget them."

Evan nodded. "Yeah. That makes sense."

For a while, they didn't talk. They just listened to the wind rushing through the tall grass. Evan felt strangely calm sitting next to someone who wasn't asking for anything, not answers, not explanations, not apologies.

After a few minutes, Lena spoke again, her voice quieter. "I come up here because of my sister. She loved this hill. She said it made her feel like she could see the whole world."

Evan's heart tightened. He didn't know what had happened to Lena's sister, but he didn't have to. Pain had a way of showing itself without being explained.

Lena watched the wind sweep across the road. "Sometimes," she whispered, "I feel like she's still here."

Evan swallowed, feeling the wind tug at his jacket. "I wish I felt that way about my father. I feel he is nowhere. Did you always feel that way about your sister after she left?"

Lena nodded, holding onto the notebook in her lap. "Always."

The word drifted between them, gentle and warm.

Evan didn't know why, but hearing that settled something inside him. Like he wasn't alone in carrying memories he didn't know what to do with.

They sat in silence again, watching the sunlight spill across the town. Evan thought about his father, about the mistakes, the hurt, the things he still didn't understand. He thought about his mother, trying her best to keep life stitched together. He thought about the corner he kept returning to, and why he kept ending up there.

Maybe he didn't have all the answers yet, but perhaps he didn't need them right now.

The wind brushed across his face again, steady and honest. He let out a breath he didn't realize he'd been holding.

Lena stood up and slung her backpack over her shoulder. "You heading back?"

"Yeah," Evan said. "Eventually."

She gave him a small smile and started down the hill. After a moment, he followed.

As he walked, Evan felt lighter, not fixed, not healed, but finally moving. The hillside no longer felt like a graveyard of memories. It felt like a beginning, and the wind, carrying echoes of voices past, sounded almost like hope.

Chapter 9

Evan didn't go back to the village that night. For the first time in a long while, he didn't feel the pull of the noise, the lights, or the strange comfort of being lost in a crowd. Instead, he walked around town slowly, taking in everything he usually ignored.

Porch lights glowing on quiet streets. Sprinklers leaving tiny rainbows on front lawns. A dog barking in the distance. Kids' bicycles lying on a driveway.

The town hadn't changed, but Evan had.

The wind carried the smell of dust and ocean air, brushing past him like a reminder of the hillside. He felt that same softness in his chest, that same sense of letting go. It wasn't perfect or complete, but it was real.

When he finally reached the familiar street corner, the one he had stood on so many nights before, he stopped. The streetlight flickered above him, just like always. The sidewalk still had the same long crack running across it. Cars passed with the same low rumble. But the corner didn't feel like a trap anymore. It felt like a memory.

Evan stood there for a moment, letting the night air settle around him. He thought about the past few months, about the emptiness that had wrapped around him like a heavy blanket. He remembered the long nights staring at the ceiling, wondering what he was supposed to do now that everything had fallen apart.

He remembered Captain Jack's voice, too:

"You're standing on the edge of something."

At first, Evan thought that meant something dark, an escape, a mistake, or a fall. Now he wondered if Jack had meant something else. Maybe the edge wasn't a cliff. Perhaps it was a new beginning.

A soft gust of wind blew across the road, bending the weeds at the base of the lamp post. Evan closed his eyes, feeling the breeze move through him. It reminded him of Lena's words, her quiet "Always," and how that moment on the hillside had made everything inside him shift, even just a little.

He didn't need to forget anything. He didn't need to run. He just needed to move. For the first time in months, he didn't feel stuck.

He stepped away from the corner, his hands loose at his sides, his shoulders lighter. The street stretched ahead of him, ordinary, familiar, but somehow new. He didn't have a plan, but he had a direction, and that felt like enough.

As he reached the end of the block, he looked back once more. The corner stayed where it was, part of the past but no longer part of him.

He whispered, barely loud enough to hear, "I'm ready." Not ready for everything. Not prepared for the whole world. Just ready for the next step.

Evan turned and walked toward home, the wind brushing gently at his back as if guiding him forward. For the first time in a long time, he didn't fight it.

Chapter 10

Evan woke before the sun rose again, something that hadn't happened in months. The sky outside his window was still pale and gray, and the house was silent except for the soft hum of the refrigerator downstairs. He lay there for a moment, breathing in the quiet, letting it sink in that today felt different. Not perfect. Not fixed. But different.

He sat up and rubbed his eyes. His chest didn't feel as heavy as usual, and the emptiness that once filled his mornings had thinned out. It was almost like the wind from the hillside had followed him home and swept some of the darkness away.

When he stepped into the hallway, he heard soft movement in the kitchen. His mother was already up, standing at the counter with her hands wrapped around a mug of tea. The early light made faint shadows under her eyes, but she looked calmer than usual, like she'd slept a little better.

She turned when she heard him. "Good morning," she said gently.

"Morning," Evan replied. His voice didn't crack or feel tight. It came out steady.

His mother blinked, surprised by how normal it sounded.

Evan poured himself a glass of water and sat down at the table. For the first time in a long time, he didn't immediately look away or stare at his hands. He met her eyes. Not long, but long enough.

"How was your walk last night?" she asked carefully.

Evan took a slow breath. "Good," he said. "I…needed it."

His mother nodded, as if she understood more than he was saying. "I'm glad you came home early."

He hesitated, then added, "Yeah. Me too."

A soft smile tugged at the corner of her mouth. It wasn't the forced kind she had been giving for months. It looked honest, small, tired, but real.

They sat in comfortable silence for a moment. It felt strange, but in a good way. Like the space between them wasn't filled with fear or worry anymore, just quiet understanding.

After a minute, Evan cleared his throat. "I was thinking today...Maybe I could look for some places hiring part-time. Something simple. Something to start." He didn't know why he said it. The words just slipped out.

His mother froze for a second, eyes wide, like she was afraid to break the moment. "That sounds...wonderful," she said softly. "I think that would be really good for you."

Evan nodded, not because he felt pressured, but because he actually meant it. He wasn't sure what kind of job he'd find. He wasn't sure how long the motivation would last. But it was a step. A real step.

And that mattered.

As he stood, his mother spoke again. "Evan?"

He looked back.

"I'm proud of you," she whispered.

The words landed gently but deeply. They didn't feel heavy or guilt-filled. They felt honest. He swallowed hard and let them settle inside him.

"Thanks," he said. And for the first time in forever, he meant that too.

He stepped outside into the cool morning air. The sun was beginning to rise, stretching warm colors across the sky. The breeze moved through the trees, brushing his face like a familiar hand.

Evan closed his eyes for a moment and let the wind wash over him. He didn't think of the corner. He didn't think of the village. He didn't even think of Captain Jack. He thought about today, just today. And how maybe, just maybe, it could be the start of something better.

He opened his eyes, took a steady breath, and walked down the front steps toward the quiet road. For the first time in a long time, his steps felt like progress.

Chapter 11

The rest of the morning passed slowly, but peacefully. Evan helped his mother wash the dishes and even fixed the crooked picture frame in the hallway that had been bothering her for weeks. Neither of them made a big deal out of it, but they worked side by side without that usual cloud hanging between them.

After lunch, Evan stepped outside again, feeling the warm sun on his face. The day was calm, the kind of calm he used to hate because it reminded him of everything he was missing. But today, the calm felt different, open, not empty.

He walked down the street with no real plan. The wind brushed through the trees, carrying a whisper across the neighborhood. It reminded him of the hillside again, and the feeling he had standing there with Lena, small but hopeful.

As he reached the main road, he saw a small bulletin board outside the town center. It was worn and faded but covered in flyers. Most were old or torn, but a bright yellow one caught his eye.

HELP WANTED – PART-TIME STOCK CLERK.

No experience needed. Start immediately.

Evan stared at it longer than he meant to. His first instinct was to walk away. He wasn't ready. He wasn't good enough. He didn't know what he was doing.

But then he remembered something Jack had said on the hillside:

"You're trying to move forward while dragging everything behind you. But it's too heavy."

Maybe Evan didn't have to drag everything anymore. Maybe he only needed to carry what still mattered.

Before he could overthink it, he pulled one of the tabs from the flyer with the phone number on it. The tiny piece of paper trembled in his hand. His heartbeat was faster, not in fear, but in a nervous, hopeful way he hadn't felt in years.

He walked across the street to a quiet bench and sat down. His thumb hovered over the numbers on his phone screen. He almost talked himself out of it, nearly, but then he hit "call" before he could stop.

A woman answered on the second ring. "Town Market. This is Rachel."

Evan's voice wavered at first, but he pushed through it. "Uh…hi. I'm calling about the stock clerk job."

"Are you available to come in today?" she asked.

He hesitated for only a second. "Yeah. I can."

"Great. Come by any time before four. Ask for me."
The call ended.

Evan sat there in stunned silence for a moment, staring at the phone in his hand. He wasn't sure whether he felt brave, scared, or both. But he had done something. He had taken a step.
A real, solid step.

He stood up and headed toward the store, each footstep feeling strangely light. As he passed by the old street corner, the one he had stood on for so many lonely nights, he slowed.

The flickering streetlight was still there. The long crack in the sidewalk was still there. Nothing about the corner had changed, but he had.

Evan stepped closer and looked at the space beneath the lamp post. He half-expected to see Captain Jack standing there with that knowing smile, waiting for him to fall back into his old habits. But the corner was empty.

Quiet.

Still.

Evan gave the corner one last look. Not with sadness. Not with fear. Just...recognition. A silent goodbye.

"That part's over," he whispered.

The wind rose gently, blowing across the road and brushing against his back as if giving him a slight nudge forward.

Evan didn't resist.

He walked past the corner without slowing down, heading toward the market with a small spark of something new glowing in his chest.

Maybe it was hope. Perhaps it was just courage. Maybe it didn't matter which.

For the first time in a long time, he felt like he was choosing his own path, not because someone pushed him, but because he was ready to walk it himself.

And that was enough.

Epilogue

It had been three months since Evan first walked into the town market to start his new job. His days were still simple, unloading boxes, stocking shelves, learning how to deal with customers, but for the first time in a long time, "simple" didn't feel like failure.
It felt like progress.

He didn't visit the old street corner anymore. He took different roads now, ones with sunlight and noise and people who smiled without pretending. His life wasn't perfect, some mornings were still heavy, some nights still lonely, but he kept moving. Step by step.

One evening, after a long shift, he decided to take the scenic route home. The sky was turning orange and pink, fading toward night. A soft wind brushed against his face, carrying the scent of warm pavement and blooming flowers. He felt calm.
But when he turned onto a familiar street, he slowed.
The corner.
His corner.

The one he had spent too many nights standing on. He hadn't planned on passing it, but now that he was here, he couldn't stop looking.

Under the flickering streetlight, a boy stood alone, arms crossed, head down, shoulders tight. Evan recognized the posture instantly. He had once stood the same way.

The boy kicked at the sidewalk as cars rolled by. He looked like he was waiting for something he couldn't explain. Something heavy. Something dangerous.

And then Evan saw him, Captain Jack.

He leaned casually on the lamp post, half in the shadows, watching the boy with sharp, knowing eyes. He looked the same as before, calm, patient, confident, like he had all the time in the world.

Jack flicked open a lighter, then clicked it shut. The sound carried across the street, sharp and cold. Evan felt a chill move down his spine. For a moment, Jack's eyes lifted and met Evan's. Neither of them moved.

Jack didn't smile. He didn't nod. He didn't speak. He just looked at Evan with a quiet understanding, as if saying, "You walked away. But not everyone does."

Evan's heart pounded, but not from fear, but from clarity.

He realized something he had never understood before: Captain Jack hadn't disappeared. Evan had walked far enough to be free.

After a few seconds, Evan looked away from Jack and toward the boy standing beside him. The kid looked so lost. So tired. So close to falling into the same trap Evan once had.

Evan thought about crossing the street, about warning the boy, telling him to go home, to leave before it was too late. But he didn't move; the boy would have to make his own choice, as he had. Evan just hoped it would be the right one.

He remembered how he had been back then, broken, confused, unreachable. Words from a stranger wouldn't have saved him. He had to save himself just like this boy would have to.

Evan took a steady breath, eyes soft with understanding. "Not my corner anymore," he whispered.

The wind stirred, brushing the hair at his forehead, gentle but firm, like a hand guiding him forward.

Evan turned and walked away, his steps strong and sure. He didn't look back.

The corner stayed behind him. So did the shadows. And the future, his future, stretched quietly ahead.

Even went to the hill often to clear his head. He knew he would cross paths with Lena, and he felt deep down that it would be a good thing for both of them.

Author's Note

When the Streetlight Flickered is a story that sits close to my heart. I didn't plan it that way at first, but as I wrote Evan's journey, his loneliness, his struggle to understand himself, and the quiet pull of escape, I realized I was putting pieces of my own past on the page. Initially, I was going to have Evan follow my path, but I decided to have him make better choices than I did.

I am a recovering alcoholic and drug addict. I spent many years fighting battles that most people never saw. I tried to hide my pain behind jokes, behind smiles, behind long nights where I didn't want to feel anything at all. And like Evan, I stood on a lot of "corners", places where I felt stuck, lost, or unsure if I even wanted to move forward, but I made different choices.

When I wrote about Captain Jack, I wasn't thinking about one specific person. I was thinking about the voice of addiction itself, the whisper that tells you it has the answers, that it can take the pain away, that it can give you a "special island." Anyone who has battled addiction knows how convincing that whisper can be. And they also know how hard it is to walk away. I intended to have Evan follow that path, but as I wrote, I realized that wasn't Evan's path; it didn't feel right. Captain Jack helped him because that was what Evan really wanted; he chose to resist the other path Jack offered.

If you have ever felt stuck, lonely, or pulled toward something you know will hurt you. You can walk away. You can step forward. And you deserve better than the corner that holds you.

Make the right choice, the right decision, and if you have already started down the other path, it isn't too late to change your course.

I am sober today because I reached a point where I finally believed that truth for myself. I am grateful I did. My life, my family, and my writing all exist because I chose to keep moving, one step at a time.

Thank you for reading this story. Thank you for letting Evan find his way. And if you are on your own journey, I'm rooting for you.

—Brett C. Persson

What Remains of Me Without Her

The kitchen light hummed the way it always had, a faint electrical buzz that never quite faded into silence. It had done that for years, long before the house became this quiet, long before the sound felt like company.

Jack sat at the table with his elbows resting on the worn wood, shoulders slightly hunched as if bracing against a cold no one else could feel. The overhead bulb cast a warm, tired circle of light that stopped well short of the room's corners. Everything beyond it seemed to retreat, waiting.

In front of him lay a framed photograph. The glass was cool beneath his fingertips, smooth and unyielding. In the picture, his wife stood beside him in a sunlit field, her hair caught mid-laugh by the wind. He remembered that day, the way the grass had brushed against their ankles, the way she had leaned into him without thinking, as if that were the most natural thing in the world.

Now, the only movement in the room came from the blinking red light on the answering machine.

Jack pressed play.

Her voice filled the kitchen, bright, casual, alive.

"Hey, love, just wanted to say I miss you today. I'll be home soon. I just got done at the store. Picked up your favorite soup, but they didn't have that rye bread you like. I'm going to stop by that little bakery on Walnut, then I'll be home. Love you. See you soon."

The message ended with a soft click.

For a moment, Jack could almost believe it again, that she was just late. That she'd walk through the door carrying grocery bags, apologizing for traffic, already telling a story before she'd set anything down.

His mind betrayed him, replaying the memory whether he wanted it or not.

She had called from the car, the sound of her turn signal faint beneath her voice. She said the store was out of the bread he liked, laughed about it, and promised to check another place on the way home. He remembered standing right here, leaning against the counter, listening to the message, half-listening while the kettle boiled. He had just missed her call while he was taking out the garbage.

"See you soon," she'd said.

Soon had stretched into hours.

The knock at the door hadn't been loud. That was the detail that stayed with him, the way it had been polite, almost hesitant. Two officers were on the porch. Their words were delivered carefully, professionally, as fragile objects passed from hand to hand.

An accident at an intersection he knew well. A truck that hadn't slowed. Jack's knees grew weak as the kettle began to scream, matching the thoughts in his mind. Now, the silence had returned, heavier than ever before. The house without her was empty and hollow.

Jack closed his eyes. His chest tightened, not sharply, but slowly, like pressure building behind his ribs. He exhaled through his nose, a long breath that seemed to carry more weight than air. The smell of old coffee lingered faintly, mixed with lemon cleaner and something else, time, maybe.

He didn't cry, not yet. Tears didn't come easily anymore. They waited until he was alone, until his body decided he had earned them.

He stood, the chair legs scraping softly against the floor, and moved into the hallway. The house responded to him the way it always did now, with small, reluctant sounds. A floorboard creaked under his heel. Somewhere deep inside the walls, pipes ticked as they cooled. The hallway smelled like fabric and dust, the kind of scent that settled into old coats and forgotten corners.

Photographs lined the walls. Their frames caught slivers of light as he passed, reflecting them in dull flashes. Wedding day. A camping trip. A photo from his recovery anniversary, her arm around his waist, his smile cautious but real. Jack paused in front of that one longer than the others.

He could still remember how nervous he'd been that day. How she had squeezed his hand and whispered, "You did this," as it mattered more than anything else.

The liquor cabinet sat at the end of the hall, used only when company was over. It hadn't opened by his hand in years, but tonight it felt like it had been waiting for him to return, longing for his touch like a lost lover.

Jack stopped in front of it, his hand hovering just short of the handle. The air here felt colder, or maybe that was his imagination. A thin layer of dust coated the wood. When he touched it, the dust smeared beneath his thumb, leaving a dark crescent behind.

The cabinet door opened with a soft groan, as if it resented being disturbed. Inside sat a bottle, unopened, untouched. Johnnie Walker Blue, his old friend.

Jack stared at it for a long moment, his jaw tightening. He could feel his pulse in his throat. He closed the cabinet, then opened it again, as if confirming it was still there.

It was.

He carried the bottle back to the kitchen. It felt heavier than he expected, the glass solid and cold against his palm. When he set it on the table, it made a dull, hollow sound that echoed just a little too loudly in the quiet room.

Jack retrieved a glass from the cupboard. It clinked softly as he placed it down. He unscrewed the cap. The smell hit him first, sharp and sweet, a familiar burn that crawled into his sinuses. His mouth watered before he could stop it. He hated that part most, the way his body remembered before his mind could intervene.

Jack poured a small amount into the glass, and then a little more, three fingers' worth in total. The scotch glugged slowly into the glass, thick and deliberate. His hands trembled, the shaking traveling up through his wrists and into his arms. He tightened his grip until his knuckles whitened.

"Twenty years," he murmured, the words barely audible. "Twenty damn years."

The glass radiated faint warmth where he held it. He stared down into the amber liquid, watching the surface settle.

"For her," he continued softly. "For us. For me."

Jack remembers an old message from almost a year earlier. The voicemail was left while he was working, and he heard it just before that meeting. Her voice was soft and happy. Her laughter filled his head, warm and full of life. "Happy twenty years, babe. I can't believe it. I'm so proud of you. You showed me that real strength isn't loud, it's quiet, it's this, it's you."

Jack remembered how she was when he returned from his meeting. He saw her standing in this same kitchen, sunlight spilling through the window, dust motes floating like they had nowhere better to be. He remembered how nervous he'd been, how his fingers had fumbled in his pocket before he finally pulled the coin out and placed it in her open palm.

P a g e | **57**

Twenty years.

She had turned it over slowly, tracing the ridged edge with her thumb like it might disappear if she didn't hold it firmly enough. The metal had caught the light, dull but solid. Real.

"You did this," she'd said, her voice softer than usual. I was not celebratory; it was just certain.

Then she smiled, the kind that didn't need words, and closed her fingers around it like it was something sacred.

The memory slipped out of Jack's mind just as easily as it had entered. His throat tightened, and a tear slipped free, then another.

Jack pressed his thumb hard into the edge of the table. The wood bit back, grounding him in something solid and real. His throat tightened, swallowing suddenly difficult, like dragging something rough downward.

Another tear slipped free and traced a warm line down his cheek. He brushed it away roughly, but another followed.

He lifted the glass.

The smell of the scotch intensified: oak, alcohol, memory. His lips hovered just above the rim. He could feel the ache in his chest sharpen, the promise of relief humming just beneath the surface. One drink. One quiet erasure. Sleep without dreams. Forgetting.

"It would be so easy," he whispered.

Images surfaced uninvited. Early mornings sober with his coffee in one hand, while her other hand slipped into his other without ceremony. The steady rhythm of days built on effort and love.

His hands shook harder. A drop spilled over the rim of the glass and darkened the table. Jack froze, "What remains of me without her?" he asked the empty room. "Am I still the man she believed in?"

The glass trembled. His teeth ground together softly. He lowered the glass. The ache diminished at the thought. It didn't vanish, but it settled some.

Jack stood and carried the glass to the sink. The light above it was harsh, almost clinical, illuminating every flaw. He tilted the glass and watched the whiskey spiral down the drain, amber twisting into darkness, and then the contents of the bottle followed.

The smell lingered stubbornly as he turned on the water. It rushed loudly, filling the sink, rinsing the glass until it squeaked clean beneath his fingers.

Jack set the glass upside down on the counter, and he dropped the empty bottle into the trash. His hands still shook, but less.

Jack picked up the sobriety coin off the table. The metal was cool, familiar. Its ridged edge pressed into his palm as he closed his fist around it, grounding himself in something earned. He slipped it into his pants pocket without looking, the motion practiced, almost unconscious.

He grabbed his keys, with the worn leather tag, the one she'd bought him years ago after his first year sober, the stitching frayed now, softened by time.

Jack pulled on his jacket and stepped outside. Cool night air washed over him, sharp and clean, clearing the stale smell of whiskey from his lungs. Somewhere down the street, a car passed. A porch light clicked on. Life continued without asking permission.

Jack locked the door behind him. As he walked toward his car, his hand returned to his pocket, fingers feeling the coin again.

He felt the stamped words, each letter as if he were reading them in the dark.

One day at a time.

Jack sat in the driver's seat for a moment, engine off, breathing. "She's gone," he said softly to the empty car. Then, after a beat, "But I'm not."

Jack turned the key and the engine caught.

Headlights cut through the dark as he pulled away from the house, leaving the empty bottle behind in the trash, exactly where it belonged.

Familiar Faces

Chapter 1 – The Observer

Claire, 50,

The train arrives at 6:42 a.m., like it always does, humming low, silver, and tired.

Claire boards without thinking, her feet moving the way they've been trained to move after seventeen years of the same job, the same route, the same seat. Third car. Window side. Forward-facing. Second row from the back. No one ever argues for that spot. It doesn't scream comfort or power. It's simply... forgotten, just like her.

She settles in, her scarf pulled tight around her neck even though it's not that cold today. She doesn't read. Doesn't scroll. Doesn't doze off. Claire watches.

She knows the rhythm of this ride better than her own breath. Knows when the wheels screech too long. Knows which doors stick. She knows the faces too, the ones that file in like sleepwalkers, quiet ghosts in wrinkled coats and heavy shoes.

There's the boy with the hood always pulled up. **Ghost Boy**, she calls him. Sketches in a spiral notebook with a chewed-up pen. His backpack is ripped on the left side, but no one tells him. No one talks to him.

There's **The Music Man**, mid-thirties maybe, suit too big for his frame, constantly tapping his thumb against his thigh in perfect rhythm. The cord from his headphones dangles like a lifeline. He never looks up. Not once.

The Quiet Lady comes in at 6:47, two stops later. Tired eyes. Smells faintly of antiseptic and lavender. A nurse, Claire thinks.

Or maybe a night janitor at one of the big hospitals. She clutches a poetry book as if it's made of glass.

There's also **The Man with the Notebook**, who sometimes smiles at no one; he just smiles. Writes with his head down, like he's afraid of being caught. He holds a lunchbox with a glittery rainbow sticker peeling off the side. Claire imagines a child packing it for him.

The Old Woman who is always looking at a letter, always sad. Something always seems empty or lost within her. She can tell she is hurting, but doesn't know why, and can't tell what the source of her pain and sadness is exactly, but she feels that she must be lonely.

None of them speaks. That's the rule on the morning train. No small talk. No eye contact. Just the lull of tracks and the occasional screech that reminds you you're still awake.

Claire has ridden this line for so long that she sometimes feels like she belongs to the train more than the city. She's watched seasons change through this scratched window. Watched buildings crumble, and new ones rise. Watched her reflection grow older in the glass, line by line.

She never writes anything down, doesn't take photos, and doesn't keep a diary. But she remembers it all. The way people shift when they're about to cry but won't let themselves. The twitch in a finger. The slow fold of arms across a stomach full of nerves. The way grief wears people like oversized jackets.

Everyone here is carrying something invisible. Claire sees it. She always has.

The conductor's voice crackles overhead, distant and flat, like a memory you're not sure you dreamed or lived. "Next stop: 12th and Rose."

She traces a finger along the condensation gathering on the window. Draws a small spiral. Watches it disappear.

In her mind, she counts them all. Ghost Boy. Music Man. Quiet Lady. Notebook Man, and the Old Woman. She adds herself to the list: **The Observer.**

Claire leans her head against the glass. It's colder than she expected. "One of us," she whispers, "soon one of us won't be riding anymore." And the train carries them forward, silent, tired, and together in a world that never seems to be noticed.

Chapter 2 – The Music Man

Marco, 34, Corporate Burnout

The headphones go in before the train arrives.

It's not about the music anymore. Not really. It's about the wall it builds between him and everything else, the screeching brakes, the mumbled apologies, the fluorescent lights that buzz like a hangover that never ends. Music makes the ride feel less like a funeral procession.

Today's track is the same as yesterday's. Gary Jules, *Mad World*. The cover version. Softer. Sadder. More honest.

Marco adjusts the volume until it's just loud enough to blur the edges of the world. He boards without looking up, his feet following the muscle memory of routine. Third car. Middle door. Left side. End seat.

Across from him, The Observer, that older woman in the window seat, glances at him. She always does. He never returns it. Not because he's rude. He just… doesn't know what to do with kindness.

He settles in, knees too long for the space, tie already loosened, thermos of bitter coffee clutched like a lifeline. His phone buzzes, and he doesn't look. It's either his boss or his mother. He's not sure which is worse.

Welcome to another beautiful day at Halberstam & Klein, where dreams go to be quietly euthanized.

His calendar is packed. Sales check-in at 9. Product sync at 10:15. Some performance review at 1. He'll nod and smile. Say, "absolutely" at least twelve times. Maybe thirteen if someone throws a pie chart at him.

He used to write music. Real music. Played synth in a shitty band with a name no one remembers. They once had a song go mildly viral. 80,000 views. For a week, he let himself believe it could be something.

Then rent came. Then debt. Then a girl he thought would stay. Then a job that paid too well to walk away from.

He opens the Halberstam spreadsheet app on his phone and closes it ten seconds later. Instead, he opens his Notes app and types three words:

"Dreams in cages."

That's it. That's all he has today.

Across the aisle, the boy in the hoodie is sketching again. Marco tries not to look, but he always peeks. The kid draws like he's trying to trap something beautiful before it disappears. Marco envies that kind of hunger. His own fire flickered out years ago. Now he's just ash in a tailored shirt.

The train jerks. Marco doesn't brace. He likes the sway, the unpredictability. It reminds him he's still in a body. Still capable of falling.

Claire, the woman in the window seat, coughs lightly, and Marco wonders if she's sick or just tired of being quiet. He wonders what she listens to, or if she listens at all. Maybe she watches. Some people do that. Sit there and soak up the world, even when the world is trying to forget them.

All around me are familiar faces…

The song repeats.

He thumbs over to his texts. Starts one. Stops.

Hey, do you ever think about that weekend in Montreal?

He deletes it.

He'll never send it. She's getting married next spring. He saw the post, big diamond, fall leaves, smiling too wide. She left him a long time ago, but sometimes he likes to pretend there's still a version of him out there she might have stayed for.

The train slows at 12th and Rose. The doors hiss open like an exhale. A few people shuffle in. No one speaks.

The Quiet Lady boards next. Smells like tired flowers. She reads poetry, and he's seen the book before. Whitman. Or maybe Plath. Something lonely.

He pulls his coat tighter. Not because he's cold, just because he can. Because control is rare these days, and wrapping himself up feels like something.

The doors close. The train rolls on.

He closes his eyes.

For a moment, he imagines a different life. One where the band made it. Where the music still mattered. Where he rides this train with headphones in, not to hide, but to *listen*.

But that world isn't this one. And as the gray tunnel rushes by, Marco opens his eyes, lets the song start again, and lets the world blur out once more.

Chapter 3 – The Ghost Boy

Jaden, 17, High School Dropout

Jaden boards through the back door and keeps his head down, just like always.

The hoodie's up. Earbuds are in. Backpack's slung low so it doesn't show the rip in the strap. No one looks twice, not that they ever did. That's the trick, right? Look like you belong and they won't question it. Look like nothing and you might as well be invisible.

He takes his usual seat, right behind the pole where no one can really see him unless they try. And no one tries.
That's fine.

He's got his sketchbook in his lap, thumb holding the page where he left off yesterday, a half-finished drawing of the lady with the scarf who always sits by the window. Her eyes are wrinkled in the corners, like they've seen too much or not enough. Her hands look like they've never held anything heavier than silence.
He flips past that one. Not today.

Today he's working on the man that has the notebook and the glittery lunchbox. There's always a little curve in his lips, but it never reaches his eyes. Jaden knows the difference. You learn early in places like his how to spot fake smiles. You either learn or you get hurt. Again.

Pencil scratches softly against the paper. It's the only sound that matters. The train's hum, the track's screech, they're just white noise. Drawing is the only thing that slows his brain down. When the world gets too loud, he can disappear into lines, into shading, into eyes that don't look away.

They told him he had "behavioral issues." That he was "unfocused." No one ever asked why he stopped turning in homework. No one asked what happened behind closed doors when the yelling started. No one asked about the bruises under the sleeves. So he stopped asking too.

Instead, he comes here. Every morning. Rides the train from end to end with nothing but his sketchbook, a broken pair of earbuds, and a whole lot of quiet.

Sometimes he draws the people around him. Other times, he draws monsters. But they usually end up looking the same.

Like the guy with the headphones, who's across from him now, head bobbing to something in his headphones. He's always listening to the same song. Jaden doesn't know the name, but he can almost hum the melody now. It's soft. Sad. Like a lullaby for people who forgot how to sleep. Then his eyes close, like he's trying to block the world out from the inside.

The train jolts—pencil slips. A line cuts across the page. He swears under his breath and erases too hard. The paper tears a little, but it doesn't matter.

Across the aisle, the lady with the poetry book boards. Book in hand, eyes already on the page. Her face is soft, but there's something heavy in the way she carries herself. Like she's wearing a coat made of bad news, he's drawn her too, but not today, today is the man with the notepad and lunchbox. A few times. Her hands especially. There's grace in them, even when she's holding nothing.

Sometimes he wants to show them his drawings. Slide a page over. Say, "Look. I see you." But his mouth never works the way he wants it to. It's like his voice got stuck somewhere around the sixth grade and never found its way back.

So, he draws.

Because if he can't talk, maybe he can at least prove he was here. That he existed. That he saw things. That he *felt* things.

The page fills slowly. Shading under the eyes. The lines of a fake smile. A tiny crack in the corner of the mouth, like something breaking but still pretending it's not. That's the thing about being a ghost. You see what others don't.

He presses his pencil down hard to finish the outline. Then flips to a blank page. He knows what comes next.

Tomorrow, he'll draw the woman with the scarf again. Maybe add color this time. Not because it matters but because she *looks,* and for a moment, he thinks that might be enough.

Chapter 4 – The Quiet Lady

Amina, 43, Night Nurse

The poetry book in her hands is more for comfort than reading.

She holds it like a relic, dog-eared and weathered, pages stained with coffee and pen ink and years of sleep-deprived underlining. She's read the same page three days in a row but can't remember a single line.

Her body aches in quiet places. Ankles. Lower back. The soft spot where grief settles behind the ribs.

Twelve hours on her feet at Mercy General. Four codes called. One lost. A man in his seventies who smiled when she held his hand and said, "It's okay, sweetheart. I'm not afraid." He died with that smile still curling his lips. Amina doesn't cry anymore, but she feels something settle behind her eyes like fog.

She boards the train just past 12th and Rose, her usual stop. Her feet know where to go: the third car, the middle bench, and the far end. She's taken the same seat for months now. Maybe years. Time gets slippery when you live in a cycle of fluorescent lights, alarms, and hallway whispers.

She adjusts her coat and pulls the book open again. Plath today. She doesn't always choose the darkest ones, but somehow, they always find her.

Across the aisle, the boy in the hoodie, whom she has seen before, pretends not to look at her. But he *is* looking. Always is. Sometimes she feels his eyes like a tap on the shoulder. Not in a bad way. More like he's asking a question with his silence, she never minds. He never talks. That's rare. People always want something from her: information, help, forgiveness, or attention.

The boy watches like he's waiting to see if she'll fall apart.

Not today, she thinks. She lets her eyes drift to the others.

The man with the headphones is mouthing lyrics again. She's close enough now to faintly hear the song, a slow piano melody she recognizes but can't place. He looks like he'd rather be anywhere else. She understands that kind of quiet desperation.

The woman by the window, older, still. Her scarf is the same pale green as always. She looks like the tunnel has something worth seeing. Amina envies her calm. Or maybe it's well-practiced.

She closes her book, mid-poem. Can't concentrate. Not with the hospital still clinging to her skin, to her thoughts. She smells antiseptic even when it's gone. Sometimes she forgets how to speak gently because she's spent the night shouting over heart monitors and begging people not to die.

And then there's the guilt.

Guilt for the patients she couldn't save. Guilt for the son she hasn't spoken to in six months. Guilt for wondering if it was easier to let the silence grow instead of risking the pain of trying again.

He used to love when she read poetry to him. When he was small enough to still sit on her lap, he'd rest his head on her shoulder and whisper, *"Reread the one about the stars."* Now his number is still in her phone, but the messages go unread.

She's written out drafts of what to say, apologies wrapped in metaphors, and hope. She never sends them, but she closes the screen, clutches the poetry book tighter, and waits for something to change.

A soft rustle breaks her thoughts.

The boy across the aisle is sketching. She catches a glimpse, a pair of eyes, drawn in pencil. The man with the notebook, it's in his eyes, she's sure of it.

He looks up for just a second. Their eyes meet.

Amina doesn't smile. She gives a slight nod. Because she *sees him*, too. And somehow, in the hush of the subway car, that feels like enough.

Chapter 5 – The Man with the Notebook

Connor, 28, Widowed Father

Connor always sits on the inside, near the window, but he never looks out.

It's not that the view isn't worth seeing, it's just that everything out there reminds him of what's been *before*. Before the accident. Before her. Before he became someone people looked at with tilted heads and lowered voices, like tragedy might be contagious.

He carries two things every day: a metal lunchbox with a peeling rainbow sticker his daughter slapped on without asking, and a soft-covered notebook that's nearly full. He writes in it every morning, not because he has anything important to say, but because it's how he keeps from unraveling.

Today, he writes:

"People wear silence like armor on this train. But it's thin. One crack, and it might all come spilling out."

He likes to write little things like that. Observations. Lines that feel like poems but aren't. Sometimes he turns them into stories for Emma, his six-year-old daughter who still thinks her mom lives "somewhere in the stars." He hasn't told her the truth yet. Doesn't know when he will. Or if he can.

The train rocks gently, and he tightens his grip on the notebook. It gives him something to hold. Something that won't disappear in the middle of the night.

Across from him, the boy in the hoodie is sketching again. Connor's seen him a lot lately. Never talks, just like all the others. But he watches, always watches. There's something sad in his face, something Connor recognizes. It's the look of someone carrying too much for his young age.

He wonders what the boy would look like as a character in a story. Probably call him "The Smiling Boy," the way writers do when they want to be ironic. A character who never speaks but draws what he can't say. A character who knows more than the adults around him.

Connor flips to a fresh page and scribbles a title: "The Smiling Boy and the Woman in the Scarf."

He doesn't know what it's about yet, but he's getting used to not knowing.

The nurse is on the train too. The one who reads poetry. He's seen her hands, always so gentle, even when they're tired. He once imagined her as a guardian angel in a story for Emma. In that version, she wore scrubs and a glowing halo, carrying a little girl through the dark. He never finished that one.

And then there's the older woman by the window. Claire, he thinks her name is. She hasn't told him that, but it feels right. Something in the way she sits, perfectly still, like she's bearing witness. She doesn't pretend the world isn't broken. She watches it fall apart with grace.

He writes a line about her, too:

"The woman by the window doesn't speak, but I think she remembers everything."

Emma would like that line.

The train slows. His stop is three away. He considers staying on longer—just one extra stop. To write. To breathe.

He looks down at the lunchbox. Inside is a juice box, two granola bars, a ham-and-cheese sandwich cut into a heart, and a folded napkin with a crayon drawing from Emma. The picture is of him and her. And a third figure, smaller, floating above them with long hair and a blue dress.

He blinks hard.

Across from him, the boy catches his eye. For a second, neither of them looks away. Connor gives a superficial nod. The boy doesn't return it, but his pencil pauses.

That's enough.

The train moves again, and Connor goes back to his notebook.

He writes:

"We're all strangers on this train. But maybe we don't have to be."

And for the first time in a long time, he lets himself believe it.

Chapter 6 – The Old Woman

Evelyn, 68, Widow

The letter is folded into fourths and creased from too many mornings like this one.

Evelyn runs her fingers along the edges as the train doors close behind her. She doesn't need to unfold it to know the words. She's written them three times already, each version slightly different, each one still unsigned.

It begins:

Dear Daniel, I saw someone who looked like you yesterday. Same kind eyes. Same crooked smile. For a moment, I thought maybe you'd come back.

She takes her usual seat, window-side, near the middle of the car. The metal is cold beneath her hands. The world outside is still dark. Her reflection in the window is softer in this light, blurry enough to pretend she's someone younger. Someone less hollow.

Evelyn used to be the kind of person who filled rooms. She laughed loudly. Danced in the kitchen—writing lists for everything. Daniel used to say she was like a lighthouse, always shining, even in storms.

But when he died, the light didn't go out all at once. It flickered. Dimming slowly, month by month, until only embers remained.

She opens the letter, smoothing it carefully on her lap. The ink is smudged in the corner, where she cried last week. Or the week before. It blurs the word *"remember."*

I still see you in little things. Coffee cups. Traffic lights. Socks left inside-out in the laundry. Do you remember the subway rides we used to take together? You always gave up your seat for someone, even if it meant you stood for thirty minutes. I hated that about you. I loved that about you.

Her throat tightens.

Across from her, the boy in the hoodie looks up from his sketchbook. She notices but says nothing. His eyes are kind. Too kind for someone so young. He reminds her of her grandson, whom she hasn't seen in months. Not since her daughter stopped calling.

The nurse, the one with the poetry book, watches too. Their eyes meet for just a moment. Something wordless passes between them.

Evelyn tries to blink it away, but the tears come anyway. Slow. Unstoppable.

She folds the letter in half again, quickly, trying to hide it. But her hands are shaking now. Her chest feels like it's caving in. The sob escapes before she can swallow it.

Just one. Just loud enough to make the train go still.

She covers her mouth, ashamed. She tries to shrink herself, to become invisible, but it's too late. The silence has been broken.

A tissue appears in front of her. The nurse. She's holding it gently, like it's not just paper but permission.

Evelyn takes it. She nods; her voice is gone. The woman doesn't speak either. She doesn't need to.

The boy in the hoodie flips his sketchbook to another page and lowers it and, slowly, turns it around. A pencil drawing of her, her scarf, her eyes, even the slight curve of her lips, reminding her of what she looked like before the moment she broke. It's stunning. Too much. She presses her hand to her chest. The boy tears the page out and hands it to her.

Across the aisle, the man with the headphones pauses his music.

The man with the notebook looks up. "I'm sorry for your loss," he says softly. She is not sure how he knew that, but he does. And just like that, the train is different.

The air shifts. It's still quiet, yes, but the silence isn't as sharp anymore. It's softer. Warmer. Held together by small, invisible threads between strangers.

Evelyn exhales. Not all the pain leaves, but some of it lifts. For the first time in years, she feels something stir in her chest that isn't sorrowful.

Hope, maybe. Or the faint outline of it. The train rolls forward. And for once, she doesn't feel alone.

Chapter 7 – The Ripple

The subway rolls into its final stop like it does every morning, brakes squealing, lights flickering overhead.

But something is different today.

It isn't loud. It isn't apparent. There's no applause. No grand declarations. Just a ripple, a soft change in the current, like wind over still water.

A moment of shared humanity that lingers after the doors open.

Claire (The Observer)

She remains in her seat after the others file out, her gaze no longer fixed on the window.

Back home, she sits at the kitchen table remembering all of them deeply, their familiar faces and the unique aspects of each one of them. Today was different, and soon things will change for them again.

Marco (The Music Man)

The melody of *"Mad World"* no longer loops in his ears as he pushes through the office doors. The music is different now, a variety giving hope and inspiration.

He opens a spreadsheet and stares at it. Then closes it again.

In a moment of hesitation or courage, he opens a browser tab and searches "inexpensive keyboards."

He hasn't played in years. But maybe he's allowed to start again.

Jaden (The Ghost Boy)

He doesn't take the train all the way home. Gets off two stops early and walks the long way.

The sketchbook in his hand feels different. He runs his fingers over the drawing he gave the older woman, the one who tried to hide her cry but didn't.

He didn't expect her to thank him with her eyes, or for her tears to make him feel *seen*, but both happened.

That night, he adds color to one of his drawings for the first time in a long time.

He picks orange, the color of a new day's sunrise.

Amina (The Quiet Lady)

She returns home, kicks off her shoes, and sits at the small table by the window. She stares at her phone. Her son's name is still pinned at the top of her messages.

Her thumb hovers. She doesn't have the right words. But maybe she doesn't need them.

She types:

Hi. Just wondering how you've been. I'd love to talk sometime. No pressure.

She sends it, then she begins to breathe again.

Connor (The Man with the Notebook)

He walks Emma to school, hand in hand, same as always. But something in him feels lighter.

At the door, she turns and asks, "Can you write me a story with me in space, Daddy?"

He nods. "Only if you're the captain."

Later, on the train ride back, he opens his notebook and titles the next   story:

"Captain Emma and the Stardust Widow."

He doesn't cry. Not this time.

Evelyn (The Old Woman)

At home, she unfolds the letter and reads it one last time. Then, with a steady hand, she adds the final line:

I miss you, but today… I felt less alone.

She walks to the park bench, the one she and Daniel claimed every spring.

She leaves the letter under the armrest, held down by a smooth stone.

She doesn't look back as she walks away.

Chapter 8 – The Boy Speaks

Jaden, 17, The Ghost Boy

The sketch is carefully folded in thirds and tucked inside the cover of his notebook, like a secret.

Jaden didn't sleep last night, not really. He stared at the ceiling and thought about the older woman's eyes after he showed her the drawing. About how they didn't just cry, they *changed*. As if, for a moment, she remembered she wasn't made of glass.

He boards the train two stops early. Just to be sure. To make sure she's there. Third car. Middle section. Window seat.

She is. Her scarf is a different color today, deep blue, almost ink-black. Her eyes look clearer. Less folded in on themselves. She watches the window, the tracks, the people. She notices things as he does.

He takes his usual seat across from her, not quite facing her. His hands tremble a little, but he doesn't let himself stop. He pulls the folded paper out of his notebook. Waits until the train jerks forward.

The car isn't crowded yet. The lady with the poetry book isn't on yet. The man with the headphones has earbuds in, head leaned back, listening to something different. The lady by the window is watching quietly.

No one says anything. Jaden steps forward and holds out the sketch. The woman by the window blinks. Her fingers brush his as she takes it. She unfolds it slowly. Her mouth opens, but nothing comes out.

"I thought…" he says, voice cracking. "You looked like you needed to be remembered."

It's the first sentence he's spoken out loud in years. Claire looks up at him, hand to her heart. Then she does something that breaks him. She stands and hugs him.

It's awkward. Too tight. A little shaky. But real. Warm. Solid. Not something drawn, not something imagined.

Jaden freezes. Then slowly, hesitantly, he lets himself lean into it. The train sways beneath them, but he doesn't care. When she lets go, he doesn't say anything else. He nods and returns to his seat.

No earbuds. No sketchbook. He sits and breathes. Across the aisle, Claire smiles softly to herself.

A few stops later, Amina boards. Her poetry book is gone. She meets his eyes. They both nod. No words, but it's enough. The silence has changed. It's no longer the kind that hides pain.

Chapter 9 – The Stranger's Smile

Marco, 34, The Music Man

The same song starts again. But today, Marco turns the volume down.

Not off. Just lower. Just enough to hear the train's hum beneath the piano. The metallic rattle. The faint murmur of passengers breathing in rhythm. It's not a conscious choice, really; it just *happens*.

He boards at the usual time. Third car. Middle door. Left side. But for the first time in… he doesn't know how long… he hesitates.

The teenage boy in a hoodie, sitting upright, sketchbook closed on his lap. Not hiding in his sketchbook. Marco pauses, thinking the boy is different in some way.

Then he sees her, the woman with the scarf by the window. The one who watches everything as it matters. She's in her usual spot by the window; hands folded neatly over a worn book he hadn't noticed before. She meets his gaze, and she *smiles*.

Not wide. Not dramatic. Just a small, human thing. A smile that says, *I see you, and I remember you.*

Marco doesn't know what to do with it. So, he smiles back. It's awkward. Half a twitch, more with his eyes than his mouth. But it's the first one he's meant in weeks.

He finds a seat nearby. The train starts to move.

The headphones are gone, and he wears his new earbuds, but the music fades into the background as his mind lingers on yesterday, the older woman crying, the boy handing her the sketch, the way everyone *saw it happen,* but no one turned away. No one pretended it didn't matter.

And maybe, Marco thinks, *that's* the thing that matters.

He reaches into his coat pocket and pulls out his phone. Opens the same email app. Scrolls past the work messages, past the newsletter subscriptions, past the promotional trash. Opens a blank draft.

To: *himself.*

Bought a keyboard. Should be here Thursday.

He smiles again.

Across from him, the woman by the window is watching. Not in a creepy way, just soft, steady. The kind of watching that makes people feel less alone.

Marco sits down, lets the music fade completely, and watches the tunnel blur past with a strange sense of peace.

One stop early, he gets off. To walk. To feel the city again. To remember that it's not all spreadsheets and bottled-up sighs.

He breathes deep. Then he pulls out his phone again. Searches: *"How to play piano again after 15 years."* And clicks the first video.

Chapter 10 – The Handwritten Poem

Amina, 43, The Quiet Lady

The train is half-full when Amina boards. She's running late; the shift went long. A patient coded, came back, and coded again. Death hovered, indecisive. She left before it made up its mind.

She carries no book today. No poetry to retreat into. Tucked inside her coat pocket is her phone with the response from her son, one short text, twelve words:

I've been okay. I'm glad you reached out, Mom. Let's talk soon.

She's read it at least twenty times. She doesn't need to anymore; it lives in her now, but she will still read it many more times.

As she moves to sit, her eye catches something unusual, something folded and carefully placed on the seat next to hers. A single sheet of paper. Cream-colored with worn edges. Ink faded just enough to make it feel… lived in.

She hesitates and looks around, but no one seems to claim it. She picks it up and unfolds it gently. It is a handwritten poem. Not a famous one copied from a book. Something original. Something someone *felt*.

The silence on the train is not empty,
It's full of things we don't say.
Grief clings to coats like static.
Love hides in folded napkins and nods.
We are strangers, yes.
But only for now.

Amina stares at it.

Her chest tightens, not in the way it does at the end of a brutal shift, but in a way she can't name, like her heart recognizes something her mind hasn't caught up to.

She looks across the aisle, and the woman by the window is watching her. There's a softness in her expression, a hint of knowing. Amina folds the paper again. Gently. Almost reverently. She slides it into her pocket.

Later that night, after another long shift, Amina returns home. She sits at her kitchen table, tired but not numb, not tonight. She opens a fresh notebook, one she bought last month and never used, and begins to write, not about bloodwork, or procedures, or regrets, but about the train.

About strangers who cry and boys who draw and poems left like seeds between the cracks of the world. She doesn't know who wrote the one she found, but she knows it meant something. And tonight, she decides she will finally write one of her own.

Chapter 11 – The Morning After

Claire, The Absent Observer

The train arrives at 6:42 a.m.

Third car. Middle section. Window seat, second row from the back.

Empty.

No scarf today. No gentle nod. No folded hands or thoughtful eyes watching the world pass by.

Just a vacant space where Claire always sat.

No one says anything. Of course they don't.

But they *notice*.

Marco

He boards with his earbuds in but doesn't play music. Not right away. He glances toward the window seat and frowns, just slightly. Checks the time, as if maybe she's running late.

When the train starts to move, he finally presses play, but the volume stays low. Almost respectful.

Jaden

He opens his sketchbook. The page he planned to start stays blank. Instead, he flips back to the portrait he drew of Claire last week. Adds shading around her eyes. She always carried a softness. He doesn't show anyone, but he holds it as if it matters.

Evelyn

Evelyn settles into her usual seat, smoothing her skirt, ready to fold and unfold her thoughts the way she always does. But something feels off before she even realizes why.

The window seat is empty. The woman with the soft eyes and the quiet watchfulness isn't there. Evelyn waits for a moment, as if the woman by the window might appear late, scarf trailing behind her, but the train doors close and the space remains hollow. She feels a slight ache in her chest, unexpected but familiar.

Amina

She clutches her notebook now and writes in it every morning. Today, she pens just one sentence:

The woman in the window seat didn't come today, and I miss her. She then begins to work on a new poem about the woman by the window.

Connor

He notices immediately. He flips to a page in his notebook marked *Familiar Faces.*

Beneath a short story about a woman who saw everything, he adds a new line: *Absence isn't silence. It's a different kind of presence.* He reads it twice. Then smiles, just barely.

The train rolls on.

People come and go. The doors open and then close again. Conversations are absent, as usual. But the air feels changed, tilted just slightly, as though the universe has made room for a missing piece.

And somewhere on that ride, in the space between one stop and the next, every passenger who's shared that third car, middle section, morning after morning, feels the same quiet thing:

Someone is gone, and it matters.

Chapter 12 – The Window Seat

The train arrives on time. 6:42 a.m. Same metal groan. Same doors sighing open. Same rhythm. Third car. Middle section. Second row from the back. The window seat is still empty.

Marco

He stands near the seat for a long moment, coffee in one hand, phone in the other. He nods toward it, just once, and sits across instead. He adds a new lyric to his phone:

"She saw the world, so we didn't have to look away." He doesn't hit save. Just leaves it open.

Jaden

He leaves something behind when he exits, a sketch. Claire's face, drawn in delicate pencil lines, eyes focused on something just out of frame. Beneath it, he writes: *"The woman who watched."* He folds it in half and tucks it between the seat and the wall. Not hidden. Just waiting.

Amina

She touches the seat as she passes, almost like a prayer. In her notebook, she copies yesterday's poem, the one she found, the one she believes Claire wrote. Then she writes another underneath it:

We carry her in our stillness now.

She signs it: *– A Fellow Passenger.*

Evelyn

Evelyn pauses when she steps into the car, her gaze drifting automatically to the familiar window seat. Still empty. Still waiting. She presses her lips together, not in sadness exactly, but in recognition absence settling into something steadier, something she can carry without breaking.

Connor

He takes the seat for a moment, just a moment long enough to place a flower on the window ledge. A daisy. Simple. White. His daughter helped him pick it. He whispers something that no one hears, then returns to his spot by the aisle and begins a new story. The title: "The Woman by the Window."

The train moves forward, and though the silence remains, it is no longer the silence of strangers. It's the silence of understanding. Of people who saw one another in the spaces between glances. In gestures, in grief, and in humanity.

They don't know if the woman by the window will return. Maybe she's just sick, or she moved, but they all feel that she won't be back, but it doesn't matter. Because now they know what it means to be *seen*. To feel less alone in a world too fast, too cold, too distracted to care.

Because of her, the window seat is no longer just a place to sit. It's a memory, it's a marker, it's a beginning.

The world is still mad, but not as lonely as it was before.

Author's Note

The seed of *Familiar Faces* was planted the first time I heard Gary Jules' cover of "Mad World."

Something about that song, the slow, aching piano, the fragile vocals, the lyrics that quietly unravel despair and isolation, stuck with me. Every line felt like a window into someone else's sadness. The kind people carry on the bus, or in elevators, or sit alone at lunch. The kind we hide behind routines and polite nods.

"All around me are familiar faces... Worn-out places, worn-out faces..."

That lyric haunted me.

I began to wonder about the people we see every day but never *really* see. The strangers we pass in silence, the ones sitting next to us on the train or across from us in waiting rooms. What are they going through? What would happen if the invisible lines between us were crossed, even for a moment?

Familiar Faces is my attempt to bring that question to life.

This story is meant to feel like a whispered conversation amid a noisy world. It's about grief, routine, silence, small kindness, and what happens when people begin to look up and notice each other.

For anyone who's ever felt unseen in a crowded room, or who has smiled through the pain no matter the cost, or who has ever heard *Mad World* and quietly nodded along with understanding, this story is for you.

—Brett C. Persson

The Edge of the City

Chapter 1

The diner was almost empty, the way it always was after ten. The hum of the soda machine filled the silence, broken now and then by the clink of silverware in the kitchen. Outside, the parking lot glowed under two flickering streetlights, the rest fading into darkness.

Casey wiped down the counter with slow circles, her rag catching on the cracks in the old laminate. She'd been on her feet for twelve hours, but her body had gotten used to that kind of ache. The smell of coffee, burnt from sitting too long, hung in the air.

Liam sat on one of the stools, a half-eaten slice of pie in front of him. His black hoodie was faded at the elbows, and his hands were smudged with pencil lead from the small sketchbook he carried everywhere. He looked up from his drawing and gave a little smile.

"You ever think about leaving this place?" he asked, like he was asking about the weather.

Casey glanced out the window, past her reflection in the glass, to where his old car sat alone in the lot. The thought of it made her chest feel tight, like wanting something too much could hurt.

"All the time," she said. Her voice was quiet, almost lost under the hiss of the coffee machine.

He nodded, like her answer didn't surprise him. "If I had enough saved up, I'd just... go. Tonight. No goodbyes."

Casey didn't answer right away. She thought about the peeling paint on her father's front porch, the way the house smelled like beer, the sound of his cough echoing through the thin walls. She thought about her tips tonight, small, crumpled bills in her apron pocket, and how far they wouldn't take her.

But she also thought about the open road she'd only seen in movies. The way streetlights might blur into stars if you drove fast enough.

"Yeah," she said finally, with a slight smile that felt both real and impossible. "Me too."

Outside, a truck rumbled past, its headlights washing the diner in a brief, golden glow. For a moment, the place didn't look so worn down. For a moment, it looked like it could be the start of something.

Chapter 2

Casey's street was darker than the diner parking lot. The only light came from the TV's pale glow through the front window. She climbed the porch steps, careful to skip the third one, which squeaked loud enough to wake the dead.

Inside, the air was heavy with the smell of stale beer and cigarette smoke. Her father was on the couch, shoes still on, his head tipped back, mouth slightly open. An empty can was balanced on the armrest beside him, ready to fall.

Casey closed the door softly, her eyes adjusting to the dim light. The news flickered across the screen, voices low and distant, talking about a storm somewhere far away. She set her purse down on the kitchen counter, the jingling of coins in her apron pocket sounding too loud in the stillness.

She walked over and took the can from his hand before it spilled, setting it on the coffee table with the others. For a moment, she just stood there, looking at him, his jaw unshaven, his work shirt wrinkled from the night before. The man she remembered from when she was little, who used to take her to the park on Sundays, was buried somewhere deep inside.

Reaching for the blanket draped over the back of the couch, she shook it out and laid it over him. He stirred, mumbling something she couldn't understand, then went still again.

In the kitchen, Casey opened the fridge. A half-empty carton of milk, a pack of cheap lunch meat, a jar of mustard. She took the milk and smelled it, still good. She poured a glass, drank it standing up, and stared at the calendar on the wall. The same picture of a lighthouse had been hanging there for three months because no one had bothered to flip it.

Her tips from the night felt heavy in her pocket. She knew exactly how much she had. She also knew how quickly it could vanish, to the gas bill, to groceries, to whatever mess her father got himself into next.

Upstairs, in her small bedroom, she sat on the edge of the bed and looked out the window. The street was quiet. Somewhere out there, Liam's old car sat in the diner lot, waiting for morning. She wondered what it would feel like to get in and go.

Chapter 3

The night was cooler than usual, the air carrying that faint smell of rain even though the sky was clear. Casey slid into the passenger seat of Liam's car, the old vinyl creaking under her weight. The dashboard was cracked in places, but the heater hummed softly, warming the small space.

They sat in the glow of the streetlight; the world outside was just shapes and shadows. Liam leaned back in his seat, his hands resting loosely on the steering wheel. The faint sound of a guitar came from the speakers, a slow, steady rhythm that filled the quiet without pushing it away.

"Figured you'd be asleep by now," he said.

"I couldn't," Casey replied. She didn't explain why.

Liam reached over to the glove compartment, pulling out his sketchbook. He flipped to a page showing a rough drawing of a coastline, waves curling toward a shore lined with tall grass.

"This is where I'd go first," he said, tapping the page. "Somewhere with the ocean. You can start over when the horizon's that big."

Casey smiled faintly, tracing the lines with her eyes. "Never seen the ocean," she admitted.

He glanced at her, a little surprised. "You'd like it."

They fell into silence again, the song on the radio fading into another. Casey looked out the windshield, imagining the highway stretching ahead of them, mile after mile. She pictured small towns blurring past, the lights of gas stations and diners fading in the rearview mirror.

"You think it's really that easy?" she asked. "Just… leave?"

Liam shrugged. "Might not be easy. But it's better than staying somewhere you don't want to be."

Casey turned the thought over in her mind. She could see it so clearly in that moment, his hand on the gearshift, her head leaned back against the seat, the hum of tires on asphalt carrying them somewhere far enough away that nothing could follow.

Outside, a gust of wind sent leaves tumbling across the lot, catching in the light before vanishing into the dark.

Chapter 4

Casey came home late from another shift, the night still clinging to her coat. She could tell something was wrong before she even reached the porch. A police car sat out front, its lights off, but the blue-and-white paint seemed to glow under the streetlamp.

Two officers stood by the door, their voices low. One of them turned when she stepped onto the curb.

"Are you, Casey Miller?" he asked.

She nodded, her stomach tightening.

"It's your father," the officer said. "Got into a fight outside Murphy's Bar. Disorderly conduct, resisting arrest." He paused like he was waiting for her to react, but she just stared at the porch steps.

"He's at the station. Bail's two hundred." The officer said.

Two hundred. It was everything she'd earned this week. She didn't argue, didn't ask questions. Just said she'd be there in twenty minutes.

At the station, she signed her name on the paperwork and handed over the bills, small, worn, and folded from her apron pocket. The clerk counted them twice, then slid the form back toward her.

When her father came through the door, he smelled like beer and cheap cologne, his eyes glassy.

"Thanks, kid," he muttered, not quite meeting her eyes.

The ride home was quiet except for the sound of his cough. Once inside, he dropped onto the couch and reached for the remote, as nothing had happened.

Casey stood there for a moment; her fists curled in her coat pockets. Something inside her felt hollow, scraped clean. She wasn't angry, not in the way that burned hot. This was colder, heavier.

She went upstairs, shut her bedroom door, and sat on the edge of the bed. Outside her window, the street was still. She thought about Liam's car in the diner lot, the sketch of the ocean, the hum of the heater.

Casey reached for her phone and sent a single message: Pick me up. She set the phone down and quickly stuffed a duffel bag full of some clothes and personal items she wanted.

Chapter 5

Liam's car pulled up ten minutes later, headlights cutting across the dark street. Casey was already on the porch, coat zipped, the duffel bag slung over her shoulder.

Liam leaned over and pushed the passenger door open. "You sure?" he asked. His voice wasn't teasing this time.

She nodded once, climbed in, and closed the door.

They didn't speak as he pulled away, the tires crunching over loose gravel. The houses slid past, porches sagging, windows glowing dimly, a few dogs barking as the car rolled by. Casey kept her eyes forward, not looking back at the narrow strip of light spilling from her bedroom window.

The radio was low, just a faint hum beneath the engine's sound. Liam's hands stayed steady on the wheel, eyes fixed on the road ahead.

They crossed the old bridge on the edge of town, the wooden planks rattling under the tires. Beyond it, the road opened into a long, black ribbon lit only by the twin beams of their headlights.

Casey rested her head against the cool glass of the window. Every mile felt lighter, like each turn of the tires was pulling a thread loose inside her.

"You got anywhere in mind?" Liam asked after a while.

"No," she said. "Just... away."

He smiled faintly at that, the corner of his mouth curving in the dark.

A green highway sign flashed by, names of cities neither of them had been to, numbers counting down miles.

Casey imagined the lines on the road stretching all the way to the ocean he'd drawn in his sketchbook. She didn't know if they'd ever get there, but for the first time in a long time, the idea didn't feel impossible.

The car moved on, swallowed by the dark, leaving only the hum of the engine and the quiet hope hanging between them.

Chapter 6

By the second day, the air in the car smelled like takeout wrappers and the faint scent of gasoline from the old engine. Casey and Liam had been trading shifts behind the wheel, stopping only for gas and whatever food they could get fast and cheap.

The first night, it had felt like freedom, windows cracked, music drifting out into the dark, the two of them laughing at nothing. But by now, the hum of the tires had turned into a low, steady reminder: they were running on less than half a tank, and the wad of bills in Casey's purse was thinner than she wanted to admit.

They pulled into a small town in the late afternoon, and the sun was low enough to paint the brick buildings gold. Liam parked near a faded motel sign that buzzed faintly in the quiet.

"This place is cheap," he said, glancing toward the office.

Casey dug through her purse, counting out the bills. "We can afford one night. After that... I don't know."

Liam leaned back in his seat, tapping the steering wheel with his fingers. "We'll figure it out."
She didn't answer.

Inside the room, the carpet smelled faintly of bleach, and the bedspread was stiff from too many washes. Casey dropped onto the mattress, staring at the ceiling fan spinning slow circles. She thought about the lighthouse calendar at home, how it hadn't changed in months. She thought about how far away the ocean still was.

When Liam came back from the vending machine with two sodas and a bag of chips, he tossed them on the bed between them.

"We just need a plan," he said. "I can find work, construction, maybe. You could wait tables again."

Casey took a sip of soda, the carbonation burning her throat. "Feels like we left just to end up right where we started."

Liam looked at her, something unreadable in his eyes. "Maybe. But at least it's not there."

She didn't argue. She wasn't sure if he was right or if he just needed her to believe he was.

Outside, a train passed in the distance, its whistle carrying long and low through the twilight. It sounded like it was going somewhere farther than they could afford to go.

Chapter 7

By the fourth day, the road had thinned to two lanes, cutting through flat land and stretches of pine. The air felt different here, cooler, touched with salt. Casey could smell it before she saw the water.

Liam's car rolled over a small rise, and suddenly the horizon opened into endless blue. The ocean spread out under a pale sky, waves curling white where they met the shore. Casey leaned forward, hands on the dashboard, as if getting closer might make it feel real.

They stopped at a gas station on the edge of a coastal town. The place was small, two pumps, a dusty window full of faded postcards, the faint hum of an old soda cooler inside. While Liam filled the tank, Casey wandered toward the road, drawn by the sound of the waves.

A short walk brought her to a weathered fence, the ocean just beyond. The air was sharp and clean, tasting like something she'd been missing without knowing it. She gripped the top rail, staring at the horizon, the wind pulling at her hair.

Behind her, she could hear Liam calling, "We can keep going south if you want. Warmer there. Cheaper, too."
She didn't answer right away.

It would be easy to get back in the car, to let the road carry them until the money ran out again. Maybe they'd find a place where they could stick, jobs, a cheap apartment, something that felt like a fresh start. Or perhaps they'd keep moving, chasing an idea that was always a little farther down the highway.

Casey took a deep breath, the ocean air filling her lungs. She thought about the diner's hum at night, the smell of burnt coffee, the hollow quiet of her father's house. She thought about Liam's sketch of the shore and how, for once, she was standing in it.

When she turned back, Liam was leaning against the car, one hand shading his eyes from the sun. "I think we might stay here for a while," she said when she reached him.

He studied her for a moment, then nodded. "We can do that."

"I think we can make this work." Casey said, "I finally feel free."

Liam smiled, "That's because we are. This is our life now, we live for us and no one else. This is our time, our life."

They took each other's hands and turned toward the ocean, letting the sound of the waves swallow the rest, both knowing they were going to be just fine.

Authors Note

This story was born out of a late-night listen to Tracy Chapman's *Fast Car*. I've heard the song more times than I can count, but that night it hit differently. It wasn't just the melody; it was the ache in her voice, the way the lyrics carried both hope and heartbreak in the same breath.

I wanted to capture that feeling of being caught between where you are and where you want to be, of dreaming about escape without knowing what you'll find on the other side. For me, *Fast Car* isn't just about driving away, it's about the quiet courage it takes to believe there's something better out there, even when you've never seen it.

Casey and Liam aren't the people in Chapman's song, but they carry that same restless hunger. They're chasing something they can't quite name, caught in the space between running from and running toward.

Writing their journey reminded me that sometimes leaving is only the first step, and that the harder part is deciding what to do when you finally arrive.

—Brett C. Persson

Where the Light Didn't Reach

You wake before the day commits to being morning. The room smells used, old fabric, dust, your own breath lingering too long in the air. Nothing fresh. Nothing rotting. Just spent. You sit up because staying down feels like consent. The mattress releases you with a tired sigh, as if relieved to be done holding you.

Light slips through the blinds in thin gray bands. It doesn't fill the room. It marks it. Dust drifts lazily through the narrow beams, unhurried, as if time itself has slowed to accommodate the quiet. You stand. The floor is cold. Your joints register it without complaint. You don't stretch. There's no need to prepare for anything.

The quiet doesn't lift when you move. It adjusts.

In the bathroom, the light clicks on and hums faintly. The mirror is fogged. You splash water on your face, cold and abrupt, then drag your palm across the glass. Your reflection appears in fragments before settling. Your face looks intact. Older. Thinner around the eyes. You brush your teeth. The mint cuts sharply across your tongue. The sound is too loud in the small room, a small violence you can't avoid. You watch yourself spit, rinse, repeat. There's no satisfaction in finishing, just completion. The mirror doesn't react. It doesn't accuse or reassure. It shows what's left. You turn off the light before leaving, as if darkness might undo what you just saw.

The kitchen smells like yesterday. You make coffee and take one sip. Bitter. Metallic. You leave the mug on the counter. Steam fades quickly. The house makes its small sounds, pipes ticking, wood shifting. You move quietly, not out of politeness but habit. Noise feels wasteful, like a resource you've already used too much of.

In the living room, the couch bears the shallow impression of repeated use. The fabric is worn smooth there, dulled by evenings that never resolved into anything memorable. A child's drawing hangs crooked on the wall. The paper has yellowed. The colors hold, dulled but intact, stubborn in a way you aren't. You don't touch it. Touching would make it real, and real would require something from you.

The study is dimmer. The light thins again, filtered through blinds that never quite open all the way. Dust floats in the narrow beam. You stop at the desk. Your hand rests on the drawer longer than necessary. The wood is warm from the room, scratched from years of use. The drawer sticks when you pull it open. The sound lands hard in the quiet, louder than it should be, and for a moment, you wait to see if the house will object.

It doesn't.

Inside, the gun waits. Clean. Familiar. Uninterested in ceremony.

You lift it. The weight settles into your hand without surprise. Not heavy enough to feel dangerous. Not light enough to feel trivial. The metal is cool, the cool that doesn't change no matter how long you hold it. You close the drawer with your foot. It slides shut quietly this time, cooperative, as if it understands its part is done.

At the table, you set the gun down. The wood creaks faintly, a small protest that goes unanswered. You sit across from it, hands on your thighs, posture careful. The room feels smaller now. Not visibly. Just closer. The air thickens, loses some of its give.

You don't rush.

This isn't impulse. Impulse would have been easier to explain later, easier to regret in the way people understand. This feels more like accounting, numbers checked twice, errors acknowledged but ignored when they don't change the outcome.

You consider the space you take up. The way conversations soften when you enter them, edges rounded off in anticipation. The effort people spend pretending not to notice how tired you are, how distant, how often you trail off mid-thought. You think of roles, father, husband, words that arrive stripped of warmth, labels that no longer attach cleanly to anything living.

You frame it as subtraction. One less weight. One less adjustment others have to make. The logic holds because it's quiet. It doesn't argue. It doesn't ask you to imagine a future that feels hypothetical at best.

You lean forward. The smell of metal sharpens, clean and unforgiving. The numbers don't align perfectly. They never do. They don't need to.

The bullet changes the room.

The sound is slight. Precise. It echoes longer than expected, bouncing once, twice, then settling into a heavier silence. Your ears ring faintly, a thin, persistent note that makes the quiet feel crowded. You notice your breathing, shallow, controlled, measured as if depth might invite complication.

This is where fear should arrive.

It doesn't.

The absence of it settles in your chest, heavier than panic would have been. Your finger hovers where it shouldn't be. Not on it. Near it. You stay there, suspended, long enough for the position to feel normal.

Time loses its edges. Seconds stretch, then blur. The room presses closer, the air warm and used, already cycled too many times. Your heartbeat becomes audible, steady, and unhurried, a metronome you didn't ask for. You stare at a chip in the wall. You don't remember when it appeared. You imagine it's been there longer than you have, enduring without explanation.

You imagine the room without you in it. The chair empty, the table cleared eventually by someone who won't know how long things sat there untouched. The house continuing its small routines. The thought doesn't comfort you. It organizes things.

The phone rests on the table, dark. You hadn't noticed it until now.

Then it buzzes.

The sound cuts through the room, sharp and invasive. You flinch before you mean to. You let it stop. The silence rushes back in, thicker, offended by the interruption.

It buzzes again.

Longer this time. Insistent.

You pick up the phone. It feels heavier than it should, not in your hand but in your attention, the screen lights.

Dad, can we talk later today?

You read it once. Then again.

There's no urgency in it. That's the problem. Just an assumption, quiet, untested confidence that there will still be a later. That time hasn't already narrowed itself down to this room, this table, this arrangement of objects.

The gun stays where it is. The phone stays in your hand. For the first time, the certainty you've been building feels brittle, like something that might fracture if pressed too hard. You don't reply. Replying would require deciding what kind of 'later' you're agreeing to.

You set the gun down. Carefully. The sound it makes against the table feels too loud, though it isn't; your breath fractures. Your shoulders tighten. No sound comes out. This isn't hope. It's an interruption, an unplanned pause in a sequence that was otherwise moving cleanly toward completion.

You place the phone face down beside the gun. The space between them is small. Smaller than it should be. Your hands shake now, finally catching up to the effort it took to stop. You let them. You stay seated, long enough for the shaking to dull into something manageable.

You don't go to the window.

You remain where you are, hands on the table. The marks they leave fade as you watch, darkening and then disappearing, evidence that refuses to stay. Light shifts somewhere behind you. The phone stays face down. Silent. The gun doesn't move. Your breathing slows too much. You correct it. In. Out.

The house resumes its small sounds. Pipes tick. Wood settles. Something switches off automatically, a system correcting itself without instruction. You don't look at the clock. This moment doesn't sharpen into meaning. It flattens, blending into the others.

You stand.

Not with purpose. Not suddenly. Just enough to change position.

You leave the room without touching the table, without closing the door. The chair stays pulled out. The objects remain precisely where you left them.

The day continues.

Author's Note

Where the Light Didn't Reach began as a short film created for a film class. The original work was built around stillness, limited space, and a single character, relying on silence and interruption rather than resolution. When adapting the film into prose, I wanted to preserve that restraint while exploring what the story's interior might reveal.

This adaptation marked my first time writing in the second-person point of view. That choice was intentional. I was interested in removing narrative distance and allowing the reader to inhabit the moment directly, without commentary or reassurance. The second person felt closest to the camera's fixed gaze in the film, present, unblinking, and unwilling to soften what unfolds.

Rather than expanding the story toward explanation or recovery, this version remains focused on pause, delay, and continuation. The adaptation was less about translating images into words and more about finding a prose equivalent for what the film left unsaid.

—Brett C. Persson

The Wind Takes All Things

Chapter I

Daniel had never liked silence, but the silence in the house today felt sharp, like broken glass on the floor. It cut into him every time he breathed. He stood in the middle of the living room, holding the small wooden box that contained everything left of his wife.

The box felt too light. Too easy to lift. A whole life shouldn't weigh so little. He ran his thumb across the carved lid, tracing the lines he had memorized in the past year. Every time he touched the box, it felt as if time folded in on itself, pulling him back to the moment he watched Mara's chest rise and fall for the last time. He had held her hand until it grew cold. He had whispered words he could barely remember now. And then someone had taken her away. Now she sat on a shelf, quiet as dust.

Daniel took a shaky breath. The room was dim, even though it was only late afternoon. He hadn't opened the curtains in weeks. He didn't want the light to come in, didn't want the world to keep going when Mara had stopped.
Behind him, the floor creaked.

Holly stood in the hallway; her dark hair tangled from sleep she never seemed to get anymore. Her face held too many expressions at once: anger, sadness, confusion, and fear. Because in the past year, Daniel had just lost his wife. Holly, on the other hand, lost her mother and, in many ways, her father, too.

She stared at the box in his hands. "Why are you holding it?" Her voice was flat, but Daniel heard the tremor underneath.

He opened his mouth, but the words were trapped behind the same wall he'd built since the funeral. Instead, he lifted the box slightly and said, "We need to let her go."

Holly's eyes flashed. "We already did."

"No." He shook his head, clutching the box tighter. "We didn't. We just… stopped talking about her. Stopped talking about everything."

"That was your choice," Holly whispered.

Daniel felt those words hit him like a punch. She was right. After Mara died, he had folded into himself like a closing door. Every time Holly tried to talk, his grief had crushed his voice. He had told himself he was protecting her by staying strong, but all he had done was disappear into silence.

He looked at the box again, then at his daughter. "We should scatter her ashes. At the places she loved. Before… before the anniversary comes."

Holly took a slow step forward. "Why now?"
Daniel thought he knew the reasons why, because I'm afraid I'll never be able to say goodbye. Because I can't breathe in this house anymore. Because I'm scared, you'll grow up remembering me as a ghost.
None of the words made it from his throat to his mouth.

"Because she deserves it," Daniel said instead. "And because we can't keep hiding from her memory."

Holly turned her head away, and for a moment, he thought she would refuse. But then she wiped at her eyes and whispered, "Fine."

Daniel nodded, though the simple word carved a deep line of guilt into his chest. Holly wasn't going because she wanted to. She was going because she didn't trust him not to break without her.

He placed the box gently on the table and went to gather their coats. The wind outside slammed against the house, rattling the windows like something alive and angry. It felt like the world was telling them to move. Or warning them about what might happen if they didn't.

When Daniel returned, Holly was still staring at the box. Not with anger. Not with fear. Just with a kind of hollow sadness that made her look older than she was.

"It's so small," she whispered. "Too small."

"I know," Daniel said softly.

They stood there for a long moment, two people with one loss between them, a loss too significant for either of them to carry alone.

Outside, the wind howled across the yard, lifting dust and dead leaves into the air. It scraped against the side like fingernails dragging along a door.

Chapter II

The next morning, the sun rose slowly and colorlessly, as if the sun wasn't sure it wanted to take part in the day. A thin fog crawled along the street, clinging to mailboxes and front lawns like it didn't want to let go.

Daniel loaded the trunk while the wind whipped at his jacket. The air was sharp, cold enough to sting. Each slam of the trunk echoed louder than it should have, bouncing off the quiet houses around them.

Inside the car, Holly sat stiffly in the passenger seat. Her backpack lay at her feet, untouched. She stared at the dashboard as if it were the only solid thing in the world.

Daniel opened the back door and gently set Mara's ashes on the seat. The wooden box creaked when it touched the fabric, a small, tired sound like something old waking up.
Holly flinched at the noise.

Daniel closed the door softly, almost like he was afraid of disturbing whatever was left of his wife inside the box. When he got in the driver's seat, the air between them felt even colder than the wind outside.

Daniel buckled his seatbelt. "Ready?" he asked.

Holly didn't look at him. "Does it matter?"

Daniel gripped the steering wheel. "It matters to me."

She let out a humorless laugh. "Since when?"

The words sank deep, heavy as stones. He didn't argue. He didn't defend himself. He just turned the key, and the engine buzzed to life.

As they pulled away from the house, the fog shifted in the rearview mirror, swallowing the doorway, the windows, the home they had stopped calling home months ago. It looked like the mist was erasing it, piece by piece.

Maybe that was for the best.

On the Road for the first few miles, they said nothing, not a word, not even a sigh. The highway stretched ahead like a long scar carved into the earth. The wind blew across the fields in harsh, uneven gusts, bending the tall grass low. It almost looked like the land was bowing to something they couldn't see.

Finally, Holly broke the silence, "Where's the first stop?"

Daniel kept his eyes forward. "Red Bluff."

She pressed her forehead against the window. "She used to take me there when I was little. I barely remember it."

"She loved it," Daniel said.

"She loved a lot of things," Holly muttered. "Didn't stop any of this from happening."

Daniel felt a sharp twist in his stomach. "Holly…"

"No," she said, shaking her head. "I don't want comfort. I want answers."

He swallowed. "So do I."

A truck roared past them, sending a violent burst of wind against their car. The vehicle shuddered and drifted slightly. Holly gasped and grabbed the door handle.

"Sorry," Daniel said quickly. "The wind…"

"It's fine," she snapped, cutting him off. However, her hand stayed tight on the handle.

He could see her reflection in the window, her eyes wide, her jaw clenched. She looked like a person bracing for an impact.

"We don't... we don't have to talk right now," Daniel offered.

She snorted. "We haven't talked in a year. Why start now?"

He opened his mouth, but she kept going.

"You think this road trip is going to fix everything? Like scattering ashes across a bunch of places is suddenly going to make us... normal again?"

"It's not about normal," he whispered. "It's about letting your mom rest."

"And what about us?" Holly asked, voice cracking. "When do we get to rest?"

Daniel's breath caught. He didn't have an answer. He hadn't rested since the night Mara died, just existed in a fog, waiting for something to change.

"I don't know," he said finally. "But maybe this is a start."

Dark clouds thickened on the horizon, rolling in like bruises across the sky. Gusts of wind grew stronger, pushing against the car in angry bursts.

"Storm's coming," Holly said quietly.

Daniel nodded. "Yeah."

"It's heading the same direction we are." Holly noticed.

Daniel glanced at her. "So, we'll face it, together."

Holly stared at him for a long moment, searching his face. "You really think we can handle it?" She meant more than just the storm.

He didn't lie. "I think we have to."

The car continued down the highway, swallowed slowly by the darkening sky. Behind them, the fog closed in, erasing any sign of where they'd been.

Ahead of them, the storm waited.

Somewhere in the back seat, the box holding Mara's ashes shifted slightly with each bump in the road, like something inside was trying to remind them:

Nothing stays still forever. Not grief. Not memory. Not even the dead.

Chapter III

The road to Red Bluff twisted upward through a forest of bare winter trees. Their branches clawed at the sky like they were trying to hold something back, or drag something down. The wind whistled through them in thin, icy tones that sounded almost like voices. Daniel tried not to imagine what they were saying.

Holly sat curled against the door, her hoodie pulled tight around her face. She hadn't spoken for nearly half an hour. The silence between them grew thicker with every turn in the road.

When they reached the lookout, Daniel parked the car and killed the engine. The sudden stop made the wind feel even louder, pounding against the windows as if it wanted inside.

"We're here," he said.

Holly didn't move.

Daniel opened his door. The wind slammed it back against his leg, making him wince. It was colder here, higher, sharper, a kind of cold that sank into bones.

He walked around to the passenger side and opened Holly's door. She slowly stepped out, arms wrapped around herself.

The cliff stretched out in front of them, dropping into a wide valley painted in faded shades of brown and gray. The wind rushed up the cliff face, pulling at their clothes, tugging at their hair, tugging at everything.

Holly shivered. "It's worse than I remember."

Daniel nodded. "She loved it here anyway."

"Why?" Holly asked, her voice barely carried through the wind.

Daniel stared out over the edge. He took a long breath before speaking. "She said the wind made her feel small in a good way. Like she didn't have to hold everything together all the time."

Holly looked down, kicking a piece of gravel with her shoe. "Funny. She always seemed like the one holding us together."

Daniel's chest tightened. "She did. Until she couldn't anymore."

Holly flinched at that.

He reached into his coat and pulled out the wooden box. The wind pushed at his hands, almost as if trying to take it from him.

Holly's fingers dug into her sleeves. "Do we have to do this part?"

"We don't," he said softly. "But I think she would want us to."

Holly stared at the ground, then at the valley, then at the sky. Finally, with a shaky breath, she nodded.

Daniel opened the box. The ashes looked wrong, too pale, too soft. Too small. He pinched a small handful and held it out over the cliff.

The wind didn't wait. It ripped the ashes from his hand, carrying them upward in a frantic swirl. For a moment, they hung in the air, trembling like they were confused. Then the gust took them farther, scattering them across the valley floor like gray snowflakes.

Holly gasped. "She's... she's gone so fast."

"She always moved fast," Daniel whispered.

Holly stepped closer to the edge, eyes following the fading trail of ash. Her voice cracked. "It's like she's running away."

"No," Daniel said, almost too quickly. "That's not..."

Holly cut him off. "She didn't tell me she was sick before she got worse. She kept it hidden. She pretended everything was fine. And now she's dust in the wind, and I didn't even get to say goodbye."

The wind screamed past them, loud enough to drown their breath.

Daniel wanted to reach for her, to put a hand on her shoulder, but something in her posture stopped him. She wasn't ready to be touched, not yet.

"I didn't know how sick she was either," he said, his voice shaking. "She hid a lot from both of us."

"Why?" Holly's eyes filled with tears that the wind quickly carried away. "Why hide something like that?"

Daniel swallowed hard. "Maybe she didn't want us to worry."

Holly stared at him, hurt glowing behind her eyes. "Or maybe she didn't trust us enough to tell us."

The wind seemed to hold its breath.

Daniel felt something crumbling inside him at her words, something old, something he'd been holding together with a thin thread.

"I wish I could ask her," he said.

"Yeah," Holly whispered. "Me too."

They stood side by side, watching the valley as the last of the ashes dissolved into the air. The world looked bigger from here, too big, too empty.

Finally, Holly spoke again, her voice quiet but steady. "Do we have more places to go?"

Daniel nodded. "A few."

Holly wiped her sleeve across her eyes. "Okay." She turned away from the cliff, pulling her hood tighter, and walked back toward the car.

Daniel followed, carrying the box that seemed a little heavier now, even though it held a little less.

As they drove away, the wind continued to chase along the cliff edge, whispering through the dead trees. And though neither of them said it out loud, both felt the same thing:

This was only the beginning of the pain they'd been avoiding, and the road ahead was going to be long.

Chapter IV

The lighthouse stood alone at the end of a narrow road, rising from the rocks like a cracked tooth. The sky above it was bruised purple, and waves slammed against the cliffs below with a steady, angry rhythm.

Holly stared at the leaning structure as Daniel parked the car. "This place looks like it's about to fall over."

Daniel swallowed. "It almost did once."

She raised an eyebrow. "And Mom *liked* this?"

He didn't answer. The truth tasted strange in his mouth.

Together, they stepped out of the car. The wind here was different, sharper, almost metallic. It carried the smell of saltwater and something else... something old and sour.

As they approached the lighthouse entrance, Holly kicked aside a broken piece of driftwood. "Why did you bring us here?"

Daniel hesitated. "This is where I asked her to marry me."

Holly froze. "Here? Seriously? This place looks like a haunted movie set."

He managed a weak smile. "It wasn't always like this."

She didn't respond, but her shoulders relaxed slightly.

Inside, the lighthouse was colder than the outside air. Their footsteps echoed across the cracked concrete floor. Rust stains streaked the walls like old tears. A broken lantern lay in a corner, surrounded by seaweed and sand.

Holly shivered. "Why does it smell like everything's rotting?"

Daniel touched the wall gently. "Salt eats everything over time."

"Even people?" she asked, bitterly.

Daniel didn't answer.

The staircase was narrow and winding. Each step groaned under their weight. Holly held the railing tightly, knuckles white.

"Mom really came up here?" she asked.

"Yes." Daniel said, "She had no fear."

"Was she crazy?"

"No," Daniel said quietly. "She was brave."

Holly let out a soft scoff. "Brave doesn't mean climbing a death trap."

Daniel didn't argue. He understood that her sarcasm was just another way she was trying to protect herself.

When they reached the top, the wind blasted them from the open windows. The view was vast and wild, endless ocean crashing against jagged rocks.

Holly leaned back instinctively. "It feels like the whole world could swallow us."

Daniel looked out, voice distant. "She said this place made her feel fearless."

Holly glanced at him. "And you believed her?"

He closed his eyes briefly. "I did. Until the night I asked her to marry me."

A long silence stretched between them.

"What happened that night?" Holly finally asked.

Daniel took a deep breath, the wind pulling at his jacket as he spoke. "She almost said no."

Holly turned sharply. "What? Why?"

"Because she didn't think she'd live long," he said. "She was afraid she wouldn't be here for us. Afraid she'd break our hearts."

Holly's voice cracked. "She *knew*? You mean... she knew she might die young, even before I was born?"

Daniel nodded slowly. "She didn't tell me at first. She didn't tell anyone."

Holly put a hand over her mouth. Tears filled her eyes, but they dried instantly as the wind snapped them away.

"So, she lied," Holly whispered. "All those years, she smiled and laughed and told me everything would be fine. And she *knew*."

"She didn't lie," Daniel said softly. "She just felt it in her soul that something was going to make her time here short. It was a feeling she had felt since she was a child. She didn't talk about it after she accepted my proposal. She knew I thought it was silly to think like that, and she wanted you to have a normal childhood."

Holly shook her head violently. "She should've told me. She should've told us both. I wasn't a baby forever. If she felt that way, she should have shared it."

Daniel looked down at the water below. "I didn't know how to tell you after she got worse. I thought if we pretended nothing was happening, maybe it... maybe it wouldn't."

Holly stared at him with disbelief. "You pretended? That's your plan? Just ignore everything and hope the world doesn't end?"

Daniel's voice broke. "I was trying to protect you and myself."

"Well, it didn't work!" Holly shouted. "Now she's gone, and I didn't even get a chance to say goodbye."

Her words hit him like thunder. The truth of her words stung as much as his wife's death.

Neither spoke for a long time. The only sound was the ocean crashing below, loud, relentless, powerful. Finally, Daniel reached into his coat for the wooden box. He opened it and held it between them.

Holly's hands trembled. "I don't want to watch this."

"You don't have to," Daniel said gently.

But she did. She moved closer, despite everything.

Daniel took a handful of ash and held it out toward the open window. The wind once again didn't wait.

It whipped the ashes sharply, so sharply that some blew right back, brushing Holly's cheek like a cold hand.

She gasped, stepping back. "It touched me."

Daniel swallowed hard. "It's just the wind."

"No," she said quietly. "It felt like her." Her voice cracked on the last word.

For a moment, the wind died down. Then it rose again, softer this time, swirling the remaining ashes outward into the gray sky. The tiny particles drifted away like pale smoke, vanishing into the distance.

Holly wiped her face with her sleeve. "I don't understand why she'd bring a child into this world if she thought she wouldn't be here."

Daniel looked at her, eyes filled with a pain he'd been hiding for too long. "She told me once… that loving you would be worth any amount of time she had."

Holly's breath hitched.

Together, without speaking, they descended the staircase, both shaken, both hurting, both carrying more truth than they had been ready to face.

When they stepped outside, the wind was still fierce, whipping their clothes and hair. But something had changed between them. They weren't talking. They weren't healed, but they were no longer hiding.

The lighthouse behind them creaked loudly, as if releasing a secret it had held far too long.

Chapter V

By late morning, the storm had passed, leaving behind a world that felt washed-out and exhausted. The highway was wet and streaked with mud. Fallen branches littered the shoulders. The clouds hung low and heavy, like they were too tired to move on.

The car, after getting gas, wouldn't start, but a jump from a passing trucker brought the vehicle back to life, though it sounded weaker than before. Daniel didn't know how far it would make it, and neither did Holly, but neither said a word about turning back.

The silence between them was different now, not sharp, not angry. Just tired. Just real.

After two hours of quiet driving, the sunflower farm appeared at the edge of the horizon, a long stretch of land bordered by a faded fence and a crooked wooden sign that read *Bright Haven Farm*. The letters were chipped. Some were missing.

"Your mom volunteered here in college," Daniel said quietly, breaking the silence.

Holly stared through the window at the fields. The sunflowers weren't standing tall or proud the way she remembered from picture books. Many were bent or snapped from the storm, their yellow petals scattered like torn pieces of sunlight across the muddy soil.

"It looks… broken," she said.

Daniel nodded. "A lot of things are."

They parked near the barn. An older woman stepped out, wiping her hands on her apron. Her gray hair was tied back in a loose bun, and her eyes were tired and yet kind. She had the eyes that had seen things grow and die too many times to count.

She squinted toward them. "Can I help you?"

Daniel cleared his throat. "I'm Daniel Walker. My wife... Mara... used to volunteer here."

The woman's face softened instantly. Her eyes glimmered with recognition. "Mara Jennings?"

Holly's breath caught. Hearing her mother's maiden name spoken out loud felt like being hit in the chest.

"Yes," Daniel said. "Her."

The woman walked forward slowly, placing a warm hand on Holly's shoulder without asking. "Your mother was a bright one. Always smiling. Always helping. Even when she was hurting."

Holly blinked. "Hurting?"

The woman nodded sadly. "She came to us one afternoon in tears... wouldn't say why. But she still spent the whole day planting sunflower seeds with the kids who worked here. Told them that even broken soil can grow something beautiful."

Daniel closed his eyes. He had never heard that story.

Holly's bottom lip trembled. "Why didn't she tell us that?"

The woman gently touched Holly's cheek. "Some people hide their pain because they think they're protecting the ones they love."

Holly stepped back, overwhelmed.

The farmer didn't push. "Take your time," she said softly. Then she pointed toward the field. "That spot over there, that's where she planted her first row."

The field she pointed at was a mess of snapped stems and scattered petals.

Perfect, Holly thought bitterly. Even the place that held Mom's memories looked ruined. But maybe… that made it honest.

Daniel and Holly walked through the soft mud, their shoes sinking with each step. The sunflowers rustled in the light breeze. Even bent and broken, they reached toward the sun.

Daniel said, "Everything always reaches for the light. Mom used to say that."

Holly couldn't remember the last time *she* had reached for the light; she guessed it was over a year ago, before Mom died.

When they reached the place, the farmer had pointed out that Daniel opened the wooden box. The wind here wasn't violent; it was soft, manageable, almost warm.

"Do you want to do this part?" Daniel asked gently.

Holly stared at the ashes. For the first time, she didn't feel angry at them. She felt sorry for them.

"It doesn't feel right," she whispered. "Throwing pieces of her away like this."

"We're not throwing her away," Daniel said, voice steady. "We're giving parts of her back to the places she loved."

Holly looked out at the broken sunflowers, their heads drooping but still standing, still there.

"Okay," she whispered. "Okay."

Daniel passed her a small handful of ash. Holly held it in her palm, surprised by how fine and soft it felt, like gray flour, like something that shouldn't exist.

Her voice cracked. "I don't know if I can."

"You don't have to be perfect," Daniel said softly. "Just honest."

Holly stepped forward. She let the ashes slip between her fingers and fall onto the muddy soil. The wind lifted a few grains and carried them into the fields, allowing them swirl among the broken flowers.

For a moment, she imagined each gray speck becoming something new, a petal, a leaf, or a seed.

Her tears fell silently, mixing with the earth below.

Daniel knelt beside her and scattered some ashes of his own. His hands shook. "She'd like this," he whispered. "She always said sunflowers were the bravest flowers."

"Why?" Holly asked, wiping her face.

"Because they turn toward the sun even after storms."

Holly closed her eyes. "I'm tired of storms."

"Me too," Daniel said.

As they walked back toward the car, Holly brushed her fingers along the broken sunflower heads. Many were snapped, but root-deep, they were still alive.

When they reached the barn, the old woman called out, "Come back in the summer. They'll rise stronger than before."

Holly nodded, though she wasn't sure if she believed it.

When Daniel opened the car door for her, she hesitated, then placed her hand lightly on his arm. Not much. Barely there, but it was more than she'd given him in months.

Daniel looked at her, surprised by the gentle touch.

She didn't look away this time. "We still have places to go, right?"

"Yes," he said.

"Then… let's keep going."

It wasn't forgiveness. It wasn't healing. But it was a step, and sometimes, one small step toward the light was enough to break the darkness open.

Chapter VI

The hillside came into view just as the sun dropped behind the mountains, painting the sky with thin streaks of red and fading gold. Daniel slowed the car as they approached the narrow dirt road that wound up toward the crest. Weeds and tall grass grew wild on both sides, bending in long arcs beneath the steady push of the wind.

"This is it," Daniel said softly.

Holly stared out the window. "It looks empty."

"Yeah, I guess it always was," he replied.

He parked at the bottom of the slope. They stepped out, the wind tugging at their clothes like impatient hands urging them upward. The air here felt different, older, heavier, almost sacred.

Holly wrapped her arms around herself. "Why this place?"

Daniel looked up at the hill. "Because this is where I met your mother."

Holly blinked, surprised. "Here? On a random hill in the middle of nowhere?"

Daniel smiled faintly. "It wasn't random. It was a hiking trail once. She'd come up here to clear her head. I was doing the same."

"What were you clearing your head from?"

"Life," he said. "And then... I saw her."

They began the slow climb. The grass brushed against their legs, whispering in soft, dry sounds. The wind blew steadily, never letting them walk in silence. As they reached the top, the world opened around them, rolling fields stretching in every direction, the sky enormous above.

Holly breathed out slowly. "It's... beautiful. In a sad kind of way."

Daniel nodded. "She said this place made her feel understood." He looked at Holly. "She said the wind never loses the things it carries."

Holly didn't answer at first. She just stared at the horizon, her hair whipping across her face. Something about the vastness made her feel small, but not the same way Red Bluff had. This was different. This was like standing inside a memory.

Daniel set the wooden box down gently in the tall grass. "This is the last stop," he said. "She wanted part of herself to stay here forever. She told me that once."

Holly's voice trembled. "When?"

"Before she got worse," Daniel said, keeping his eyes looking at the ground, in shame.

"And you didn't tell me?" Holly questioned.

He swallowed. "I thought I was protecting you. I didn't want you to feel like you were losing her, and I was too scared to tell you, too scared to face your pain."

Holly stepped back, tears forming in her eyes. "It wasn't right." But the anger was no longer in her words. She appreciated her father being honest about why he kept silent. She still didn't fully understand it, but she understood it better than she had before.

Daniel's face twisted. Pain. Regret. Love. "I know," he whispered. "And I'm sorry. For all of it."

The wind roared across the hill, louder than before, swirling around them like a restless tide.

Holly wiped her cheek. "I want to understand her. I want to forgive her. But it's so hard."

Daniel opened the box. The ashes glowed faintly in the dying light. "You don't have to feel everything today," he said softly. "Grief doesn't work like that."

Holly stared at the ashes. They looked softer here, almost peaceful, not like what she had seen at the lookout or the lighthouse.

"They look like dust," she whispered.

"Dust that meant something," Daniel replied. "Dust that lived and loved and made you."

Her voice broke. "I miss her."

Daniel touched Holly's hand. "So do I."

It was the first time he'd allowed himself to say those words without shame.

Holly took a handful of ash. Daniel did the same. Together, they stepped to the edge where the grass sloped downward into the valley.

"Ready?" Daniel asked.

Holly shook her head. "But I'll do it anyway."

They opened their hands.

The wind didn't snatch the ashes this time. It lifted them gently, as if it finally understood the weight they carried. The gray particles rose, turning and twisting in the light until the sunset colored them gold.

Holly watched them swirl into the sky, her breath catching. "It's like she's…" She couldn't finish the sentence.

"Still here," Daniel finished in a whisper.

The ashes drifted farther, scattering across the hilltop, the fields, the sky, soft as smoke, fragile as breath.

Holly closed her eyes and let the wind wash over her. For the first time since her mother died, the wind didn't feel cruel. It didn't feel like it was taking something away; it felt like it was giving something back.

After a long silence, Holly whispered, "Dad?"

"Yes?"

"She's everywhere, isn't she?" Holly asked.

Daniel looked at her with tears in his eyes, the wind blowing his hair back like it was pulling the truth out of him.

"Always," he said.

Holly leaned against him. He wrapped an arm around her, holding her as the sun slipped behind the hills. Above them, the last of the ashes glittered faintly in the fading light, then disappeared, not gone… just part of everything now, and for the first time in a long time, the space between father and daughter felt whole enough to breathe.

Chapter VII

The road away from the hillside wound gently downhill, curving between fields the color of faded gold. The storm clouds from the night before were long gone, leaving behind a soft blue sky brushed with pale streaks of sunlight. The air felt lighter than it had in days, as if the world itself had unclenched a fist.

Daniel drove slowly, not wanting to rush the moment. Beside him, Holly leaned against the window, watching the countryside pass in long, quiet waves. Her eyes were red, her face tired, but there was something new there too, something softer, steadier.

A kind of peace was trying to grow roots. For a long time, they didn't speak. They didn't need to.

The wind outside the car rolled across the tall grass, bending it in smooth ripples. It didn't howl or scream the way it had earlier in the trip. It simply moved, gentle, steady, guiding.

Holly exhaled against the window, watching her breath fog the glass. She dragged her fingertip through it, tracing the outline of the hills far ahead. "Feels strange," she murmured. "The wind, I mean. It's different now."

Daniel glanced over. "Different how?"

"It's not tearing everything up anymore," she said. "It feels like it's... carrying things instead."

He relaxed his grip on the wheel and nodded. "Wind can be both."

They fell quiet after that, not the heavy kind of calm, but the sort that settles around you like a warm blanket.

Holly looked out again. The grass bent in long waves, dust lifted in thin little spirals at the roadside, and the sunlight stretched across the fields like it was reaching out to touch them. She thought about her mom at Red Bluff. About the lighthouse. The storm. The yelling. The hurt. The sunflowers that snapped in half, and the few that somehow stayed standing. She thought about the hillside where the ashes rose like a tiny galaxy before disappearing into the sky.

Those memories still stung, but not as much as before. They were sharp, yes, but the kind of sharp you can touch without bleeding.

After a while, she whispered, "She's everywhere, isn't she?"

Daniel's throat tightened. He kept his eyes on the road, blinking once, steadying his voice. "Yeah," he said softly. "She is."

Holly's smile was slight but real, like the first bit of sunrise after a storm finally broke.

A breeze pushed across the fields, stirring up another little twist of dust. It curled in the air, turned once, twice, and slowly came apart. The particles didn't drop hard; they just drifted away, folding back into the world like they'd been part of it all along. Holly watched until they vanished.

People don't disappear, she realized. They change how we see them. They become the wind, the dust, the sunlight… the stories we hold onto.

Daniel reached over and gave her hand a gentle squeeze. He didn't need to say anything.

The road ahead glowed under the afternoon sun, stretching out wide and open. For the first time since Mara's death, the future didn't feel like something to fear.

It felt possible. It felt big. It felt new.

The wind softened against the car, almost like a promise, and father and daughter kept driving, carrying not only what they'd lost, but everything they still had.

Author's Note

This story began as a simple idea about grief and memory, but it quickly became something much more personal. All of us, at some point, learn what it means to carry the weight of losing someone we love. Grief changes how we see ourselves. It changes how we move through the world. Sometimes it turns us silent. Sometimes it makes us angry. Sometimes it teaches us how deeply we can love.

The Wind Takes All Things is about that journey. It is about the pieces we lose, the pieces we keep, and the painful, beautiful ways we learn to keep going. I wanted to write an honest story, one that didn't pretend grief is clean, simple, or gentle. Loss breaks us in strange ways, but it also pushes us to grow in places we never expected.

Holly and Daniel's journey is fictional, but the emotions behind it are genuine. They represent what happens when two people try to hold onto each other while standing in the shadow of the same loss. Their story is about learning that healing is not forgetting; it is remembering with less fear.

If you've ever lost someone, if you've felt that ache in your chest, that silence in the house, that strange heaviness in the air, I hope this story reminds you that you are not alone. Grief doesn't disappear, but it becomes something we can carry. Something that shapes us rather than destroys us.

And sometimes, when we least expect it, the wind softens, and it brings back pieces of the love we thought we lost.

—Brett C. Persson

When the Sea Calls:

A Journey Beyond the Shore

Chapter One

The sea was quiet that evening, except for the soft lapping of waves against weathered wood and the occasional call of a distant gull. Dennis stood at the edge of the pier with his hands in the pockets of his faded jacket, staring at the horizon like it might finally answer the questions he hadn't found the words for.

The sky was bruised with pinks and purples; the kind of sunset that used to make him believe anything was possible. But tonight, it just made him feel old.

He hadn't been back to Haven Rock, Washington, in over fifteen years. Not since the funeral. Not since the town stopped feeling like home. But something had pulled him back, something he couldn't name. He told himself it was to settle the estate, to finalize the sale of the house, to finally close the door on a chapter he had long since stopped reading. But the truth had more weight than that. He missed the feeling of hope that once lived on this shoreline.

Out on the water, tied to the very end of the dock, sat 'Faith'—his father's old sailboat. Still bobbing in place like a forgotten dream that refused to sink.

It looked smaller now, almost sadder. The paint had peeled back in long, curling strips, and the name stenciled on the stern had faded to a whisper. But it was still here. Still waiting.

He ran his hand along the railing as he stepped onboard, the wood warm from the day's sun and rough beneath his fingers. Everything inside was just as he remembered, cramped and musty, but oddly comforting. The tiny kitchenette. The sagging bunk where he used to hide with a flashlight and comic books. And the little brass compass mounted near the helm, its needle still twitching north like a heartbeat that never quit.

Dennis sat down on the edge of the cabin and closed his eyes. Memories rolled in with the tide. He was eight again, clinging to the wheel while his father barked cheerful orders. "Feel the wind, Danny! Let her guide you. You don't fight the sea; you dance with it."

He smiled faintly at the memory. His dad always made sailing sound like magic, like the boat could take you not just to another place, but to another world entirely.

He opened his eyes, and something caught his attention, a folded piece of paper, yellowed with age, wedged between the pages of the old logbook. He pulled it free. His name was written across the front in a strong, looping script.

His father's handwriting.

Dennis's chest tightened as he unfolded the note. It was dated the day before his father died.

"Dennis,

If you're reading this, then the sea has brought you back, just like I knew it would. I never stopped believing in you. Sail away, son. The stars are waiting. There's more to this world than you can see from the shore."

—Dad

Dennis sat still for a long moment, letting the words soak in. He hadn't cried at the funeral. Not once. But now, alone on this creaking boat under the darkening sky, the tears came fast and quietly.

He didn't know what the note meant. He didn't know what he was supposed to do. But for the first time in years, he felt something stir inside him. Something that felt a lot like belief. He wiped his face with the sleeve of his jacket and looked out at the water. The tide was shifting, and maybe it was time to sail again.

Chapter Two

Dennis spent the night on his father's sailboat, *The Faith.*

Not intentionally, he hadn't planned to sleep at all, but after rereading the note, something inside him refused to leave. He curled up on the bunk with an old wool blanket still folded in the storage chest. The smell of sea salt, aged wood, and faint mildew filled his lungs. Somehow, it was comforting.

When he woke, the world outside was painted in the soft gray of morning fog. The kind of fog that made the town disappear into silence, leaving only the sounds of the harbor: the clink of rigging against metal, the splash of a fish breaking the surface, and the sighing breath of the tide.

He sat up slowly, rubbing sleep from his eyes. The note was still clutched in his hand.

The words haunted him in a way that felt... gentle. Not like a ghost dragging chains, but more like a voice you hadn't heard in years calling you by name from across a crowded room. It had been a long time since anyone said his name like that. With love. With belief.

He looked around the cabin again, this time more carefully. Everything had a layer of dust, but nothing felt abandoned. The lanterns still worked. The little stove still sparked when he turned the knob. Even the map pinned to the wall hadn't curled too much at the edges.

His father had loved this boat as if it were a second home. Maybe it was.

Dennis stepped out onto the deck. The fog rolled over the water like a blanket being pulled tighter, and for a moment, the shore behind him disappeared entirely. That's when he heard the sound, it was faint at first, like music under the surface of the sea. It sounded like humming. Notes of a lullaby? A melody without words. It came and went with the wind.

He shook his head and laughed softly. "I must be losing it," he muttered. But the fog only grew thicker. And the music didn't stop.

He glanced toward the harbor, where the dock lights flickered like lanterns in a dream. The town was there, somewhere. But right now, it felt like another world, and for the first time, Dennis didn't want to go back.

He spent the next few hours cleaning the boat. It wasn't much, but it felt like a ritual. Like waking something up. He scrubbed the deck, oiled the wood, checked the sails, and tested the motor, which coughed twice before surprisingly rumbling to life. For the most part, everything still worked like the *Faith* had just been waiting.

As he worked, memories rose of sailing under the stars with his father, pointing out constellations. Of Emily laughing beside him on the bow, her legs swinging over the water, hair blowing in the wind. Memories of that last night before she left. The way she kissed him and said, "Some dreams don't wait forever."

He hadn't followed her. He hadn't followed any dream he had after that, just drifted like they were lost on the sea, just survived.

As the sun burned off the fog, Dennis stood at the helm, hands on the wheel. The sails were rigged. Supplies were in the hold.

He'd grabbed some food from the marina shop earlier that morning and a thermos of black coffee, enough for at least a few days on the water.

The compass spun slightly before settling on a heading.

Northwest.

A direction without a destination, and yet, something in his gut told him it was precisely where he needed to go. He took a breath and untied the mooring lines. The *Faith* rocked gently, as if excited to be free again. Dennis gave the engine a push and eased the boat away from the dock. As the harbor faded behind him, the music returned.

Stronger now. Still without words. Still only for him. He didn't know where he was going, but the stars and the sea were waiting. For the first time in years, Dennis was ready to sail.

Chapter Three

By the second night, Dennis was far beyond the reach of city lights. The shoreline had long since vanished, swallowed by the sea behind him. Out here, there was only the sound of the waves, the creak of the sails, and the low hum of the *Faith* carving her way across the water.

The stars were everywhere. Brighter than he remembered. Clearer. As if they were leaning in to listen.

He stood barefoot at the bow, a cup of lukewarm coffee in his hand, his eyes tracing constellations his father had once named for him. Orion. Cassiopeia. Lyra. And just above the horizon, a new one. One he didn't recognize. Three pinpricks of light in a perfect triangle.

He blinked. They were still there. The breeze shifted, warm, strangely warm, and the music returned.

It wasn't in his ears exactly; it was in his bones. Like something deep inside him had always known this tune. A lullaby hummed by the sea itself. The rhythm matched the waves, the sails, even the thump of his heartbeat. He closed his eyes and let it wash over him.

When he opened them again, he wasn't sure what time it was. The stars hadn't moved, not really, but the sky had taken on an odd shade of blue, too rich for night and too dark for morning. The kind of sky dreams came wrapped in.

Dennis turned to check the compass. It was spinning. Slowly, but with purpose, like a dancer turning to a silent rhythm.

Dennis furrowed his brow and tapped the glass several times, but the compass didn't stop its slow, rhythmic spinning.

The *Faith* shuddered, just slightly, as if something beneath the hull had nudged it. Dennis stepped back toward the cabin, instinct prickling at the back of his neck. Not fear exactly. Not danger. But something unknown, vast and ancient, brushing close.

That's when the light appeared, not from above, like the stars or moon, but from below. It started as a soft glow beneath the surface of the water. Pale blue. Then green. Then shimmering white. It pulsed like breath. Like something alive. The water around the boat lit up, revealing what looked like an enormous circle carved into the seafloor, geometric and glowing, impossible and perfect.

Dennis stared, unmoving. The music swelled, fuller now, with voices. Still wordless. Still beautiful. He whispered, "Am I dreaming?"

The *Faith* began to slow, though he hadn't touched the sail or the wheel. It glided forward as if pulled by invisible hands. Then, something broke the surface. Not a person, not a creature, but a shape.

It rose silently, gliding upward through the mist, sleek, silver, and glowing, like a ship made of starlight. Its form shifted, part sailboat, part spacecraft, part something older than either. It hovered a few feet above the water, casting no shadow but lighting everything around it.

Dennis backed toward the mast, mouth dry. He wasn't afraid. He was in awe. The vessel drifted closer. A panel opened on its side, revealing a doorway, and beyond it, a soft golden light.

He could see figures within. Vague at first, like silhouettes behind frosted glass. Then clearer, tall, robed, glowing with the same gentle shimmer as the ship. Their faces were calm. Peaceful. Kind.

One of them raised a hand, not beckoning, but greeting. Dennis's breath caught in his throat. He didn't know how, but he understood. They knew him, and they had been waiting.

He looked down at his hands. They were trembling, but not from fear, from wonder. He took one step toward the edge of the *Faith's* deck, then another. The music surrounded him now, not outside, but within. A memory he had never lived, a promise he had never spoken.

Dennis reached out toward the light.

Chapter Four

Dennis hesitated at the edge of the *Faith's* deck, one hand resting on the rail, the other stretching slowly toward the doorway of light. The air around him shimmered like heat rising off pavement, though the night was incredible.

The glowing vessel hovered silently beside him, weightless, seamless, unreal. Yet every instinct in his body said it was more real than anything he'd ever known. And still, one small part of him clung to reason. *This is impossible,* he thought. *This is madness.* Even as Dennis told himself that, he knew he was going. Not because he had no choice, but because he had *finally* found one.

He stepped off the deck.

There was no splash, no fall. The distance between the *Faith* and the hovering ship melted beneath him, as some invisible bridge of belief had always connected the two vessels. His foot met a smooth surface, warm, solid, and alive beneath his skin.

The doorway widened to welcome him. As he passed through, the glow softened to something more intimate, like candlelight and moonlight combined. The interior of the ship was nothing like he expected. No metal walls. No blinking lights. It felt organic, like walking into the belly of a giant seashell carved from starlight: soft curves, gentle hums. Every surface seemed to breathe.

The tall beings stood before him, their eyes deep pools of silver. They didn't speak aloud, but their presence filled the air like a tide rising. One stepped forward, placing a hand over where its heart might be.

Dennis did the same, instinctively.

In that moment, a thousand memories not his own flooded through him, star maps sketched on skyless worlds, sails made of time, oceans that stretched between galaxies. He saw children laughing in languages that never needed words, and songs sung to planets as they slept.

And through it all, a profound, unwavering message:

You were never forgotten.

Dennis's eyes filled with tears. He didn't know why, only that something inside him had been waiting to hear that his entire life.

The being extended a hand. Not demanding, and not urgent. It was an invitation, and Dennis took it.

The room shifted, or maybe the ship itself did. Walls peeled away to reveal the sky, not just the stars he'd seen before, but a sky full of movement and colors he couldn't name. Constellations began drawing themselves in real time, like a cosmic ocean.

Below, the *Faith* still floated on the sea, now almost motionless, gently bobbing in place, a small, faithful friend who had carried him to the edge of something greater.

He whispered, "Thank you," to her, to his father, and to the sea.

Then the vessel began to rise. There was no sound, no jolt. Just a feeling, like being lifted by a memory too beautiful to hold. As they ascended, Dennis saw the Earth curve beneath him, the stars unfolding above.

He was no longer drifting. He was *sailing*. Not away, but *toward*.

Toward something he didn't understand yet, but somehow, it understood him.

Chapter Five

There was no sense of time aboard the ship. No ticking clocks. No rise or setting sun. Only the pulse of the vessel, slow and steady, like the heartbeat of the universe itself.

Dennis stood by a wide, curved window, watching galaxies spill across the void like spilled paint on a black canvas. The Earth was gone from view now, swallowed by distance and memory. In its place: the stars, countless and alive.

Behind him, the beings moved like light through water. Silent, graceful, and never hurried. They did not speak, but Dennis felt their thoughts as impressions, memories carried on the breeze of their presence.

They were travelers, watchers, guardians of paths long forgotten by humanity, and somehow, he was one of them now. Or at least… *chosen.*

Dennis had been given a chamber of his own, if you could call it that. It wasn't a room so much as a space that responded to his thoughts. When he thought of warmth, soft light glowed from the walls. When he longed for music, he heard a familiar, soothing melody. The same one he had heard on the sea.

Each night, or what passed for night, he dreamed vividly of oceans that glittered like glass, and of his father, standing at the helm of the *Faith*, pointing upward with a grin: "One day, Dennis, one day, the sea won't be enough for you."

He dreamed of Emily. Her voice, her laughter, the look she gave him when he first kissed her. Regret pulled at his chest like an undertow. He had let her go, too afraid, too rooted in the safety of the harbor, but now, everything was changing.

On the third "day" aboard, or the third shift in awareness, perhaps, one of the beings brought him to what he could only describe as a *hall of echoes*. The room was enormous, with arches that stretched into infinity and a floor that shimmered like still water. In the center, a sphere floated, glowing, rotating, alive with images.

As Dennis approached, the sphere reacted. Scenes appeared from his life.

Moments long buried: His mother rocking him to sleep, humming the same melody he heard in the fog. His teenage self, standing frozen at the train station, watching Emily disappear into the blur of departure. His father's last sail, alone, as storm clouds gathered. Then… moments that *hadn't* happened or hadn't happened *yet*.

He saw himself older, standing on a distant world with a sky the color of fire. He saw children running around him, laughing, bright-eyed, calling him by name. He saw himself reaching out a hand to someone cloaked in light.

Dennis turned to the being beside him. "Are these... real?" he asked.

The being didn't speak, but the answer bloomed in his mind like a whisper in his head, *"They are the paths you've touched. The lives you've shaped. The ripples you never saw."*

Dennis sank to his knees. All this time, he had thought he was small and didn't matter. Lost. Forgettable, but the stars remembered.

As he lay in his chamber that night, staring up into a ceiling that shimmered with nebulae, he realized something profound. This journey wasn't about escape. It was about connections.

He hadn't been pulled from Earth to leave it behind. He had been chosen to *understand it better*, to see his life not as a closed book, but as a single chapter in a much greater story, one still being written.

Yet… a new thought gnawed at the edge of his mind. If he had been brought here to understand, to remember, then perhaps there was something else he had to do. Something he had to choose. Something waiting for him… back on Earth.

Chapter Six

Dennis awoke with tears on his cheeks. He wasn't dreaming. He had seen too much, *felt* too much, for this to be a dream. The ship drifted silently through a river of stars. The same being that had shown him the sphere now stood near the entrance to his chamber, radiant as ever, but… solemn.

It was time. Dennis knew without words.

He stood slowly, casting one final glance around the chamber that had begun to feel like home. His fingers trailed the curve of the wall, and the ship hummed softly in response, like it, too, was saying goodbye.

He followed the being through the corridor, down toward the chamber where the great window opened once more. Below them: Earth. Blue and fragile. Beautiful and broken. Waiting.

The same doorway that had opened once in the fog now stood before him again, no longer glowing, but open wide with quiet promise.

Dennis turned to the being standing by the door and asked, "Why me?"

The answer came, not in speech, but in feeling, *"Because you listened. Because you remembered."*

Dennis swallowed hard, nodded once, and stepped through.

Dennis woke up in the sunlight. Warm and golden against his skin. The sound of gulls overhead and wood creaking gently beneath him. He could taste the salt in the air.

Dennis sat up slowly, rubbing his eyes. He was back on the *Faith*. Moored at the dock. The sail was furled. The coffee thermos was empty beside him. The fog was gone.

And yet… something in him knew he hadn't imagined it, he had lived it. He looked down at his hands. Clean. Callused. Steady.

In his palm, he found something strange, a small, silver token etched with a pattern that shimmered faintly in the light. It didn't match any currency. It didn't belong here. But it pulsed softly in his hand, like a heartbeat.

He smiled.

Two weeks later, Dennis stood beside a FOR SALE sign, a clipboard in hand. The marina manager raised an eyebrow.

"You sure about this?" the man asked. "She's a good boat."

Dennis nodded. "She got me where I needed to go."

That night, he boarded a bus out of Haven Rock, Washington. No destination, just a direction.

Northwest.

He'd given away most of his things and packed only the essentials: clothes, journal, the silver token tucked deep in his pocket. There was no plan. No map. Only a feeling. A sense of purpose he hadn't felt in years. He was no longer chasing ghosts or running from regret. He was sailing forward, on land now, but still guided by wind and stars.

The stars weren't just in the sky anymore; they were in him, a part of him.

Epilogue:

Ten Years Later

Haven Rock, Washington Marina

The dock had changed over the years, the old wooden boards replaced by composite planks, and the marina office now a sleek little café with wi-fi and oat milk lattes.

But the *Faith*, she was still there.

Fresh paint. New sails. A new name stenciled neatly on her stern: *Emily's Grace*.

A young woman stepped aboard, her sandals tapping softly against the deck. She moved with the ease of someone who belonged on water, though her eyes searched like someone hoping to find something lost.

She opened the hatch and climbed into the cabin. Everything was neat and cared for; clearly, someone had loved this boat since Dennis left. But it was the old box tucked behind the bunk that drew her in.

A weathered journal. Wrapped in twine. She hesitated before opening it. Inside were sketches of stars, maps with no labels. Passages written in a hand both rushed and deliberate.

"They told me the stars remember. I believe them now. The journey didn't end when I stepped off their ship; it began. The rhythm of that music has guided every step I've taken since the song I first heard in the fog."

"I used to think I had wasted my life. That I had let her go, and that made me broken. But it wasn't too late. It never is, not if you listen. Not if you sail."

"If you're reading this, maybe it's your time now. Maybe the sea has whispered your name, too. If so, don't hesitate. The world is wider than you know. And somewhere out there, the stars are still waiting."

At the bottom of the page was a silver token, tied with a ribbon. The same symbol etched in its center glowed faintly under the cabin light.

The woman smiled softly, tears in her eyes. She knew this handwriting. She knew this man, and even though she hadn't seen him in decades, she understood what had happened now.

She stepped out onto the deck and looked toward the horizon. *"Come sail away,"* she whispered.

And she did.

Author's Note

I've always been fascinated by stories that begin quietly, where nothing explodes, no one runs, and yet, something inside a person shifts. Styx's *Come Sail Away* has always felt like that kind of story to me. It's more than a song about a voyage; it's a quiet invitation that becomes a cosmic leap of faith. A journey that starts with sorrow and ends in something almost holy.

That idea stuck with me.

When the Sea Calls was born from that feeling: the sense that sometimes the sea (or life, or grief, or memory) calls us to leave behind everything we thought we knew and trust something deeper, something unseen. Like the narrator in the song, Dennis doesn't know exactly where he's going, only that he must go. And once he listens, everything begins to change.

This story isn't an adaptation of the song; it's more of a spiritual echo. The same ache. The same wonder. The same whispered invitation to believe in something greater, even when you don't fully understand it.

—Brett C. Persson

The Things We Try to Outrun

Chapter I

The gate buzzed, jerked, and slid open with a sound he would never forget. It was the last noise he heard as an inmate, and somehow it felt louder than anything in the twelve years before it. He stepped through carrying a plastic bag that held everything the state said belonged to him: a folded pair of jeans, a wallet with no money, a bus pass, and his release papers wrinkled from being handled too many times the night before.

The sky looked too big. Colors felt sharp. The air tasted like dust and sunlight, things he'd forgotten how to name. He stood there for a second, staring at the open space ahead of him, half expecting a guard to call him back and tell him there'd been a mistake.

No one called after him, and no one followed. The gate locked behind him, and with that quiet click, the world he had known since he was seventeen became memory.

His parole officer, a tired-looking woman with a clipboard and soft eyes, met him by the sidewalk. She didn't congratulate him, and she didn't smile. She handed him a packet of rules and reviewed some of the details in a monotone voice, indicating she had done it a thousand times before.

"You have a curfew," she said. "Job search logs are due every Friday. Mandatory N.A. meetings twice a week. No contact with anyone who has a record. Weekly check-ins. You violate any of this, and you go back. Clear?"

He nodded. Words felt heavy in his throat, so he kept them inside.

She watched him for a moment longer, as if checking whether he understood the weight of freedom, or the weight of losing it. Then she walked away, her heels clicking on the concrete until she disappeared around the corner of the administration building.

He stood alone.

The bus arrived fifteen minutes later, wheezing to a stop like it resented being there. He climbed aboard and sat near the back, gripping the plastic bag in his lap. His reflection in the window startled him, older, harder, the boy he used to be erased under years of fluorescent lights and metal bars.

City streets rolled by in a blur of color and motion. People crossed intersections without looking at him. Cars honked. Dogs barked. All of it felt too fast, too loud, too alive. He tried to breathe slowly, tried to let the noise settle somewhere inside him, but his pulse kept skipping like it wasn't sure how to behave out here.

When he stepped off downtown, the smell of coffee and car exhaust wrapped around him. He had an address for a halfway house and three job applications printed from the prison computer lab. He walked into the first place, a hardware store, trying not to look like a man who'd forgotten how to talk to strangers.

The manager shook his hand until he reached the question on the form about felony convictions. The handshake loosened. The smile stiffened. The interview ended five minutes later.

The second interview ended faster. The third didn't even pretend.

He walked blocks without thinking, the city stretching in every direction, vast and unfamiliar. Hunger gnawed at him, so he turned toward a convenience store on the corner. The bright lights glared through the glass windows, the same kind of lights that had flooded his life with violence twelve years earlier.

He stopped.

His breath hitched. His feet refused to move. The door, the windows, the glow, they snapped him backward into memory, into the night when fear and drugs and desperation had fused into a single, irreversible moment.

He closed his eyes. Counted three slow breaths. Told himself he was no longer that seventeen-year-old boy.
But another truth whispered back: the world still saw him as that boy, or worse, a felon.

A car horn jolted him out of his memory. He stepped away from the store, forcing himself to keep walking, one foot in front of the other. The sidewalk felt uneven under his shoes. The city felt too bright.
His first day of freedom had barely begun, and he already felt exhausted.

Ahead, a bus stop came into view. He sat down, the plastic bag crinkling against his leg, and stared at the traffic moving steadily past him. He wasn't sure what waited for him next. All he knew was this: freedom wasn't easy. It wasn't light. It didn't erase the past. It was just a different kind of weight he had to learn to carry.

Chapter II

The afternoon sun slid lower, throwing long shadows across the street as he waited for the bus. The city moved around him like he wasn't even there. People were hurrying home from work, laughing into their phones, sipping iced coffees they couldn't afford. He watched them the way someone watched fish through glass: close enough to see clearly, but not close enough to touch.

He rubbed his hands over his face, trying to shake off the sense of failure already settling in. Three rejections in a single morning. A panic attack outside a convenience store. Twelve years behind bars, and the world still felt like a door that wouldn't open.

A gust of wind stirred the litter near the curb. A shadow passed in front of him. "...Is it really you?"

The voice was soft, unsure, and it brushed against something deep in his memory. He looked up.

She stood a few feet away, the strap of a messenger bag across her chest, the same shade of green jacket she used to wear in high school, faded now, but unmistakable. Her hair was shorter, her eyes sharper, but the moment he met them, he felt seventeen again, standing on a cracked sidewalk with a girl who believed he was better than the world he kept falling into.

He swallowed hard. "Yeah," he said quietly. "It's me."

For a moment, she just stared, like she was piecing together the boy she remembered with the man sitting on the bus bench. Then she stepped closer. "I heard you were getting out today. I wasn't sure if it was true."

He nodded. "Got released this morning."

She hesitated, shifting her bag on her shoulder. "How are you holding up?"

He let out a breath that wasn't quite a laugh. "Still figuring that out."

Her eyes softened. She sat down beside him, leaving a polite few inches of space, but close enough that he could feel her warmth. "I'm glad you're out," she said.

For a moment, neither spoke. Cars hummed past. A cyclist rang his bell. Somewhere across the street, a kid dragged a stick along a fence, the clacking sound oddly comforting.

"I'm sorry," he said finally, the words heavy and awkward. "For the way I left things. For… everything. You didn't deserve any of it."

A small, sad smile pulled at her lips. "We were kids," she said. "Kids trying to outrun things we didn't understand." She brushed a loose strand of hair behind her ear. "I'm not here to make you explain yourself."

That alone nearly undid him.

"What are you doing now?" he asked.

"I work at the Glenwood Community Center," she said. "Most days with people in recovery or re-entry programs." She glanced at him. "People trying to rebuild their lives."

Of course she did. Even back then, she had been the one who checked on her neighbors, who wrote essays about wanting to change the world. He used to wonder how someone like her had ever fallen for someone like him.

"It's a good place," she added softly. "We help with job training, housing leads, and support groups. Stuff that makes the transition a little easier."

He looked down at his empty hands. "I don't think anything about this is easy."

"No," she agreed. "But it doesn't have to be impossible."

The bus pulled around the corner, rumbling toward them. He felt a sudden, irrational fear that, when it came to a stop, she would vanish, as if this moment were too fragile to survive movement.

She stood as it approached. "If you want," she said, "you can stop by the center. I'm not promising miracles. But we have people there who understand what you're carrying."

He didn't answer right away. The thought of stepping into a place full of strangers who might judge him, or worse, pity him, made his chest tighten. But something in her eyes, steady and patient, made him want to try anyway.

"Yeah," he said. "Maybe I will."

The bus doors hissed open. She took a step inside, then paused and looked back at him.

"It really is good to see you," she said.

He nodded, unable to speak past the sudden thickness in his throat.

And then she was gone, the bus pulling away, her silhouette shrinking into the blur of the city. He watched until the movement swallowed her completely.

For the first time since walking out of prison, the weight pressing on his chest loosened, just a little, just enough to breathe.

Maybe the world wasn't ready to forgive him. Perhaps it never would, but someone had seen him today and really seen him. And that, he realized, was enough to take one more step forward.

Chapter III

The next morning, he stood across the street from the Glenwood Community Center, hands in his pockets, nerves knotting in his stomach. The building wasn't intimidating; it was just an old brick structure with a yellowing banner that read "Second Chances Start Here." But stepping through that door felt harder than facing prison gates.

He almost turned around twice. Once, when a group of people walked out laughing, as they belonged in a world he didn't. And once, when a woman pulling a toddler by the hand glanced at him with the wary look people give men who look like trouble.

But he'd told her, *Maybe I will.* And for some reason, he wanted to keep that almost promise. He took a breath, crossed the street, and walked inside.

The lobby smelled like old carpet and donated coffee. A corkboard on the wall overflowed with job postings, support group flyers, and scribbled notes offering rides or spare rooms. Behind a desk sat a woman with silver hair and a sharp, assessing gaze.

"Can I help you?" she asked.

He cleared his throat. "Yeah. I… uh… was told someone here could help with job placement. Re-entry stuff."

Her expression softened just a little. "Name?"

He gave it to her, and she typed it into a computer. Her eyebrows twitched, just for a second, when his record popped up. He saw it. He always saw it.

"You'll want Room B," she said, sliding him a clipboard. "Fill this out and have a seat."

He sat in a folding chair that creaked under him. The form asked everything he wished he didn't have to say out loud, felony details, prison years, drug history, skills that felt small and outdated. His handwriting wobbled on the paper.

He had just finished when she walked in.

She wore the same green jacket but carried an armful of files this time. Her eyes widened when she saw him, and something warm flickered there, relief, maybe even pride.

"You came," she said.

"Yeah," he replied, trying not to sound like a nervous kid.

She sat beside him, scanning the paperwork. "I'm glad. Really. Let me show you around."

She led him past open doors and crowded rooms. In one, a counselor sat with a circle of men talking about relapse triggers. In another, volunteers helped people write résumés. At the far end of the hallway was a computer lab full of hand-me-down desktops and a dozen people typing away as their futures depended on it.

"This is where most people start," she said. "We offer workshops, job coaching… even interview practice if you want it."

He nodded slowly. "I probably need all of that."

She smiled, a slight, encouraging curve of her lips that made his chest tighten. "Good. Then you're in the right place."

The following two weeks were a blur of early mornings and unfamiliar routines. He showed up at the center every day, sometimes before it opened. The staff, cautious at first, began warming to him as he helped rearrange chairs, carried boxes, and fixed a broken shelf without being asked.

Still, he felt the stares sometimes. A glance at his hands. A whisper after reading his intake form. People said they believed in second chances, but belief didn't always look like trust.

She was different. She treated him like someone capable, not someone dangerous. She taught him how to navigate online job portals, how to answer interview questions without flinching at the past, how to breathe through the guilt when it pressed too hard on his ribs.

One afternoon, after he'd struck out yet again, "We appreciate your honesty, but we've decided to move forward with another applicant," he sank onto the step outside the center. She found him there, elbows on his knees, staring at the cracks in the pavement.

"They don't want someone like me," he muttered.

"That's not true." She sat beside him. "They don't want someone like who you *were*. They don't even know who you are now."

"Does it matter?"

"Yes." Her voice was firm. "It matters a lot."

He shook his head. "Feels like every time I take a step forward, someone slams a door in my face."

"Then we'll find the one that doesn't," she said.

He looked at her, really looked, and wondered how many people in the world had this kind of faith left in them, faith in him, of all people.

The breakthrough came three days later. She approached him, waving a slip of paper. "I talked to a friend who manages a small warehouse on the east side. They're short-staffed. He's open to meeting you."

He blinked. "Are you sure?"

"He believes in giving people chances," she said. "And I believe you'll show him he's right."

So, he shaved, borrowed a clean shirt from the donation bin, and walked into the warehouse with his shoulders squared and palms sweating.

The manager, a gruff man with gray at his temples, read his résumé and asked him one question: "Are you willing to work hard and show up on time?"

"Yes, sir," he answered without hesitation.

"Then you start Monday."

It took him a moment to understand the words; it had all happened so fast. Then it clicked, she had done all the prework for him.

His first week on the job was brutal: long nights, aching muscles, and a constant fear of messing up. But he showed up early, stayed late, and kept his head down. Co-workers kept their distance at first, but the older guys appreciated someone who didn't complain about heavy lifting, and by the end of the week, they'd started teaching him shortcuts to make the work easier.

On Friday, the manager clapped him on the shoulder. "Good work this week," he said. "Keep it up."

It was a small thing, but it felt massive.

When he walked outside into the cool evening air, she was waiting by the curb, arms crossed, jacket zipped high, smiling at him like he'd done something remarkable.

"How was your first week?" she asked.

He exhaled slowly, the breath carrying a mix of exhaustion and pride. "I think," he said, "it's the start of something good." And for the first time in years, he believed it.

Chapter IV

Life settled into something almost steady. He woke before sunrise, caught the bus to the warehouse, worked until his muscles burned, and then headed straight to the community center. The routine felt safe, like rails laid down to keep him from slipping off the edge. For the first time in years, he felt like he was building something instead of destroying it.

But stability is fragile, especially for someone whose past sits just beneath the surface of every good day.

It began with a whisper.

He noticed it first in the kitchen at the center. A group of volunteers fell silent the moment he stepped inside, their eyes flicking from him to each other. One of them, a young woman with a clipboard pressed to her chest, offered a polite smile, too tight to be sincere. He'd seen that expression a thousand times in prison, and it tightened something in his gut.

Later that afternoon, he found her in the hallway sorting paperwork. She wouldn't meet his eyes.

"Did I... do something wrong?" he asked.

She shook her head quickly. "No. Nothing like that." But her hands trembled as she stacked the papers. "I just didn't realize who you were."

There it was. The same cold punch to the ribs he'd felt a hundred times since release. He wanted to ask how she found out, a Google search? Old news article? Someone recognizing his name from the trial? But he didn't. The answer didn't matter. What mattered was that people were talking, and talking, he knew, would spread fast.

Two days later, he learned just how far it had spread. He stopped at a gas station after his shift, sweat still clinging to his shirt, dust coating his boots. He grabbed a bottle of water and approached the counter, grateful he no longer froze at the sight of the bright fluorescent lights.

But the man behind him in line spoke his name. Not a question, an accusation.

He turned.

A stocky man in his early thirties stood there, face flushed, jaw tight. His eyes burned with something ancient and raw.

"You've got some nerve being out here like nothing happened."

He stiffened. "Do I know you?"

"You know who I am," the man snapped. "My cousin was the kid you killed."

The air went thin.

The man stepped closer, crowding him toward the counter. "You stole his life. Stole everything he should've had. And now you're out here walking around? Shopping? Working? Like you deserve that?"

He swallowed hard. "I served my time."

"That wasn't enough." The man's voice cracked under the weight of grief and rage. "It'll never be enough."

The cashier shifted nervously, but neither man looked away.

"I'm sorry," he said, because it was the only truth he could offer. "If I could change what happened, "

"Don't," the man snapped. "Don't you dare say that to me."

For a moment, the man looked like he might swing. Part of him wished he would. Part of him believed he deserved it.

But instead, the man spat at his feet. "You should've stayed locked up. That's where monsters belong."

Then he stormed out, the door banging hard behind him.

The cashier cleared her throat. "Do you… still want the water?"

He put a few dollars down on the counter and left without answering.

He didn't sleep that night. His body ached from tension he couldn't shake. Every time he closed his eyes, the look in that man's face burned into his mind, the grief, the hatred, the certainty that the world would never be right if he were walking through it.

By morning, he felt hollow. He skipped the center. Skipped breakfast. Skipped everything except work, and even that felt like moving through deep water.

She noticed immediately.

"You okay?" she asked gently when she saw him that evening. He shook his head. She stepped aside with him near the doorway. "Talk to me."

But he couldn't. The words stuck. The shame stuck. The guilt stuck. "It's nothing," he said. "Just tired."

She didn't believe him, but she didn't push. "If you need anything… I'm here."

He nodded but didn't look her in the eye.

The next complication came two days later, this time at the center itself. She found him in the hallway, jaw tight, shoulders rigid.

"We need to talk," she said quietly.

His stomach dropped.

The program director had asked to speak with her that morning. Word had reached him about the confrontation at the gas station, about whispers among volunteers, about "concerns" raised by members of the community.

"He thinks you being here might be a 'disruption,'" she said carefully. "That your presence could be… triggering."

"I don't belong here," he said instantly.

"That's not what I said."

"Doesn't matter." He stepped back. "He's right. Every time I walk into a room, people look at me like I'm a threat. Like I'm a…"

"You are *not* that boy anymore," she insisted.

"Tell them that," he shot back, louder than he meant.

Her face softened. "Let me handle this. Please. This place is meant for people like you. You deserve support."

He shook his head, turning away. "Maybe support is wasted on someone like me."

"Don't say that," she whispered.

But the words were already in him, already growing roots.

He skipped the center again the next day. Didn't answer when she texted. Didn't show up for a meeting she'd scheduled with a counselor. He went to work, worked himself into a sweat, then went home and sat in the dark.

His mind replayed every moment, the whispers, the stares, the confrontation. The way her boss questioned her judgment because of him. The way he seemed to bring chaos everywhere he went.

The past, it seemed, was not content to stay where he left it. It crawled back, inch by inch, through gaps he didn't know he still had.

By the end of the week, he wasn't sure if he'd been rebuilding a life… or building a fragile illusion that was now starting to crack, and for the first time since walking out of prison, he wondered whether trying to start over had been a mistake.

Chapter V

For the next several days, he moved through life like a man underwater. Work, bus, halfway house. Work, bus, halfway house. The rest, meetings, the community center, conversations with her, fell away piece by piece.

He kept telling himself he just needed space. Time. Quiet. But the truth was more straightforward and heavier: he was ashamed to be seen. Shame had a way of tightening around him until he couldn't breathe, and lately it wrapped him like a noose.

Each night, he sat on the thin mattress in his room, staring at the wall as shadows shifted with the headlights passing outside. He thought about relapse more than once. Not because he wanted the high, but because the numbness had once been a place where guilt couldn't find him.

He didn't use it, but he thought about it. And the thought of using it frightened him. By Friday, he hadn't spoken to her in four days.

On Saturday evening, he stepped off the bus after a ten-hour shift and felt something break inside him, not a sound, not a physical snap, just a quiet collapse of whatever had kept him standing.

He didn't walk toward the halfway house. Instead, he sat down on the curb, elbows on his knees, head in his hands. Traffic passed in bright streaks; the world moved like he wasn't part of it.

He didn't cry. He didn't curse. He just sat there, empty, the weight of the past pressing so hard he wondered if maybe the people whispering were right, perhaps he didn't deserve this life he was trying to build.

Footsteps approached. He didn't look up until he heard her voice.

"There you are."

He flinched at the sound of it, gentle but threaded with worry. She crouched down beside him, her green jacket brushing the pavement.

"I've been calling you all week," she said softly.

"I know." He said.

"Why didn't you answer?"

He stared at the street. "Because I didn't want you to see me like this."

"Like what?" She questioned.

"Like someone who keeps messing everything up."

She exhaled, long and pained. "You haven't messed anything up."

"That's not what people say."

"I don't care what people say." She touched his hand, "I know the truth, you have changed."

He shook his head, jaw tightening. "You should. They're right. Every time I get close to something good, the past shows up and ruins it. I hurt people. I took a life. That doesn't disappear just because I'm trying to be better."

She sat beside him on the curb, not caring about the dirt, the traffic, or the people walking by. "What happened at the gas station wasn't your fault."

"It was," he said without hesitation. "Everything that's happening now, people talking, your boss questioning you, it's because of me. Because of what I did. I bring trouble everywhere I go." He swallowed hard. "You deserve better than having to defend someone like me."

"Stop," she said sharply, not cruel, but certain. "Don't decide what I deserve. And don't rewrite the story to make yourself the villain in every moment of your life."

He didn't answer. Couldn't.

She waited, letting the silence settle. Finally, she spoke again, quieter this time. "You want to know what I see when I look at you?" He didn't trust himself to nod.

"I see someone who made the worst mistake a person can make and then spent twelve years paying for it. I see someone who got out and didn't run back to old habits. Someone who shows up early for work and stays late. Someone who pushes through fear every single day to buy a bottle of water in a store. Someone who walked through the doors of a place designed to help people like him, even though he was terrified."

Her voice shook slightly. "I see a man trying. Really trying. And that matters."

He felt his throat tighten. "Trying isn't enough."

"It is," she insisted gently. "It's the only thing that *is* enough. Redemption isn't a moment, it's a hundred tiny choices you make every day, even when you feel like you don't deserve the air you're breathing."

He closed his eyes, the words hitting something profound and aching inside him.

She reached out and placed her hand over his, not grabbing, just resting there like a promise. "You can't outrun your past," she said. "No one can. But you can stop letting it tell you who you are."

He stared at their hands, unsure how something so small could feel so stabilizing. After a long moment, he whispered, "I'm scared."

"I know," she said. "But you're not alone in it."

He breathed in shakily, like someone surfacing after being underwater too long.

"I don't know how to keep going," he admitted.

"Yes, you do," she replied. "You go one day at a time. One step at a time. And when the past tries to pull you under, you talk to me. You come to the center. You go to your meetings. You reach for the people who want to help you instead of hiding from them."

He didn't speak. But he didn't pull his hand away either.

She squeezed it softly. "Let's start over. Tonight. Right now. No more disappearing. No more carrying this alone."

Silence stretched, heavy, but different now. Less like drowning, more like catching breath. Finally, he nodded. "Okay."

A small smile lifted the edge of her mouth. "Good."

She stood and offered him her hand. For a moment, he hesitated, not because he didn't want to take it, but because part of him still believed he didn't deserve to.
But he reached for her anyway.

As she helped him to his feet, he realized something important: Redemption wasn't a thing handed to you. It was a thing you accepted, slowly, painfully, even when you didn't think you had the right.

And tonight, he chose not to run.

Chapter VI

The following week felt different, not easier, but steadier. He forced himself back into routine. He went to work. He returned to meetings. And, most importantly, he walked through the doors of the Glenwood Community Center with his shoulders square and his heartbeat loud but controlled.

People still stared. Some still whispered. But now he stayed. Now he refused to disappear. She stood beside him, not shielding him but walking with him, quiet, steady, present. That alone made each step feel possible.

On Thursday afternoon, the program director called her into his office. He waited outside, pretending to read a flyer on the bulletin board while anxiety crept up his spine. When the door opened ten minutes later, she gave a modest nod that meant *Come in.* The director, a man in his fifties with deep lines around his mouth, gestured toward a chair.

"I won't sugarcoat this," he began. "There's been concern."

Concern. The word tasted like judgment wrapped in politeness. He folded his hands in his lap. "I understand."

"I know you've been trying," the director said. "You show up on time. You're respectful. But some members of this community, clients and volunteers, feel uneasy. And after the incident at the gas station…"

He felt heat rise in his chest. "I didn't start that."

"No," the director agreed. "But it stirred emotions, old ones, painful ones. We can't ignore that."

He nodded. He wasn't here to argue. He was here to listen, even if the words hurt.

"We're hosting a community forum next week," the director continued. "A space for people to express concerns, ask questions, talk openly about re-entry work." He hesitated. "Some have asked if you'd be willing to speak."

His stomach dropped. "Speak?"

"Yes. About your experience. Your past. Your goals. Why programs like ours matter." The director folded his arms. "But let me be clear, you don't have to. It's not required."

He could barely breathe. Speak? In front of strangers? In front of people who already judged him? In front of people who might hate him?

She stepped forward gently. "You don't owe anyone an apology speech," she told him softly. "You don't owe them anything you're not ready to give."

He knew it wasn't about owing. It was about owning his story, his truth, the man he had become. His voice felt thin when he spoke. "If it helps… I'll do it."

Her eyes widened slightly, surprise, pride, fear for him all at once. The director nodded. "Very well. We'll add you to the schedule."

The night of the forum, the center buzzed with energy. Folding chairs filled the main hall, and people spilled into the back. Some faces were familiar. Some weren't. Some looked curious, others wary.

He stood behind the curtain near the podium, palms sweating, heart hammering. His mind flicked through every possible disaster: shouting, accusations, someone recognizing him from the trial, someone telling him he didn't belong.

She stood beside him, gently touching his arm. "Just breathe. Tell the truth. That's all."

He nodded, even as fear shook him to the bone.

The director stepped up to the microphone, gave a brief introduction to the event's purpose, and then gestured toward him.

"Our next speaker has agreed to share his journey with honesty and courage. Please welcome..."

He didn't hear the rest. His ears rang. He forced his legs to move.

The room fell quiet as he approached the podium. Every eye was on him. Every breath caught. He gripped the edges of the lectern to steady himself.

He stood at the podium, his hands gripping the sides like they were the only thing keeping him upright. His shoulders rose and fell as he tried to breathe.

"My name is Michael," he said, his voice already unsteady. "I, um... I didn't write this down because I really didn't know what I was going to say. A friend told me to tell the truth."

He swallowed hard and stared at the floor for a second too long.

"When I was seventeen, I robbed a convenience store for drug money, and I killed an eight-year-old boy."

The words hit the room and just stayed there.

"He was eight," Michael said again, quieter this time, like he needed to hear it himself. "He should've been worried about school. About cartoons. About growing up. Instead, he died because of me."

His hands began to shake. He pulled one away from the podium and wiped his face, embarrassed but unable to stop.

"I see him all the time," he said. "I see his face when I wake up. I see him when I try to sleep. I see him in grocery stores, at bus stops, everywhere. Every kid that age feels like a reminder that won't let go."

He took a breath that turned into a sharp, broken sound.

"I don't have words big enough for that kind of regret. I don't think anyone does. Twelve years in prison didn't make it go away. It didn't make it lighter. It just gave me more time to understand how much I destroyed."

He paused, pressing his lips together. The silence stretched.

"There were nights in my cell when I wished I wouldn't wake up," he admitted. "Not because I wanted to escape punishment, but because I didn't know how to carry what I'd done anymore. Knowing a child is gone because of you… It doesn't leave room to breathe."

His voice cracked fully now.

"I don't deserve forgiveness. I know that. I'm not asking for it." He shook his head. "I just need you to understand that I live with this every second of my life. I always will."

He tried to continue, but the words stalled. His mouth opened, then closed. He bent forward slightly, both hands back on the podium now, knuckles white.

"I…" He stopped. Took a breath and tried again. "When I got out, I thought maybe I could just stay quiet. Stay invisible. But the past doesn't let you do that."

A tear slipped down his cheek. He didn't wipe it away.

"I almost gave up," he said. "More than once. I thought about using again, running away from myself. I thought about just ending it, that maybe the world would be better if I were just gone.

Thought maybe the world would be better off if I didn't try to be part of it."

His voice dropped to a whisper.

"And then this place let me walk through the door."

He looked up, eyes glassy.

"The community center didn't tell me it was okay that I killed a defenseless child. They didn't pretend that what I did wasn't real. But they didn't turn me away either. They helped me learn how to live without running. How to stay clean and how to show up even when I hated myself."

His breathing was uneven now. He pressed a hand to his chest.

"I don't know if I'll ever forgive myself," he said. "I don't know if I should. But this place gave me a reason not to quit. And for someone like me, that matters more than anything."

He nodded once, like he was convincing himself.

"I'll spend the rest of my life carrying what I did to that child. Nothing will change that. But because of this place, I'm still here. I'm still trying. And I'm trying because giving up would mean that the eight-year-old boy died for nothing."

His voice failed him completely. He bowed his head, silent, shoulders shaking, unable to finish.

After a long moment, he stepped away from the podium, not looking at anyone, the weight of his truth hanging heavy in the room.

Then someone in the third row, an older woman with gray hair and trembling hands, began to clap. Slow. Soft. But steady.

Another person joined. Then a third. Not applause of celebration, applause of acknowledgment. Not forgiveness. But not rejection. Just a room full of people saying, *We heard you.*

He felt something loosen in his chest. Something old and tightly coiled began to unwind. She met him at the side of the stage. Her eyes glowed with pride, with relief, with something gentler and deeper.

"You did it," she whispered.

He let out a breath that felt like shedding weight he'd carried for years. "Yeah," he said softly. "I did."

And for the first time, he didn't feel like he was walking through the world wearing his crime like a scarlet letter. He felt like a man who had spoken his truth, a man who had faced the community and himself and survived it.

Chapter VII

Life didn't magically get easier after the forum. No one threw open doors for him. No one handed him forgiveness wrapped in soft words. But something had shifted, subtle but unmistakable.

People at the community center no longer turned away when he walked in. Some kept their distance, but others greeted him with cautious nods or quiet "good to see you" murmurs. The whispers didn't vanish, but they lost their sting. He had said his truth out loud, and it no longer controlled him the way silence once did.

At work, the warehouse felt different, too. The older guys slapped him on the back with something like respect. Even the younger workers, still wary but curious, had started asking him for tips about stacking product or securing pallets. The manager pulled him aside one afternoon and said, "Keep this up, and we'll talk about moving you to forklift certification."

It wasn't a promise. But it was a sign. A small one. A real one.

Those were the kinds of signs he was learning to look for.

The following week, he returned to his meetings more consistently. He spoke up when he felt cravings creeping in. He didn't pretend to be stronger than he was. When he talked, his voice still shook, but he didn't hide the shaking anymore.

"You're learning to trust yourself," his sponsor told him one night after the meeting. "That's harder than staying clean."

He didn't fully believe that, but he held onto the words anyway.

And then there was her.

Their conversations grew longer, easier, less tangled in fear or guilt. She never pushed him, never pried. She just walked beside him, sometimes literally, sometimes in quiet text messages sent late at night when the team at work was giving him a hard shift.

One evening, after he'd finished a long day at the warehouse, she met him outside the center with two cups of cheap hot chocolate from the machine by the front desk.

"You looked cold," she said, handing one to him.

They sat on the low brick wall by the parking lot. Leaves drifted around them in the warm autumn wind.

"I've been thinking," she said.

"That sounds dangerous," he replied, managing a small smile.

She nudged him lightly with her shoulder. "I've been thinking about how you stood up there at the forum. How brave that was."

"It didn't feel brave," he admitted. "It felt like being cut open."

"Bravery usually does."

He stared at the steam rising from the cup. "I didn't expect anyone to listen."

"They listened because you spoke honestly." She paused. "And because you're not hiding anymore."

He let her words settle. Then, quietly, he said, "It scares me."

"What does?" She asked.

"Letting myself hope for something better."

She was silent for a moment, then said, "Hope is supposed to scare you a little. It means it matters."

He swallowed thickly. "Do you think I deserve it?"

She didn't answer right away. Instead, she reached out and rested her hand on his gentle, warm, steady. "It's not about what you deserve," she said softly. "It's about what you build. And you're building something good."

A breath he didn't know he'd been holding eased out of him. He didn't look away.

For the first time, her hand didn't feel like something he had to avoid or retreat from. It felt earned, not through perfection, not through redemption, but through effort, through the slow repair of a life that had been broken for too long.

The next morning, before work, he walked into a convenience store. Not because he needed anything, though he did grab a bottle of water, but because he wanted to.

The bell above the door chimed. The lights buzzed overhead. A register hummed softly in the corner.

He felt no panic this time, no trembling hands. No ghosts rising from the past to choke him. He paid for the water, nodded to the cashier, and stepped outside into the morning air.

It was such a small act, normal, forgettable, unnoticed by everyone else. But to him, it felt like standing at the top of a mountain he had once believed was impossible to climb.

He took a drink, the water cool against his tongue, and walked toward the bus stop as the sun began to rise.

A man shaped by regret. A man shaped by love. A man shaped by effort, day after day, step after step. A man not defined by what he had done, but by what he chose to do now.

He still carried his past. He always would. But now he had his future, too, and for the first time in a long time, he felt strong enough to hold both.

The Roadside Angel

Chapter 1

The highway ran straight as a blade through the desert, cutting the world into two endless halves of sand and sky.

Ethan Carver stared through the windshield until his eyes blurred, the heat shimmering ahead making the road look like it was melting into nothing. The dashboard clock glowed 3:12 p.m., but it might as well have been midnight for how dark he felt.

The collar was in the glove box.

He could feel it there, the way you feel a pebble in your shoe even when you try to ignore it. Every bump in the road seemed to whisper, *You left. You walked away.*

His right hand twitched on the steering wheel. He told himself he was adjusting his grip, but his fingers drifted toward the glove box latch anyway. They hovered there for a second, then he yanked them back like the handle was hot.

"Don't be dramatic," he muttered.

The passenger seat was worse. His resignation letter lay there, folded and refolded so many times the edges were going soft. The church letterhead looked wrong to him now, like it belonged to someone else. *Reverend Ethan J. Carver* no longer matched the man whose name it carried. That man believed in things.

Ethan cracked the window. Dry air pushed in, hot and gritty, carrying the faint smell of dust and sunburnt sage. Nothing out here but scrub and low hills, the occasional cactus raising its arms like it had a question God had never answered.

Ethan snorted under his breath. "Get in line."

A car passed in the opposite lane, just a blur of silver and a whoosh of air, and then it was him and the highway again. The radio was off. He couldn't stand music today. Every worship song felt like a lie, and every secular song felt like a ghost of some simpler time.

He had the strange, floating sensation of being between lives. Behind him: a brick church with stained glass windows, a pulpit he'd stood behind for nearly twenty years, a congregation that still thought he had a direct line to heaven. Ahead of him: more road. That was it, just more road.

He pressed his thumb against the steering wheel, feeling the faint texture of the worn leather. His throat felt dry. He couldn't tell if it was from the heat or the words he'd choked down for years.

"Dear brothers and sisters," he whispered to the empty car, his voice rough. "Today we'll be talking about… about…"

He couldn't even finish the sentence. The words dissolved, leaving a hollow ringing in his ears. Once, he'd known what to say. Once, sermons had come like water, prayers spilling over, stories tying themselves neatly to Scripture, his voice steady and sure as if he believed every word.

Then Lorie had died. His hand tightened on the wheel.

He pushed the thought away, pressing his foot down a little harder on the accelerator. The engine hummed slightly louder, the needle creeping up the speedometer. The desert rolled on, silent and indifferent.

He drove.

Chapter 2

The sun dipped a little lower, turning the light into a deeper gold. Shadows gathered at the base of rocks and bushes, stretching like dark fingers across the sand. Ethan's water bottle was lukewarm when he took a sip. It tasted like plastic and regret.

"What's the point of faith," he said softly to the windshield, "if God doesn't show up?"

The words startled him. He hadn't meant to say them out loud. They'd lived in his chest for months, a dull ache he pressed down whenever someone said, *"We're praying, pastor. We know God hears you."*

He laughed once, a short, broken sound that didn't feel like it belonged to him.
"Does He?"

The last time Ethan had stood behind the pulpit, the sanctuary lights burning bright and unforgiving, he'd looked at the faces he'd known for years, Helen in the second pew, constantly nodding along; the Ramirez family crammed into one row; old Mr. Douglas with his hearing aid turned off half the time, and he hadn't seen the flock anymore.

He'd seen people who trusted him to explain a God he wasn't sure he recognized.

He'd preached anyway, words from some mechanical part of his brain that still knew how to string verses together. He'd talked about hope. He had spoken about endurance. He'd told them God was near to the brokenhearted, even as his own heart felt like it was on the far side of a closed door.

After the service, they'd filed past him in the aisle, shaking his hand. *Beautiful sermon, pastor. That really spoke to me. You're a blessing to this church.*

No one noticed that his eyes were glassy, that his smile didn't quite reach the corners. No one asked if he believed what he'd just said.

"Twenty years," he said into the empty car. "Twenty years of telling people, you show up. And then…"

Lorie's face came back whether he wanted it or not. A kid's face, thirteen and still mostly baby-soft around the cheeks, eyes too big for the hospital bed she'd sunk into.

They'd prayed. The church had filled with hands raised and voices cracking, begging for a miracle. Ethan had prayed as his life depended on it; maybe it had. He'd promised things, bargained in ways he would have once preached against. *Just this one, Lord. Just this one.*

Two days later, he stood at her graveside and tried to say the right words to her parents. God felt far away that day. Then he felt farther the next, and the next like radio static fading out your song, leaving only white noise.

"I used to tell people God was closer to them than their own breath," he said, fingers tapping the steering wheel. "Was that for their sake, or mine?"

The collar shifted in the glove box when the car hit a bump. Inside his head, it sounded like a tiny laugh. He clenched his jaw and looked back at the road, straight and endless and bright.

"If this is a test," Ethan said, his voice barely above a whisper, "I'm failing it."

Chapter 3

The temperature gauge nudged higher before Ethan noticed. He'd been staring at a distant shimmer on the horizon, half-convinced it was a building, half-convinced it was just more heat messing with his eyes, when the red needle caught his attention. It was edging past the middle, climbing steadily.

"Don't you dare," he muttered to the car. "Not now." As if in answer, the engine gave a faint, worrying whine.

Ethan's heart rate picked up. He eased his foot off the gas and scanned the sides of the road. No gas station. No rest stop. Just scrub and sand and rocks, the scenery repeating itself like a cruel loop.

"Come on," he said. "Just get me to… anywhere."
The needle climbed higher.

A beep sounded, shrill and accusing. A tiny red light blinked on the dashboard. "Great." He tried to keep his tone level and failed. "Fantastic."

The engine cough-sputtered, the car lurching like it was trying to shake something off. Hot air began to pump through the vents. The power steering stiffened, the wheel suddenly heavier in his hands.

"Come on, come on," he whispered.

The car wheezed, then lost power. The dashboard lights flashed once, then fizzled out like a dying heartbeat. The engine went quiet. The only sound left was the hum of tires rolling slower and slower until the car coasted to a reluctant stop on the shoulder.

Silence rushed in, thick and immediate. For a moment, Ethan just sat there, both hands locked on the wheel, as if tightening his grip might convince the engine to change its mind. The heat pressed in around him. Sweat slid down his back.

Ethan closed his eyes.

"Of course," he said softly. "Why wouldn't this happen now?"

He let his forehead tip forward until it rested against the top of the steering wheel. The plastic was warm. Everything was warm, sweat, air, the creeping anger that began to rise from somewhere behind his ribs.

When he opened his eyes again, the world looked sharper. Crueler. He grabbed the door handle and shoved the door open.

The outside heat hit him like a physical thing, dry and heavy. He stepped out anyway, slamming the door behind him. The car, a faded blue sedan with more miles on it than he wanted to admit, sat there smugly, hood pointed toward the empty road like a dog that had finally decided to lie down and not move another inch.

Ethan walked around to the front and popped the hood latch. Hot metal and steam greeted him. He squinted against it, waving one hand uselessly in the air.

He knew as much about engines as he did about quantum physics. He stared down like the tangle of pipes and parts might explain itself.

"Talk about timing," he said.

The desert stretched out in every direction, the highway a thin dark ribbon cutting through endless tan. No cars in sight. No distant rumble. Just a faint buzz of some unseen insect, the whisper of hot wind scraping across sand.

He pulled his phone from his pocket. No bars. The little "No Service" indicator glared up at him.

"Perfect," he snapped, shoving it back into his pocket. Anger flared, bright and childish. Before he could think better of it, he drew his foot back and kicked the front tire. Pain shot up his toes and into his ankle.

"Ow, " He hopped backward, cursing under his breath. The car, indifferent, sat quietly in the sun.

He stood there on the side of the road, a former pastor in dusty shoes, sweating through his shirt, glaring at a dead car as it had personally betrayed him. His heart thudded in his ears.

"Is this funny to you?" he shouted suddenly, voice bouncing off into the empty air. "Is this supposed to be some kind of object lesson?"

Neither God nor the desert answered. The sky stayed cloudless and blue. He waited, breath heaving, for some sign, a breeze, a voice, anything.

Nothing.

Of course, nothing.

He shook his head, a bitter smile tugging at his mouth. "Fine," he said. "Message received."

That's when he felt it: the prickle at the back of his neck. The sense that he wasn't alone anymore.

He turned.

Chapter 4

A man stood a few yards behind him on the shoulder, where a moment ago there had been nothing but empty road. Ethan's first thought was that he had to be dehydrated. The heat was playing tricks on his eyes. But the man didn't waver like a mirage. He just stood there, solid and still, his shadow falling long across the gravel. He was barefoot.

That detail lodged itself in Ethan's mind and refused to move. Barefoot, on hot asphalt that should have burned skin, and yet the man didn't flinch. He wore simple clothes: faded jeans and a loose, sun-bleached shirt with sleeves rolled to the elbows. A small canvas bag hung across his chest, the kind hikers carried.

He looked like he could have been in his mid-thirties or maybe even his mid-fifties; something about him resisted being pinned down. His hair was a dark, unremarkable brown, too long to be tidy, too short to look wild. His face was tanned, lined at the corners of his eyes in a way that suggested laughing more than frowning.

He regarded Ethan with calm curiosity, as if finding a stranded man yelling at the sky was mildly interesting but not particularly alarming.

"Rough day?" the man asked. His voice was gentle, with no noticeable accent, just the kind of tone people used when they already knew the answer.

Ethan blinked. "Where did you come from?"

The man tilted his head toward the road behind him. "Down that way."

"I didn't see you," Ethan said.

"You were busy arguing." The man's eyes flicked to the sky, then back to Ethan. "Easy to miss things when you're doing that."

A flush crept up Ethan's neck. "I wasn't..." He stopped himself. Lying felt pointless. "Yeah. I suppose I was."

The man took a few unhurried steps closer, stopping at a polite distance. His feet really were bare. Ethan looked for signs of blisters, burns, something, but the skin looked... normal. Dusty, but unharmed.

"Are you going somewhere in particular?" the man asked, nodding toward the car.

"Anywhere that isn't where I came from," Ethan said before he could soften the words.

The man's mouth curved in a small, almost knowing smile. "That's a big place."

Ethan exhaled, long and tired. "Look, I don't know who you are, but unless you happen to be a mechanic with a portable miracle in that bag, I'm not sure you can really help."

The man glanced under the open hood, leaned in slightly, then shook his head. "She's done for the day. Maybe longer."

Ethan bristled. "You didn't even look."

"I looked enough." The man's eyes met his eyes again. They were a clear, steady hazel. "There's a diner a few miles up the road. You can call for help from there."

"A few miles?" Ethan repeated the words, dropping like stones into his stomach. In this heat, with no shade, the idea made his skin itch. "You mean walk?"

The man lifted one shoulder in a slight shrug. "Unless you plan to push the car, or maybe 'Flintstone' it there."

Ethan opened his mouth to snap back something sarcastic, then stopped. The truth was, he didn't have better options: no service, no traffic, no ideas.

"Fine," he muttered. "Guess I walk."

The man nodded. "Good choice. Do you want company?"

The question was so simple that it almost annoyed Ethan. Did he want company? He wasn't sure he'd wanted his own company for months. The idea of walking alongside a stranger, of making small talk about the weather or directions, sounded exhausting. Still, the road ahead stretched long and featureless, and the thought of doing it alone made his chest tighten.`

Ethan studied the man again. Barefoot, calm, carrying nothing but that canvas bag. No car in either direction. No dust trail to suggest where he'd come from. Something didn't quite add up.

"What's your name?" Ethan asked.

The man smiled faintly. "You can call me whatever makes you comfortable."

"That's not an answer."

"It's the one I have." The man said.

They stood in silence for a moment, dry wind tugging at Ethan's shirt.

"Are you always this cryptic?" Ethan asked.

"Only when people ask questions they don't really want answered."

Ethan huffed out a breath that was almost a laugh. "You're not making this decision easier."

"I'm not supposed to." The man's gaze softened. "But you might find the walk less heavy if you shared it."

The phrasing scraped against something inside Ethan. How many times had he told his congregation they didn't have to walk alone? How many times had he said God would shoulder their burdens too?

Now, here he was on the side of an empty road, deciding whether to say yes to a barefoot stranger because he didn't want to be alone with his own thoughts. Ethan looked down the highway. The faint shimmer he'd hoped was a building had solidified just enough to suggest the outline of something artificial, a sign, maybe, or the curve of a roof against the sky.

He sighed. "Alright, walk with me. At least until the diner."

The man nodded as if this were the most natural outcome in the world. "Good." He stepped forward, falling into pace beside Ethan as they started down the road.

Chapter 5

The first stretch of walking was just the sound of their footsteps and the low rush of wind skimming across the pavement.

Ethan's shoes scuffed against the shoulder gravel, dislodging tiny rocks that skittered away. Beside him, the man walked with straightforward, unhurried strides, as if the heat didn't bother him at all.

Ethan tried not to look at the bare feet.

"So," he said finally, more to fill the silence than anything, "you just… walk highways for fun?"

The man smiled. "You could say that."

"I could," Ethan said, "but I'd hope for more detail."

"Sometimes people are where they think they chose to be," the man replied. "Sometimes they're where they've been led. Either way, the road is the same." He glanced at Ethan. "What about you?"

"What about me?"

"Did you choose this road, or did you end up on it because you didn't know where else to go?" The man questioned.

Ethan shifted his gaze to the horizon. The diner was still out of reach, a vague promise in the distance.

"I put gas in the car and pointed it away from town," Ethan said. "That feels like choosing."

"Pointed it away from what, exactly?" the man asked. "A place? A job? A person?"

Ethan's jaw tightened. "All of the above."

"And toward what?"

Ethan didn't answer immediately. A bead of sweat slid down his temple. "Nowhere," he admitted at last. "That's the point."

The man nodded as if this confirmed something he'd already suspected. "Pain tries very hard to convince us nowhere is safer than somewhere."

"That's a nice fortune-cookie line," Ethan said. "You practice that one?"

The man chuckled softly. "Does it bother you because it's untrue, or because it's true?"

Ethan glowered at the road. *This is why I hate conversations*, he thought. Words always seemed to find the sore spots. "You ask a lot of questions."

"Only the ones that are already echoing in your head," the man replied. "I think you've been asking yourself versions of them for a long time."

"How would you know that?" Ethan asked.

The man didn't answer right away. A crow called from somewhere in the distance, a harsh caw that cut across the quiet. Finally, the man said, "You have the look of someone who's been carrying a heavy thing for so long he's forgotten what his hands feel like empty."

Ethan's throat tightened unexpectedly. "I'm fine."

"I didn't say you weren't," the man replied. "Fine and empty aren't opposites."

Ethan wished for the car again, just so he'd have something to fiddle with, knobs, radio, window controls. Out here, there was nowhere to put his hands but at his sides or in his pockets, nowhere to look but at the road stretching ahead.

"So, who or what are you?" Ethan asked. "A therapist? Some life coach wandering the desert, offering unsolicited insight?"

The man's eyes crinkled at the corners. "Do you want me to be?"

Ethan made a frustrated sound. "I'd like you to be normal. That's what I'd like."

"Nobody out here is normal," the man said mildly. "Not the people yelling at the sky. Not the ones who walk barefoot by choice."

Ethan opened his mouth to retort, then closed it again.

They walked in silence for a while. The heat pressed down, heavy and constant. Sweat glued Ethan's shirt to his back. His calves ached.

"Why did you become a pastor?" the man asked suddenly.

The question hit like a stone hitting his ribs. Ethan swallowed. "Why are you barefoot?"

The man glanced at his own feet as if noticing them for the first time. "Shoes wear out."

"So do people," Ethan said.

The man nodded. "Why did you become a pastor?"

Ethan stared straight ahead. The diner was closer now; he could almost make out the shape of a sign.

"My father was one," he said finally. "Seemed like the family business."

The man waited.

Ethan sighed. "And... I believed it. Once. It wasn't just an obligation. I thought," He paused, searching for the right words. "I thought God had done something in me. I wanted to spend my life telling people about it."

"And now?"

"Now," Ethan said slowly, "I'm not sure what I experienced, or what I talked myself into because everyone expected me to."

The man regarded him with a quiet intensity. "Did you lose your faith, Ethan, or did you hide it somewhere you knew no one would find it?"

Ethan stopped walking. The sound of their footsteps ceased, leaving only the whisper of wind and the faint tick of cooling asphalt.

"How do you know my name?" he asked.

The man's expression didn't change. "You wear it like a coat. It's hard to miss."

"I didn't tell you," Ethan insisted. "I never said it."

"You said it out loud," the man replied. He tapped two fingers lightly against his chest. "Not with your mouth."

A chill slipped down Ethan's spine despite the heat.

"This is ridiculous," he said, turning back toward the road, forcing his legs to move. "You're messing with me."

The man fell into step beside him again without effort. "Would you rather I agree with everything you already think?"

"Yes," Ethan snapped. "That would be nice for a change."

"That would leave you exactly where you are," the man said. "On a broken-down road, yelling at a silent sky."

Ethan's anger flared again, bright and hot and familiar. "And what do you know about that, huh? About yelling and getting nothing back? About begging God for one thing, just one, and being met with silence?"

The man's face softened. "More than you think."

"You don't know anything about me," Ethan said.

"I know enough," the man replied. "I know you asked for a girl to live, and she died. I know you told her parents God was still good. I know every word tasted like ash in your mouth. And I know you've been wondering ever since if you lied to them or to yourself."

Ethan stumbled, his breath catching.

He hadn't said Lorie's name. He hadn't said "hospital," "funeral," or "parents" out loud. Those memories lived in the locked room behind his ribs.

Ethan stopped a second time, dust puffing up around his shoes. "How," he whispered, "do you know that?"

The man looked at him for a long moment, the wind tugging at his shirt, the sky bright and hard above them. "You said it out loud," he repeated gently, tapping his chest once more. "You just didn't know anyone was listening."

Ethan's pulse pounded in his ears. The diner sign stood ahead, clearer now, words still unreadable but undeniably real.

Ethan swallowed hard. "Who are you?" he asked.

The man's smile was small and unreadable. "Right now? Someone walking beside you."

Ethan stood on the hot shoulder of an empty desert highway, sweat trickling down his back, confusion and fear churning in his stomach. The road ahead shimmered, uncertain but unavoidable. He took a breath that felt like it scraped his lungs on the way in.

Then Ethan and the man started walking again.

Chapter 6

The sun drifted lower, smearing the sky with a burnt-orange haze. The air felt thicker now, as if the desert were holding its breath. Ethan's mouth was dry, and each swallow tasted like dust.

The man walked beside him with the same steady ease, hands tucked loosely behind his back, as though this endless highway were nothing more than a stroll through a shaded park.

Ethan forced his focus forward. The diner was closer, yes, but still too far for comfort. The heat pressed in from all directions, wrapping him in something heavy and oppressive.

After several minutes of strained quiet, the man spoke again.

"You're tired." The man stated.

Ethan wiped his forehead. "Good observation."

"It's not the walk that's tiring you."

Ethan snorted. "Sure, it is. It's a hundred degrees out here."

"The heat wears at the body," the man said. "But guilt wears at the soul."

Ethan stumbled a little. "I didn't say anything about guilt."

"You didn't have to." The man said, "You wear it on your soul."

Ethan clenched his jaw. Every word the man spoke felt like a blade slipped between ribs, not deep enough to wound, but sufficient to pry things open.

"I walked away," Ethan said sharply. "I left my church. My calling. My marriage. Pick one. I'm sure guilt ties into it somewhere."

The man nodded. "It's not the walking away that troubles you."

"Oh? Please, enlighten me since you seem to know everything." Ethan was growing angry.

"It's why you left," the man said softly. "And why didn't you tell the truth?"

Ethan opened his mouth to argue, then closed it again. Because the man had, unfortunately, landed too close to home.

He had left his congregation with a neat explanation of the need for rest, for stepping back for reflection. He hadn't told them the truth: that he no longer believed he could hear God in the silence. That every prayer felt like shouting into a canyon that gave nothing back.

The man watched him quietly, reading what Ethan couldn't quite voice.

"What would you have said," the man asked, "if you'd been honest?"

Ethan's throat tightened. He looked down at the road, watching the cracks and small pebbles pass under his feet. "I would've said I'm lost."

"There," the man murmured. "That wasn't so difficult."

Chapter 7

The horizon began shifting colors as the sun dipped lower, turning shadows into long, spindly shapes. Ethan squinted toward the diner sign, still too far to read, but close enough to make out its rectangular outline.

The man glanced at him. "You know what I've been wondering?"

"No," Ethan said. "But I'm sure you'll tell me anyway."

"I've been wondering when you stopped listening."

"To whom?" Ethan asked.

The man raised an eyebrow. "You already know."

"God," Ethan said hollowly. "Just say God."

"If you insist." The man said, "Why did you stop listening to God?"

Ethan let out a harsh laugh. "Listening? I tried listening. For months. Maybe years. Silence was the only thing I ever got back."

"That silence isn't punishment," the man said. "It's an invitation."

"Invitation to what? Madness?" Ethan questioned.

"To admit that you needed help."

Ethan shook his head violently. "No. That's not how it works. Pastors don't get to fall apart. We're supposed to hold up other people. We're supposed to be the ones with answers."

The man's tone was gentle but firm. "Who told you that, God, or the people who relied on you?"

Ethan felt his breath catch. "Both."

"Wrong," the man said. "Just the latter."

Ethan stopped walking for a moment, running a hand over his face. The air burned against his skin. He could feel another question coming before the man even opened his mouth.

"And when Lorie died," the man said quietly, "who comforted the comforter?"

Ethan's stomach twisted. He hated how that question made his knees weak. He hated the way it scraped across the half-healed wound he kept taped over in the dark.

"You need to stop," Ethan said. "I mean it."

The man nodded. "We can be silent."

But even the silence wasn't safe. Ethan felt things shifting inside him, small, painful cracks forming in walls he'd built months ago.

Chapter 8

They walked on in quiet, filled with tension, Ethan trying to steady his breathing, the man simply matching his pace without effort.

Then the man held out his arm, stopping them both.

Ethan looked around. "What?"

The man nodded toward the pavement ahead.

A rattlesnake lay coiled in the center of the road, its body a tense, perfect circle, its tail shaking in a low, angry rattle. Its eyes were fixed on them, dark slits that warned them not to come closer.

Ethan froze. "Great. Perfect."

The rattle grew louder, vibrating against the heat-thickened air. Ethan could feel the danger radiating from it, cold, coiled, ready to strike.

Before Ethan could speak, the man stepped forward.

"Don't," Ethan grabbed for his arm and missed.

The man knelt slowly on the road, his bare feet inches away from hot pavement, his posture relaxed and utterly fearless. He lowered his hand, palm open, like he was greeting an old friend.

He whispered something Ethan couldn't hear, soft, rhythmic, almost soothing.
The rattlesnake uncoiled.

Ethan's breath caught as the serpent's tense body loosened, its rattle slowing until it stopped entirely. Then, without any sound or strike, it slid away across the road and vanished into the scrub brush.

Ethan stared. "What," he whispered, "was that?"

"Fear listens when certainty does not," the man said, rising again. "Most creatures only strike when they feel unseen."

Ethan swallowed hard. "And you weren't afraid?"

"Not of him," the man said. "I knew he didn't want to harm us."

"How?"

"Because I asked," the man said simply.

Ethan felt a tremor in his chest. Not fear, something else. Something ancient and stirring. "Who are you?" he murmured again. But the man only smiled.

Chapter 9

They resumed their walk, Ethan's legs trembling slightly, not from the distance, but from the unnerving display he'd just witnessed.

"You believe in miracles," the man said, "or you used to."

"I used to," Ethan admitted. "Not anymore."

"Because one prayer wasn't answered?"

"Because a lot of them weren't answered, and the most recent one was the most important prayer that wasn't answered."

They continued for several yards in silence before the man spoke again.

"And you believe that means God was never listening?" Asked the man, "Or that he doesn't exist?"

Ethan clenched his fists. "Don't twist it. I prayed for Lorie. I begged. I sat by her bed and read Scripture until my voice cracked. Her parents held onto every word I said, and I," His voice broke. "I promised them God was there, that He cared. That He would act."

"And when she died?" The man asked, "How does any of that mean that God didn't care or that he didn't act?"

Ethan stopped walking, breath shaking. "When she died... I realized I'd spoken in God's place. I'd told them what I wanted to believe, not what I knew to be true."

"And what do you believe now?"

"That God wasn't listening," Ethan said. "Or worse, He was, and He did nothing."

The man looked at him with a softness that made Ethan want to look away. "You think silence is abandonment."

"What else could it be?"

"Silence," the man said, "can be presence. Or patience. Or invitation."

Ethan shook his head. "No. Silence is just silence."

The man studied him for a moment. "Then why are you talking to me?"

Ethan blinked. "What?"

"If silence is meaningless," the man said gently, "why are you so desperate to fill it?"

Ethan opened his mouth, then closed it again.

The road stretched out ahead of him, shimmering with heat. Somewhere beyond that shimmer was a diner that suddenly felt very far away.

Chapter 10

The walk grew heavier. Ethan's steps slowed, his breath becoming shallow. The weight on his chest, the old guilt, the anger, the grief, felt like it had doubled in the space of an hour. He felt stripped bare. Unraveled. Like every piece of armor he'd worn for months was being peeled off and laid out for inspection.

The man stayed beside him but didn't speak again for a long time. It was almost worse that way, Ethan was left alone with the thoughts the man had stirred up.

Finally, trying to distract himself, Ethan asked, "How far did you say the diner was? It seems like it isn't getting closer."

"We're closer than you think," the man said.

"That's not an answer," Ethan said.

"It's the one that matters."

Ethan huffed. "You know, you're incredibly frustrating."

The man smiled, "So, I've been told."

Ethan shot him a look. "By who?"

The man smiled faintly. "By people who weren't ready to hear what they already knew."

Ethan didn't bother responding. His anger had dissolved into a weary, aching sadness, not just for Lorie or for his congregation, but for himself. For the man he thought he was, and the man he realized he might have become.

The man's voice came again, softer than before. "She forgave you, you know."

Ethan froze. "Don't."

"She did."

"She's dead," Ethan said flatly.

"Dead people don't lose the ability to forgive." Said the man.

Ethan's breath hitched. He felt something crack deep inside, something he'd held shut for too long. He kept walking only because stopping would have been its own kind of collapse.

Chapter 11

The diner sign finally came into clear view, rusted metal, chipped paint, letters faded from years of sun. It sat at the end of a gravel driveway leading to a squat building with a flickering neon "OPEN" sign in the window.

Ethan exhaled a shaky breath of relief. "There," he said. "I can call a tow truck, get water, maybe even sit in the air conditioning."

"Those things will help your body," the man said. "Not your spirit."

"My spirit can wait," Ethan muttered. His feet sped up, toward shade, toward relief, toward anything that didn't require him to be vulnerable on an open road.

The man slowed.

Ethan didn't notice at first. He walked three more steps before realizing the man was no longer beside him.

He turned.

The man stood still, hands at his sides, watching him with an expression that wasn't sad, but wasn't quite neutral either.

"You're not coming?" Ethan asked.

"I've gone as far as I'm meant to," the man said.

"Meaning what?" Ethan asked.

"Meaning this part of the road is yours alone."

Ethan felt something tighten in his chest. "Wait. You, you can't just stop here."

"I can." The man said, "In fact, I just did."

"Why? What does that even mean?"

The man lifted one hand in a small gesture of blessing, or farewell. "We've spoken all the words that needed speaking today."

Ethan took a step towards him. "But I still have questions."

"You'll find answers," the man said. "But not all today, and not from me."

The wind shifted, kicking small swirls of dust.

"But," Ethan's voice cracked. "I don't even know who you are."

"You do," the man said softly. "You just don't know how to name it yet."

Ethan swallowed hard. "Will I see you again?"

The man smiled, a gentle, patient smile that held something ancient and kind. "You'll see me every time you stop running."

Without a sound, the man was gone. No footsteps. No fading silhouette. Just an empty road. As if he'd never been there at all.

Chapter 12

Ethan stood rooted to the spot, the wind brushing his shoulders, the setting sun casting long shadows across the pavement. His breath came in short, disbelieving bursts. "Wait," he whispered. "Wait!"

He walked in a quick circle, scanning the desert for footprints, movement, anything, but the man had vanished as cleanly as smoke.

Finally, shaking, Ethan turned toward the diner. His steps were uneven, his vision blurred with exhaustion and something heavier, fear, awe, grief, he couldn't tell.

The bell over the diner door jingled when he pushed inside. Cool air hit his face like a blessing. A waitress behind the counter looked up and smiled politely.

"Evening. Need a menu?" She asked.

Ethan swallowed. "Did," He stopped to steady his voice. "Did you see a man come in before me? Barefoot, carrying a little bag?"

She frowned slightly, thinking. "No, sweetheart. You're the only one I've seen for at least twenty minutes."

Ethan's stomach twisted. "Cold water, please, and a burger." Ethan slid into a booth and reached for his wallet to pay.

Something small and smooth brushed his fingers. Ethan pulled it out. It was a wooden feather, hand-carved, delicate.

Ethan stared at it, breath trembling, heart pounding. "Who," he whispered to no one, "were you?"

The feather rested quietly in his palm, impossibly light, and for the first time in months, Ethan felt something move inside his chest, not certainty, not clarity, but the faintest shimmer of something he thought he'd lost forever, hope.

Chapter 13

The wooden feather sat on the table like a question Ethan wasn't ready to answer. He turned it over in his hand, tracing the tiny grooves carved into its length. Every line felt intentional, deliberate, like someone had poured time and purpose into it. The grain caught the dim diner light, showing faint whorls and patterns that looked almost... natural.

Ethan wasn't imagining this. It was real. He could feel the weight of it, or the strange lack of weight. It was lighter than any wood should be. He wondered how it had gotten into his pocket. His fingers tightened around it as the waitress approached with a glass of water. She set it down gently.

"You okay, honey?" she asked, brows pulling together. "You look like you've seen a ghost."

Ethan let out a thin breath. "I might have," he said.

She gave a little laugh, unsure whether to take him seriously. "Well, that happens sometimes out on these highways. People see all sorts of things in the heat." She lowered her voice. "You sure you're not dehydrated?"

"I'm... something," Ethan said. It was the closest he could manage to the truth.

The waitress patted the table. "Well, your burger will be ready shortly. If you want to freshen up, you have a little bit of time. The bathroom's to your left, and if you need the phone, it's on the wall right next to it."

"Thank you," Ethan whispered.

She moved on, leaving him alone again with the feather and his trembling hands.

He squeezed his eyes shut and pressed the heel of his palm against his brow. "Who are you?" he murmured again. "What was I supposed to learn from you?"

The road had broken something open in him. The man hadn't offered answers so much as mirrors, reflecting doubts he buried, shames he hid, grief he tried to outrun. Now he had this token. This impossibility. He closed his fingers around the feather, holding it as carefully as a prayer he wasn't ready to say.

Maybe the desert air was hotter than he realized because for the first time in months, he felt something inside him begin to thaw.

Chapter 14

It took nearly an hour for the tow truck to arrive. During that time, Ethan sat in the booth, ate his burger, and drank several glasses of water. He alternated between staring at the feather and staring out the window at the empty road where the man had disappeared.

No footprints. No dust trail. No logical explanation, and yet the man's words refused to leave him.

Silence can be presence.

She forgave you.

You'll see me every time you stop running.

These were not things Ethan wanted to hear. They were things he needed to hear. He left the diner with the feather clutched in his palm and rode with the tow truck driver back to town. He barely spoke during the ride, just sat in the passenger seat, turning the feather over again, feeling something unnamed settling inside him. Not peace. Not yet.

Three Days Later

Ethan stood in the parking lot of his old church. The brick exterior looked the same as always, warm red stone, white trim, stained-glass windows glowing faintly with early morning sun. He'd walked through those doors a thousand times. He had stood in the pulpit, held hands with grieving families, baptized babies, married couples, and prayed with the living and the dying.

His entire life was woven into the walls of this place, and he had walked away. He swallowed hard. His hands trembled, the feather tucked safely in his jacket pocket like an anchor.

"You can do this," he whispered to himself. "Just go inside. Just talk." When he reached for the door, it swung open before he touched it.

Pastor Reed stood there. He was older than Ethan by at least a decade, with graying hair and a deep but gentle voice that once guided Ethan through ordination. He blinked in mild surprise, then smiled, warm and unguarded.

"Ethan," Pastor Reed said softly. "It's good to see you."

Ethan's throat tightened. "I… didn't think I'd ever walk back here."

"Most people don't walk away forever," Pastor Reed said. "Not when their heart still beats for something bigger."

Ethan shook his head. "I don't know what my heart beats for anymore."

Pastor Reed stepped aside, waving him in. "Then let's talk. You don't have to have the answers, just be willing to ask the questions."

The sanctuary was empty, quiet, washed in the soft colored light of morning. The same pews Ethan had once seen filled with faces now sat in still rows, waiting. Ethan slowly walked to the front, feeling the space breathe around him.

"I don't know if I believe anymore," he confessed quietly.

Pastor Reed nodded. "You said that before you left."

Ethan blinked. "How?"

"You didn't say it with words," Pastor Reed said gently. "But some silences speak loudly. Your eyes said what you couldn't."

Ethan exhaled shakily. "I thought walking away would fix it."

"And did it?" The older Pastor asked.

Ethan closed his eyes. "No. It broke me open."

Pastor Reed touched his shoulder, firm and steady. "Then maybe that's the beginning, not the end."

Ethan reached into his pocket. His fingers closed around the feather. He pulled it out, holding it in the morning light.

Pastor Reed's brows lifted. "That's beautiful. Where did you get it?"

Ethan stared at it, at the impossible memory of the man who placed it in his pocket without ever touching him.

"I'm... not sure," he said. "But I think I met someone I wasn't meant to ignore."

Pastor Reed didn't push. He nodded. "Come back Sunday. Speak if you feel ready. Sit in the pew if you don't. You're welcome here either way."

For the first time since Lorie's death, Ethan felt those words land somewhere inside him like truth. He wasn't done. He wasn't disqualified. He wasn't abandoned. He was being called back.

Chapter 15

Sunday Morning

The sanctuary filled slowly, voices murmuring, Pages of the Bibles and hymnals rustling, children laughing softly. Pastor Ethan watched from the side hallway, hands trembling, breath shallow. He wasn't preaching, not yet, but Pastor Reed had asked him to speak briefly. Just a few words. Honest ones.

When Pastor Reed finished the sermon, he turned to the congregation. "Before we close, Pastor Carver would like to share something."

Every head turned. Ethan stepped forward from the side of the altar. The room was quiet. Expectant. Patient. Ethan took a deep breath and held the wooden feather in his hand, where no one could see it.

"I left this place," he began, voice rough, "because I thought God had stopped speaking to me."
He paused. His eyes stung with tears.

"But I think I was wrong. Not because I heard a thunderous voice or because I got the miracle I asked for. I think I was wrong because God isn't always loud."
A hush settled over the room.

"Sometimes," Ethan said, "God walks beside us in silence, until we're ready to hear Him again." The words left him gently, like they'd been waiting.

Ethan swallowed hard. "I'm not the same man who stood in this pulpit before. I'm not sure I ever will be, and I think now deep down in my soul that it is probably a good thing. I'm here, and I believe that a true calling and journey is just starting now."

Pastor Reed stepped up beside him, placing a supportive hand on his shoulder. The congregation murmured, some nodding, some wiping tears.

Ethan looked at the stained-glass cross above the altar. Light poured through it, scattering colors across the floor like a quiet blessing, and for the first time in what felt like forever, silence didn't scare him; it comforted him.

Ethan reached into his pocket and closed his fingers around the feather. It warmed instantly, as if responding to his touch.

"Thank You," he whispered, not to Pastor Reed, not to the congregation, but to someone who had walked barefoot beside him on a lonely road.

No response came, and he didn't need one, because he already knew what it would be.

Author's Note

The Roadside Angel wasn't a story I planned to write. It arrived the way some stories do, quietly at first, then all at once, insisting on being told. I've never been someone guided by religious belief, but I've always been fascinated by the moments when faith and doubt meet in the same breath. There's something deeply human in the idea of losing your way, and something equally human in being offered help from the last place you expect.

This story grew out of that space. Not from doctrine, but from the emotional truth of a person standing at the edge of what they believe and wondering if there's anything left on the other side. I didn't set out to write about angels or divine intervention; I set out to write about someone hurting, someone questioning, someone finally hearing what they needed to keep going.

Whether the man on the road is taken as an angel, a stranger, a metaphor, or something else entirely is up to the reader. That ambiguity is the part of the story I love most. Sometimes the things that guide us back aren't meant to be explained; they're just meant to be felt.

I hope this piece finds you in whatever way you need, the same way it found me when I wasn't looking for it.

—Brett C. Persson

When the Stranger Comes Along

Chapter I

Briar's Hollow always felt old, even in the summer. The kind of town where paint peeled faster than anyone bothered to repaint it, where the wind carried secrets better than it carried dust, and where people had learned, generation after generation, to look away from the things they didn't want to see.

In late September of 1978, the town looked older than usual. As if something unseen had pressed its weight onto the rooftops, bending them into a sagging bow beneath the pressure of a familiar, unspoken fear.

By late afternoon, Main Street was nearly deserted. Shop windows that usually stayed open until dusk were already shuttered, boards hammered across them with a hurried, desperate rhythm. The older men who played cards outside Harris's Barbershop had vanished; only their folding chairs remained, tipped sideways as though they'd been knocked down in a rush.

Even the sky seemed to understand what week it was. The sun fell behind the tree line quicker than it should have, and the light it left behind was thin, an anemic glow that made the hills look like the crooked backs of sleeping beasts.

Lena Hart stood outside Granger's General Store, watching Mrs. Granger hang a hand-painted sign in the window:

CLOSED UNTIL FURTHER NOTICE. GOD PROTECT US ALL.

People pretended this sort of thing was normal. Lena knew better.

"Grandma says it's the season," Mrs. Granger muttered when she noticed Lena staring. "Best if everyone stays inside. Curtains drawn. Lights low." She kept her eyes down, as though speaking too clearly might summon something out of the woods.

Lena nodded even though she didn't fully understand. She had been only nine during the last cycle, too young to remember anything but the strange unease, the whispered arguments behind closed doors, and the way grown-ups startled whenever they caught their own reflections.

Now sixteen, she felt the tension in the bones of the town like a pressure drop before a storm. People weren't scared of something *new*. They feared something they'd already survived once… and weren't sure they could again.

Across the street, Mr. Hammond struggled on a ladder, hammering boards over his second-story windows. He was trembling so hard the nails shook in his grip. Every few seconds, he looked toward the woods that edged Briar's Hollow, his eyes wide and wet like a cornered animal.

At the base of the ladder, his wife whispered prayers under her breath, fast, panicked, stumbling over words Lena recognized from church but had never heard spoken with such desperate urgency.

Lena tightened her jacket and stepped away from the storefront. The September air had teeth. It bit at her cheeks as the wind picked up, rolling across town with a low whistle that almost sounded like someone calling her name.

Behind her, doors slammed. Deadbolts clicked. Curtains snapped shut. The Hollow was closing itself like a fist.

Only Lena seemed to be moving in the opposite direction, toward the edge of town, toward the line where the asphalt road broke into dirt, and the dirt vanished beneath pine needles, and the pines gathered close like watchers holding their breath.

Her grandmother would scold her if she knew, *"The week before he comes, you stay near people, Lena-girl. Don't wander. Don't tempt the dark."*

But Lena wasn't wandering. Not really. She was just… looking, seeking.

She had spent years hearing half-legends spoken in fear-thick voices. *He shows you what you hide. He steals your reflection. He turns good people inside out. Don't look him in the eyes.* No one ever spoke plainly. No one ever answered when she asked simple questions like *why*, how, or *who saw him last.*

Fear made people vague, and vague made Lena furious.

She stopped at the last streetlight on Willow Bend Road, the final one before the woods swallowed the world. The bulb flickered above her, whining with electricity that didn't seem steady enough to survive the coming dark.

The wind rushed again, colder this time. The pines shivered, and something moved between them. Not a shape exactly… more like the suggestion of one. A blur darker than the shadows around it. A silhouette with no detail, standing very still at the tree line.

Lena blinked, and the figure was gone, but the streetlight above her dimmed into a sickly orange glow, and for a heartbeat, Lena felt something she had never felt before.

Not fear. Not danger. Not even curiosity. Recognition.

As though someone far older than the town itself had turned its gaze toward her and whispered, "Seven years, and now I see you."

Lena took a step back. The pines exhaled. A low rustle slithered through the underbrush like something retreating or creeping closer.

From behind her, a voice cracked through the air. "Lena! Get away from those woods!"

She jumped. Mrs. Granger stood in the middle of the road, face pale, apron fluttering in the wind. "It's getting dark," she warned. "You don't want to be out here now. Not this week."

Lena cast one more glance at the trees. Empty. Quiet. Innocent, like nothing had ever been there, but she knew something had. She felt it in her chest like the distant toll of a bell.

As Lena followed Mrs. Granger back toward town, doors slamming behind them, streetlights dying one by one, Lena couldn't shake the feeling that Briar's Hollow was not closing itself up out of fear. It was hiding, and whatever it was hiding from had finally opened its eyes.

Chapter II

Lena's grandmother lived in the oldest house in Briar's Hollow, a narrow white farmhouse with a roof that sagged in the middle and windows that looked like drooping, tired eyes. It sat at the end of the dirt road where the streetlights no longer reached. The house didn't need them. Grandma Hart kept candles burning in every window from the first day of the "Seven-Year Week" until the Stranger was gone.

A ritual, she said. A warning, Lena suspected.

Inside, the air smelled like cedarwood and peppermint tea. A kerosene heater buzzed in the corner, flickering shadows over the walls. Lena shook off her jacket and boots, trying to ignore the way her grandmother watched her through the glow of the flames, sharp-eyed despite her age, as if she already knew Lena had been somewhere she shouldn't.

"You wandered too far," Grandma murmured without looking away from her knitting needles. "The woods are restless tonight."

"They're just trees," Lena said, more defensively than she meant to.

Grandma let out a humorless breath. "Nothing in Briar's Hollow is ever 'just' what it seems."

The needles clicked faster.

Lena sat across from her, the air thick between them. She had waited years to ask, waited for the right age, courage, and moment. Tonight felt like all three.

"Grandma," she began softly, "what really happened last time he came?"

The needles froze mid-stitch. The house seemed to be still. Outside, the wind scraped long fingers across the siding, searching for cracks.

Her grandmother set the knitting aside, hands trembling only slightly. She took a slow sip of tea before speaking, as if words needed warming before they could be safely let out.

"People tell stories," She said. "But stories… they rot. They twist. Folks shape them to avoid truths they don't want to face."

"That's not an answer."

"It's the only answer worth giving," Grandma said.

Lena leaned forward. "I saw something tonight."

Grandma's eyes snapped up, bright, frightened, ancient. "Don't say that."

"But…"

"Not this week. Not tonight."

Lena whispered, "I think I saw him."

The old woman shut her eyes, shoulders slumping as though Lena had confirmed a terror she'd hoped was still far away.

When Grandma spoke again, her voice was a cracked whisper, "He didn't come to hurt us. Not the first time. Not ever. People did that to themselves."

Her gaze drifted to the window, where the candle flame sputtered as if disturbed by a breath no one took.

"Your great-grandmother was a girl when he first appeared. 1908, she said, before the coal mine caved in. Before the Frost Family vanished. Before the Hollow closed in on itself and forgot its own beginnings."

Lena swallowed. "What did she say he was?"

Grandma shook her head slowly. "A mirror. Not made of glass. Made of... knowing."

A chill, thin but sharp, crept along the back of Lena's neck. "How can a person be a mirror?"

"He isn't a person, and he isn't a person either. That's the part people lie about. They call him a demon because demons are easier to blame than guilt."

The heater hummed louder. Outside, a tree branch scraped the house like a fingernail across skin.

Lena's voice was barely a whisper. "Then what does he want?"

Grandma's hands curled into fists. "He wants nothing. That's the part that drives men mad. Evil wants something. Anger wants something. Greed wants something. But a mirror? A mirror waits."

A hollow quiet filled the room, and Lena felt it settle into her bones.

"I remember the last cycle," Grandma continued, her voice trembling. "Your father came home shaking. Wouldn't talk. Wouldn't eat. I found him standing in front of the bathroom mirror in the dark. No lights on. Just... staring at himself. Like he expected to see someone else staring back."

Lena stiffened. She had never heard this part. "What happened to him?" she asked.

Grandma's eyes flicked toward the old hallway, toward the door that had been shut since 1971. "He stopped seeing himself," she whispered. "And once you can't see yourself anymore... You lose yourself."

The house creaked as if agreeing. Lena felt her heartbeat thrum through her chest, slow, heavy, too loud.

"But why did he stop?" Lena asked. "What did he see?"

Her grandmother's breath shuddered out of her, thin as paper. "You must understand this, Lena-girl. He does not show you monsters. He doesn't have to. The monsters we fear most are the truths we refuse to look at."

She reached for Lena's wrist, gripping tight, almost painfully.

"When he comes," Grandma said, voice quivering with ancient fear, "do not meet his eyes. Not even once. Because in them… you will see the face you've been hiding from every day of your life."

Lena swallowed hard. "And what if I'm not scared of what I'll see?"

Her grandmother shook her head with a pity so deep it hurt to look at. "Everyone is scared," she whispered. "Even the ones who swear they aren't. Especially them."

Just then, the candle in the window flickered wildly, then extinguished. The room fell into a dim, wavering darkness.

Grandma's grip tightened until her knuckles went white. "Pay it no mind," she breathed.

However, Lena minded, because, through the window's reflection, she saw, just for a second, a shape standing at the tree line. Tall. Still. Watching. Though it was only a heartbeat, it felt like the Stranger wasn't looking into the house at all. He was looking into her.

Chapter III

The next morning dawned colorless and thin, the kind of morning that felt scraped bare. Most of Briar's Hollow stayed indoors, curtains pulled tight enough that no one could see out, or in. Even the birds seemed to avoid the sky.

Lena stood in the kitchen, filling the kettle, when she noticed her grandmother hadn't touched her breakfast. The old woman stared at the window, at the soot mark where last night's candle had burned itself black before going out.

"He's closer," Grandma murmured, almost to herself.

Lena didn't ask how she knew. The fear in the woman's voice told her everything. By noon, news had already traveled through the Hollow, quietly, through whispers, through phone lines full of static. Someone had seen him. Someone always saw him first, and it was never in the same place twice. Near the Frostridge barn. Behind the abandoned gas station. Standing on the ridge overlooking the cemetery.

Each sighting had similar, if not precisely the same, details: no footsteps, no face that you could remember clearly. No movement except for the way the shadows bent around him, and always, always, he was looking. Not at a home, not at a person, at the place where someone *was going to be.*

That afternoon, a thin layer of fog rolled in, not thick enough to hide in, but enough to blur the edges of things. The trees were silhouettes. The sidewalks were smudged. Even the sky looked like someone had erased half of it.

Lena couldn't sit still.

Her grandmother dozed in the armchair, a Bible sliding from her lap. The room was too warm, too quiet, too full of the kind of heaviness that made breathing feel burdensome.

Lena slipped out the back door. She told herself she wanted air, that the house was suffocating her. But the truth was simpler; she wanted to see him again.

The fog curled low along the ground, swirling around her sneakers as she walked. The town felt abandoned. A swing in the park creaked back and forth, though there was no wind. A lawn sprinkler sputtered weakly, unfixed, forgotten. Somewhere far off, a dog barked once, then yelped as if something had startled it into silence.

Lena crossed Maple Street and made her way toward Willow Bend Road, the road where the pavement stopped, and the woods began. The fog thickened as she approached, turning everything into a watercolor wash of gray and white.

Her heart thudded louder with each step. *You shouldn't be here.* Her grandmother's warning echoed in her head like a hymn. *Not this week. Not tonight.* But the Stranger wasn't waiting for night. A shape slowly emerged through the fog ahead. Tall, dark, and perfectly still.

Lena stopped walking. The fog parted around the figure, swirling at his feet like mist swirling around a stone. His coat hung loose, old-fashioned, the fabric heavy and dark, as if it had soaked up a century of storms. His boots touched the ground, but somehow didn't disturb it.

He did not turn to face her. But she felt him noticing her and seeing her without really looking. Like the way a mirror doesn't choose who stands before it, it simply reflects.

Lena swallowed hard. Her breath fogged in front of her, though the air wasn't cold enough for that. The Stranger's presence changed the temperature, the sound, the weight of the world itself.

"Hello?" she said, voice cracking more than she expected. The Stranger didn't move.

She took one cautious step forward. The silence deepened, pressing around her like something physical. "Who are you?" she whispered.

At that, the Stranger's head tilted, slowly, deliberately, like an animal sniffing a scent in the wind. But his face remained just out of clarity, like a half-remembered dream. She couldn't see his eyes. She couldn't see his mouth, but she felt them.

A pressure built in her chest, tight, hot, like she was being pulled toward something buried deep under her ribs. For one terrifying second, she felt like she might step forward again without meaning to.

Voices carried faintly behind her. Townspeople coming closer down the road, older women clutching rosaries, Mr. Hammond whispering frantic prayers, Sheriff Laughton shouting for folks to keep their distance.

The Stranger straightened.

The fog thinned.

Then, without a sound, he was suddenly farther away. Ten feet. Twenty. Thirty. Not walking and not fading.

Just *elsewhere*.

As if the world had blinked.

Lena gasped and stumbled backward, heart hammering so hard she felt it in her throat. Sheriff Laughton reached her, grabbing her elbow roughly.

"What were you thinkin'?" he snapped. "You don't get closer to that thing!"

Lena jerked away. "He wasn't doing anything."

"He never does," one of the women whispered, eyes wild. "That's the part that scares us."

Behind them, the fog swallowed the Stranger's silhouette until it was nothing but mist again. Lena stared into the blankness, breath trembling. He hadn't touched her. He hadn't spoken. He hadn't moved.

Yet she felt shaken open, as if something in her had been quietly examined, turned over, and placed back where it came from. Not harmed. Just known.

The sheriff pulled her away, muttering orders and curses, but Lena barely heard him over the ringing in her ears. Because somewhere beneath the fear, beneath the confusion, beneath the instinct to run… Lena felt a strange and terrible certainty.

The Stranger hadn't come to the Hollow; he had come for *her*.

Chapter IV

By the next morning, Briar's Hollow felt wrong in a way that no one could quite name, but everyone recognized.

The fog didn't lift.

Fog always burned away by mid-morning, but not today. It clung to the ground like a living thing, twisting between porch steps and telephone poles, swallowing the road until it seemed the whole Hollow floated on a sheet of milky-white nothing.

The sheriff's cruiser crawled up and down Main Street, its headlights cutting through the haze in thin, useless beams. No sirens, no one wanted to draw attention, not during The Stranger's week. Lena watched from her porch.

Across the road, Mrs. Granger was standing in her yard barefoot, her nightgown damp from the grass. She hadn't noticed her door hanging open behind her. She just stared at the fog, lips moving as if in conversation with someone no one else could see.

Lena stepped off her porch. "Mrs. Granger?" she called gently.

The woman didn't answer. Her eyes were hollow; her cheeks streaked with tears she didn't seem to know she'd shed. As Lena got closer, she saw scratches on her arms, fresh ones, angry red, as though she'd clawed at herself in the night.

"Are you okay?" Lena asked.

Mrs. Granger blinked, slowly, like waking from a long sleep, and finally turned toward her. Lena recoiled without meaning to. Her pupils were blown wide, swallowing nearly all the color from her eyes.

"I saw my reflection," the woman whispered. Her voice trembled like a child's. "In the kitchen window. Before dawn, but it wasn't me. She smiled at me, Lena. Smiled... like she'd been waiting."

Lena felt her stomach knot. "Where's Mr. Granger?" she asked softly.

Mrs. Granger's lip quivered. "He's... gone." Her breath fogged the air. "He left without his shoes. Didn't take his truck. Just walked into the fog and..." Her voice cracked into a wild, broken laugh that didn't sound human. "And I think he was smiling too."

Before Lena could respond, Mrs. Granger stumbled backward and slammed her door shut, leaving nothing but silence and the echo of her shuddering cry.

Lena wrapped her arms around herself and hurried away. Something was unraveling.

By afternoon, the schoolyard was littered with shattered glass.

Someone, or perhaps multiple someones, had smashed every classroom window. Shards glittered in the gray light like frozen tears. The police roped off the area, but no one believed it was vandalism.

Not now. Not this week.

Principal Reeves stood in the middle of the chaos, muttering to himself, sweat darkening his collar. Lena heard snippets as she walked past:

"I didn't mean to." "It wasn't me in the glass." "I only wanted to scare it away..." "...but it wouldn't stop staring."

He flinched when he saw Lena, as if afraid she might reflect something at him.

Lena quickened her pace. Everywhere she went, she saw signs of cracks forming beneath the Hollow's surface.

That evening, the quiet was shattered by a siren, not an ambulance, not a police car, but the volunteer fire bell.

It rang wildly, frantically, as though someone were yanking the rope with shaking hands. Lena ran with half the town to the edge of Miller's Field, where they found Calvin Price, the local drunk, dangling from the wooden ladder that led up to the water tower. Dead. Neck twisted. Bare feet swinging.

He'd carved words into the tower with a rusted pocketknife, letters uneven and frantic: I SAW MYSELF, AND I WASN'T ALONE.

A collective gasp fell over the crowd. Someone crossed themselves. Someone else vomited. Sheriff Laughton barked orders, trying to regain control, but it was no use. Fear had already taken hold. Mrs. Price collapsed to her knees, screaming Calvin's name, her voice hoarse and raw.

Lena looked away, only to notice the fog swirling thicker around the base of the water tower, like something had been standing there recently.

Watching. Waiting. Breathing.

That night, Lena couldn't sleep. She lay awake listening to her grandmother mutter prayers in the next room. The candles flickered violently, their flames stretching thin and tall, as if pulled upward by invisible fingers.

Just past midnight, someone screamed outside. Lena bolted upright.

Through the window, she saw Tommy Maher, a quiet teen from school, dragging himself across the street on his elbows, his legs useless behind him. He was babbling through bloody lips.

"Get them off," he sobbed. "Get them off me, get them, get…"

But there was nothing on him. Nothing except the marks. His back was covered in scratches that formed two words, carved into his skin deep enough to bleed:

LOOK CLOSER

Lena's breath hitched. She backed away from the window.

Her grandmother burst into the room, clutching her rosary tightly enough that her knuckles had gone white. "Lena," she rasped, "listen to me. This is only the beginning. When he arrives, the town sees what it has buried, and some things", her voice broke, "some things should have stayed buried."

Lena trembled.

Her grandmother reached for her face, cradling it with shaking hands. "Promise me," she whispered, "you will not let him see you. Not your eyes. Not your truth. Promise me, Lena-girl."

But Lena couldn't answer. Because even as her grandmother pleaded, Lena heard the softest sound outside. Not footsteps. Not a voice. Just a faint, deliberate *shift* in the fog.

A presence settling into place, and Lena knew, with a cold certainty that hollowed her ribs, the Stranger was close. Closer than he had ever been.

Chapter V

Lena barely slept.

When she did drift off, her dreams were not dreams at all but flickers, flashes of the tree line, the fog, and the faint outline of a man who didn't move even when everything else did. She would wake gasping, unsure whether she had just dreamed of him, or whether he had simply been waiting at the edge of sleep for her to arrive.

By morning, Briar's Hollow felt muted, as if someone had wrapped the entire town in cotton. Doors stayed locked. Voices stayed low. Even the few cars on the road drove slowly, their headlights cutting through the fog in dim, watery beams.

Lena stepped outside only long enough to realize she had no intention of staying indoors. Her grandmother pleaded, begged, yelled, but none of it mattered. The fear in her grandmother's voice felt like background noise now, a hum beneath the louder, sharper pull tugging at Lena's ribs.

She needed to see him again. Not because she wasn't afraid. But because fear had begun to feel secondary to something else. Curiosity. Recognition. Something that tasted almost like hunger. She pressed her jacket tight and walked toward Willow Bend Road.

The fog was thicker today, dense enough to blur the houses into vague silhouettes. Lena stepped carefully, avoiding the patches where puddles had frozen over, not from temperature, but from something colder.

A strange quiet clung to everything. The kind that made even the sound of her breathing feel intrusive. As if the fog carried a memory of every sound ever made within it, and resented the addition of a new one.

Lena slowed near the old Miller Bridge, where planks had rotted for decades. The fog here felt heavier, swirling low and purposeful. Someone had been scratching at the wooden railing. Deep gouges in the wood lined either side, fresh enough that the splinters were still pale.

A message, carved frantically:

YOU KNOW HIM, DON'T YOU

Lena's pulse jumped. Another message below it:

WE ALL DO

She stepped back instinctively. The fog shifted behind her, cool and wet against her skin, almost like a presence brushing past. She spun around. Nothing. Just fog. And silence. And the faint impression of movement, like someone had just taken a step out of her sightline.

She found herself walking faster, toward the forest. Toward the place where she had first seen him clearly. Her heart hammered, but not with fear, but with anticipation.

A thought whispered in her mind, so quiet she wasn't sure if it was hers or not, *I'm not afraid of you.*

Another thought followed, colder and not hers, *then why do you want to see me so badly?*

Lena stumbled. That voice, that second voice, hadn't sounded external. It had sounded like a thought shaped by someone else's mouth. She clutched her stomach and forced herself to breathe. She kept walking; she couldn't stop.

At the edge of the woods, the trees loomed taller than she remembered, their branches twisted like arthritic fingers reaching for something out of reach. A shallow puddle spread across the dirt path. Lena stepped around it until something in it caught her eye.

Her reflection, but not exactly her reflection. Her reflection stood still while she moved. Her reflection watched her. Her reflection's eyes were darker than they should've been, deep, bottomless, like wells with no water left in them.

Lena's breath hitched. She crouched slowly, edging closer to the puddle. Her reflection smiled at Lena. Lena jerked back, heart slamming against her ribs. Before she could scream, a shadow shifted behind her.

She didn't need to turn to know he was there. The air changed. The fog thickened. The world held its breath.

Lena turned.

He stood at the edge of the tree line, tall and silent, coat hanging heavy around him like a shroud. He wasn't blurry this time; he was sharp. Defined. More real than the trees themselves. But his face, his face refused to settle into focus, like her mind rejected the effort to understand it. He didn't speak. He didn't approach.

She felt him examining her, peeling back the layers of her thoughts like pages of a book worn from rereading. A strange calm washed over her. A clarity she hadn't felt in years.

She stepped toward him.

Just one step. His presence grew colder and denser. The fog seemed to coil around his boots like obedient mist. Another step.

She felt a pulse, like a heartbeat that wasn't hers. "You're not…" she whispered, "…you're not what they say you are."

The Stranger tilted his head, slow and deliberate, like last time. Lena felt something shift inside her chest, something she'd buried long ago. A memory? A truth? A version of herself she'd forgotten. The Stranger lifted his chin as though acknowledging it.

Suddenly, the branches overhead snapped violently, as if something massive had brushed through them. Lena jumped, instinctively stepping back. When she looked forward again, The Stranger was gone as if he had never been there at all.

Her pulse still raced with the echo of his presence, and the fog still swirled in the exact shape of a man where he had once stood. Except she felt, deep in her bones, he had shown her something without showing anything at all, and she wanted more. Needed more.

By the time Lena returned home, her grandmother was waiting on the porch, rosary clenched so tightly the beads had left red dents in her palm.

"Where were you?" her grandmother whispered, voice breaking. "Don't lie to me."

Lena opened her mouth. The truth tried to come out: *I saw him.* But another thought, slippery, cold, and not entirely hers, rose to the surface instead: *Don't let her know.*

"I was just walking," Lena lied.

Her grandmother sobbed, a broken sound that made Lena's stomach twist. "Lena-girl," she whispered, "once he notices someone… he does not stop."

Lena looked away, unable to respond, because deep down, past fear, past the trembling, past the voice of reason, she hoped her grandmother was right.

Chapter VI

The night the Stranger finally spoke began without warning. No fog. No screams. No sirens. Just an unnerving stillness, as if the Hollow had fallen beneath a sheet of glass.

Lena lay awake long after her grandmother had shuffled off to bed. The candles in the windows burned low, their flames trembling with each shallow breath the house exhaled. Every creak of the floorboards, every whisper of wind felt amplified, as if the world had turned up the volume on silence.

Lena couldn't take it anymore. Her skin buzzed with something electric, something restless, something that felt less like fear and more like a tether pulling her toward the trees. Lena slipped outside.

The screen door groaned softly behind her, but the night swallowed the sound whole. The moon hung low, dull and exhausted, barely casting enough light to see the outline of the road, and the woods waited at the end of it.

Alive.

Listening.

Expectant.

Lena's breath fogged even though the night was warm. She wrapped her arms around herself, but it didn't help. The cold wasn't external; it radiated from somewhere deeper, somewhere being tugged forward bit by bit.

When she reached the tree line, the darkness seemed to inhale, and the world shifted.

He stood between the pines as he had always been there. As if the trees themselves had grown around him. His coat brushed the ground without disturbing the needles. His head tilted slightly, as though acknowledging her approach before she'd even made it.

This time, Lena didn't stop; she stepped into the woods. The earth felt softer here; the air was thicker. Shadows swayed on their own, moving in odd, whispered rhythms. Somewhere deeper in the forest, a branch snapped, but not the brittle kind of snap. This one was wet and heavy, and Lena didn't look away from him.

The Stranger remained still until she was only a few feet away. Not close enough to touch him, but close enough that her breath mingled with the cold aura radiating off him.

"You came," Lena whispered.

The Stranger didn't answer, but something in the space between them tightened, like a wire pulling taut.

"I know what they say about you," she continued. "But they don't know anything real. I can tell."

Still nothing. His stillness unnerved her more than if he had moved. People fidgeted. Animals twitched. Even the dead sagged. But the Stranger… He was still as if he was something not bound to muscle or bone.

Lena swallowed hard. "I saw something in that puddle yesterday," she said softly. "Was that you? Or me?"

The Stranger tilted his head further, and the faintest shift rippled through the air, like cold fingers brushing the back of her mind. Her heart stuttered.

"*You looked at yourself,*" he said.

The voice didn't echo. It didn't vibrate. It didn't even sound as though it came from him. It sounded like it rose from the soil beneath her feet.

Lena shivered. "I saw something that wasn't me."

"You saw what you refuse to see when the world is bright."

The words slid beneath her ribs, cold and exact. Lena's throat tightened. "What does that mean?"

The Stranger stepped closer. Barely a few inches, but the shift felt seismic. The shadows around him recoiled, then bent toward him again like metal drawn to a magnet. His coat whispered against the air, though no breeze moved. "People hide themselves," he murmured. "You hide better than most."

Lena took a shaky step back. "Hide what?"

He didn't answer immediately. Instead, he lifted his hand, slowly, gracefully, and for the first time, Lena saw his fingers.

They were long, pale, and slightly blurred at the edges, as if reality couldn't fully decide where they ended. He reached toward Lena, not touching her, not getting close enough for skin to meet skin, but the air thinned between them as though preparing for an impact.

When his hand leveled with her face, Lena felt a pressure behind her eyes. It felt like a sharp prick, a pull, like something inside her had been hooked.

She gasped. Images flickered, not memories, but shards of memories. Her father's hollow stare. Her own reflection smiled without her. Fog swirling in the shape of a man. Fingers scratching words into wood. Eyes, her eyes, dark and bottomless.

The Stranger lowered his hand. Lena staggered, dizzy, the world stretching at the edges.

"That is what you hide," he said quietly.

Lena's breath shook. "You showed me… something inside me."

"I showed nothing," he said. "You looked."

Her heartbeat quickened. "Why me?"

"Because you were already looking for me." He said.

A chill slid down her spine. "I wasn't…"

"You were," he murmured, voice lowering. "Long before you knew my name. Long before your father stared into himself and broke."

Lena flinched.

Her father.

Her grandmother had spoken of him like a ghost, but the Stranger spoke of him like a wound.

"What did you do to him?" Lena whispered.

The Stranger's head tilted in the other direction, almost in sadness. "I did nothing," he said. "He saw the man he could have been if he stopped lying. He could not live with the difference."

Lena's breath caught, a sharp, painful inhale. Tears stung the corners of her eyes. "You're not a demon," she whispered.

"No."

"You're not evil." She whispered.

"No."

"Then… then what are you?"

He stepped closer again, close enough that Lena felt the cold radiate from him like a quiet storm.

His voice brushed against her ear, soft and devastating, "*I am the truth you avoid.*"

Her pulse roared in her ears. Before she could respond, the forest behind her erupted with shouting, voices crashing through the trees, frantic and angry. "Lena! Get away from him!", "Where is she?", "Don't let her look at him!" Flashlights bobbed between the trunks. Branches snapped. The frantic, human noise broke the fragile stillness like a stone through glass.

Lena turned in panic. The Stranger was gone, but his voice lingered in the dark, faint as mist curling around her ankles, "*This is only the beginning.*"

Chapter VII

The townspeople dragged Lena home that night like she'd been contaminated.

Sheriff Laughton gripped her arm hard enough to leave a bruise, muttering under his breath about "damn foolish kids" and "the week of all weeks." Mrs. Hammond sobbed prayers the whole walk, as if Lena herself might erupt in flames at any second.

By the time they reached the Hart farmhouse, her grandmother was waiting on the porch with a lantern in hand. Its glow washed her face pale. "What have you done?" Grandma whispered, not angry. Terrified.

Lena tried to explain that nothing happened, that he didn't hurt her, that she'd only spoken with him. But speaking with him was the very thing no one in Briar's Hollow dared do.

Sheriff Laughton handed her over like a problem, returned her to her rightful owner, then left without looking back. The townspeople dispersed quickly, desperate to get indoors before the Stranger noticed them again.

Grandma pulled Lena inside and locked the door. Then she turned the lantern down low. "Sit," she commanded.

Lena sat at the kitchen table, heart still pounding, lungs still tasting of cold forest air.

Her grandmother lowered herself into the chair opposite her, spine trembling. "You've made this worse," she whispered. "Much worse."

Lena gripped the edge of the table. "Please, tell me what's going on. All of it. No more pieces."

Grandma's eyes glistened, not with tears, but with the sheen of long-buried truth rising too fast to contain.

"You think I've kept things from you to be cruel?" she said. "I've kept them because the past is poison. This town has swallowed it every seven years for seventy years." She exhaled shakily. "…it tastes blood again."

Lena's pulse quickened. "What happened, Grandma? What did the elders actually do?"

The old woman looked toward the dark hallway, toward the closed door that had stayed untouched since Lena's father disappeared into himself. Then she stood, slow, deliberate, and walked to the pantry.

From the top shelf, beneath folded linens and old kitschy cookbooks, she pulled out a shoebox wrapped in twine so brittle it broke in her hands. She placed it on the table.

"Your great-grandmother left this," she said. "I never opened it until after your father…" Her voice snagged on itself. "…until after he was gone in all the ways that mattered."

She pushed the box toward Lena. Inside were yellowed papers, brittle maps, torn journal sheets, and a faded photograph of nine men standing in front of the old town hall. They wore suits, but not one of them smiled.

On the back of the photo, in shaky handwriting:

THE ELDERS, 1943

Lena studied the faces. She recognized some of the surnames: Hammond. Miller. Laughton. Reeves. Families are still running the town today.

"Read," Grandma said.

Lena lifted the first journal page. It was dated September 18, 1943.

The Stranger has returned. The council fears he will expose us. The truth is too dangerous... The people must never know what we did in the mines.

Lena frowned. "What mines?"

Grandma sank back into her chair. "The Hollow didn't always survive on farms and carts. They found coal once, briefly. But the mine collapsed the same week the Stranger came the first time."

Lena flipped to the next page.

We blamed him. We told the town that his presence cursed the ground. It was easier than admitting the beams were rotted, the supports poorly built... easier than admitting we ignored the warnings because we wanted the money.

The words twisted something deep inside Lena's chest.

"They let people die?" she whispered.

"Fourteen men," Grandma said quietly. "Including your great-uncle."

Lena's fingers trembled as she lifted another page.

The Stranger did not curse the mine. He merely walked among us. Those who met his eyes saw what we had hidden. Saw the greed. Saw the lies. Some went mad. Some confessed. And the elders...

The sentence trailed off. The next sheet was torn. The ink blotched as though someone had tried to rip the truth out physically. Lena moved to the next page.

We confronted him tonight. Tried to drive him out. But he did nothing. He only watched while we uncovered our own sins. We beat him with lantern poles, but every strike landed on each other, not on him. Our own hands turned against us.

Grandma's voice dropped to a whisper. "People broke bones fighting shadows. Fighting themselves."

Lena swallowed hard. She could almost picture it, the rage, the fear, the self-inflicted blows mistaken for battle.

Another entry:

We cannot let the truth spread. If the town knows the curse is us, our greed, our cowardice, everything will collapse. The Stranger must become the villain. The story must change.

Lena's hands curled into fists. "They lied," she said, voice cracking. "For seventy years."

"They did worse than lie," Grandma whispered. "They created a legend so powerful nobody ever questioned it. They built a monster out of the one thing that could have saved them."

Lena's breath caught. "Saved them how?"

Grandma leaned forward, eyes glistening. "The Stranger doesn't punish. He reveals. He holds up a mirror until people can't look away."

Lena remembered the puddle. The smile that wasn't hers. The voice in her mind. *You hide better than most.* Her skin prickled.

"There's something else," Grandma said, pulling another document from the bottom of the box. It wasn't a journal entry.

It was a list of names, seven of them, written in the same faded hand. Next to each name, the word "BROKEN" or "GONE."

The final name on the list:

JAMES HART - BROKEN

Lena's father.

Her breath left her body in a thin, shaking gasp. "They knew," she whispered. "The elders knew what happened to him."

"Of course they did," Grandma said bitterly. "They knew exactly what he saw. That's why they kept you away. That's why they forbid anyone from talking. Because your father…" She hesitated. "…your father saw something truly terrible in himself. And they were afraid you might one day see it too."

Lena's tears blurred the paper.

"But they were wrong," Grandma whispered. "You aren't your father. You aren't any of them. You're stronger."

Lena shook her head, unable to speak. She didn't feel strong; she felt cracked open. Exposed and somewhere deep in the woods, she felt the Stranger again, quiet, patient, watching. Not hunting. Not haunting. Just waiting.

As if the truth she had just uncovered was only the surface of a much deeper wound.

Chapter VIII

Briar's Hollow did not sleep the night Lena learned the truth. Whispers moved through the fog like insects, crawling under doors and slipping through cracks in the windows.

She spoke to him. He marked her. She's letting him in. She's becoming like her father. Lena heard fragments of a rumor carried on the wind when she opened her bedroom window. People always fear what they've buried the deepest, and now those buried things were clawing their way up all over town.

By dawn, Briar's Hollow had become a hive on the verge of collapsing in on itself.

The fog clung to the ground like a film of ash. The houses leaned inward, shutters locked, every porch light burning despite the daylight, tiny flames against a much older darkness.

Lena wandered into the kitchen to find her grandmother sitting upright at the table, pale as wax, a shotgun resting across her lap. It looked wrong in her hands, too heavy, too violent for a woman who preferred sewing needles and hymnals.

"What is that for?" Lena asked quietly.

"For protection," Grandma whispered. "Not from him... but from them."

Lena's stomach dropped. "Who?"

As if in answer, a fist slammed against the front door so hard the hinges rattled.

Grandma flinched, clutching the shotgun tighter.

"Don't open it," she warned. But the pounding grew louder. More fists. More voices.

"Open up, May!" They shouted.

"We need to talk to the girl!" Another voice said.

"You can't hide her now, not after what she's done!" A woman screamed.

Lena's heart thudded painfully in her chest. '*They know.*' She thought.

The shoebox of secrets. The truth about the elders. Her meeting with the Stranger, and they feared her now.

Grandma rose shakily. "Go. Through the back. Don't let them see you."

"No," Lena whispered. "I have to…"
The door splintered.

Sheriff Laughton shoved his way inside with two deputies and half a dozen townspeople trailing behind him. Their eyes were wild, not angry, but terrified. And fear is far more dangerous than anger.

"Where is she?" he demanded.

Grandma lifted the shotgun. "You stay back."

"Put that down, May," the sheriff said, though his hand hovered over his holster. "We're not here to hurt her. We need answers."

"She's a child," Grandma snapped.

"She's not a child anymore," Mrs. Hammond said from behind him, voice trembling. "He's noticed her. And we know what that means."

Lena stepped forward before her grandmother could stop her.

"It means nothing," she said. "He hasn't harmed anyone."

A collective gasp rippled through the room.

"You see?" Mr. Reeves hissed. "That's how it starts. He twists their thoughts. He makes them defend him."

Lena's pulse quickened. "No. I read the journals. I know the truth about the mine, about the elders. The Stranger didn't curse this town. You did."

The sheriff's face darkened. "Those journals are lies. Old ramblings. Stories from a woman who went senile years before she died."

Lena felt heat flood her chest. "They're not lies. You were never cursed. You were guilty."

Gasps. Murmurs. Someone shouted a prayer. Someone else whispered, "She's turning."

Lena held her ground. "He didn't hurt my father. My father hurt himself because he couldn't face who he really was. And that scares you. That he might show you your real self, too."
The room erupted.

"She's dangerous!" Someone yelled. People started shouting, "She needs to be cleansed!" "She's becoming one of his!" "She's been chosen!"

The sheriff raised his voice. "Enough! We will take her to the church. Father Brannigan will perform the ritual. It's the only way to cut his influence before the cycle ends."

Grandma stepped in front of Lena, voice shaking. "Over my dead body."

Mrs. Hammond's eyes, bloodshot, frantic, fixed on Lena with something like pity twisted into fear.

"Sweet girl," she whispered, "once he notices you... There's no saving you."

Lena felt something inside her splinter, not from fear, but from clarity. These people weren't trying to protect the town. They were trying to protect themselves from the truths they had buried so deeply that the mere thought of being exposed had turned them rabid.

In that moment, Lena understood, The Stranger wasn't the danger. The town was. She stepped around her grandmother, shoulders squared despite the tremble in her limbs.

"You're not taking me anywhere," she said.

The sheriff reached out to grab her arm, and the world went still. Not silent, still. Like sound itself had been swallowed.

The fog pressed against the broken doorway, thickening into something almost solid. A cold draft swept through the kitchen, extinguishing the lantern and every candle in the room.

In the sudden darkness, someone whimpered. Lena felt it before she saw it, a presence behind her, familiar, heavy, patient. The Stranger stood just outside the broken doorway, shrouded in fog, tall enough that his shadow stretched across the floorboards toward her feet.

The townspeople recoiled. The sheriff stumbled back, hand shaking on his holster.

Grandma gasped and clutched her chest.

But Lena... She didn't move. She felt no urge to hide. No desire to run. Only a strange, calm certainty that this moment, this fracture between truth and fear, had always been coming.

The Stranger's voice whispered inside her mind, '*Choose, Lena.*'

Her breath caught. 'Choose what?' She thought.

'*Them.*' A pause like a heartbeat. '*Or the truth.*'

She looked at the terrified faces crowding her kitchen. The people she'd grown up around. The people who had lied. The people who had broken her father. The people who would rather destroy her than face themselves.

Then she turned her gaze toward the Stranger, still, cold, impossible, yet unmistakably honest, and the choice became clear. Lena stepped toward him.

Just one step. It was enough. A gasp tore through the room. Someone screamed. The sheriff shouted something incoherent. But Lena didn't hear any of it. Because the fog curled around her ankles like a welcome. The Stranger didn't reach for her, but he stayed. Because stepping toward him didn't feel like surrender, it felt like stepping into truth.

Chapter IX

The moment Lena stepped toward the Stranger, the fog surged, swallowing the porch, the broken doorframe, and half the kitchen in a cold, rolling tide.

"Grab her!" Sheriff Laughton shouted, voice cracking with panic.

But his deputies didn't move. They were staring at the Stranger. Or rather, staring at what the Stranger made them see.

The fog shifted around them, warped into reflections. Shapes formed, versions of themselves, twisted and distorted, stepping out of the mist like nightmares wearing familiar faces.

A deputy dropped to his knees, sobbing. Mrs. Hammond screamed. Mr. Reeves covered his eyes, shaking violently.

The fog pressed deeper into the house. The Stranger didn't lift a hand. He didn't need to. People unravel faster when they're shown the truth they've buried.

Lena's grandmother stumbled backward, clutching her chest. "Lena, don't go with him, please…"

The Stranger turned his head slightly toward Grandma Hart, and the fog softened around her, thinning enough for her to breathe. Lena felt something tighten in her throat. He wasn't hurting her grandmother. He was protecting her.

The elders, the Sheriff, the townspeople, those who'd lived on lies for decades, were choking on their own reflections.

Sheriff Laughton fired a shot into the fog, but the bullet had struck him in the chest. The Sheriff collapsed, howling, clutching his chest.

Chaos exploded.

"Run!" someone shrieked. "Get the priest!"

"He's killing us!" Someone else shouted

"No, no, NO, I see him, I SEE HIM…"

The Stranger stepped back into the fog, and Lena followed. The mist closed behind them like a curtain.

The forest swallowed their footsteps, or perhaps they made none. The tall pines rose like cathedral spires, branches creaking overhead in a cold, whispering rhythm.

The Stranger walked ahead of Lena, never touching her, never signaling for her to follow, but she didn't need guidance. She felt tethered to him, as though a thread ran from the center of her chest to the emptiness where his face should have been.

"Where are we going?" she whispered.

The Stranger didn't answer. He kept walking until they reached a clearing Lena didn't recognize. The fog here moved strangely, lifting in pieces, lowering in sheets, forming shapes that dissolved before her eyes could catch them.

In the center stood a rotting wooden platform. She knew it instantly. The old gallows. Abandoned decades ago, when the Hollow still believed punishment could scrub out sin.

The platform groaned beneath the Stranger as he stepped onto it. Lena's breath hitched.

Behind them, the trees erupted, shouting, dozens of townspeople charging into the woods, carrying lanterns, crosses, kitchen knives, anything heavy enough to feel like protection.

They surrounded the clearing in a ragged circle, breathless and shaking. Father Brannigan stepped forward first, clutching a Bible so tightly the leather creaked.

"In the name of the Lord," he shouted, voice trembling, "we cast you out!"

The Stranger didn't move. He stood in the center of the platform like something patient. Something inevitable.

Father Brannigan raised the Bible higher. "You are a corrupter! A deceiver! A curse upon this land!"

The Stranger tilted his head slightly as the lanterns flickered violently in the night.

The Stranger spoke. Not softly like before. Not inside Lena's mind. His voice filled the clearing like a storm collapsing inward. "I deceive nothing."

The crowd recoiled, clutching their ears though the voice wasn't loud, just absolute. "You look into darkness and blame the night for what you see."

Mrs. Hammond fell to her knees, sobbing. Mr. Reeves backed into the fog, muttering, "No, no, no, no..." like a broken machine.

Father Brannigan shouted, "You cannot break us! We are God's chosen!"

The Stranger lifted one hand. The fog responded like loyal hounds, circling the elders first. Their shadows reached upward. Stretched. Lengthened. Split from their bodies.

Lena watched in horror as the shadows peeled themselves into separate shapes, exact copies of the men and women they belonged to. These shadows smiled. Wide. Cruel. Knowing.

The elders screamed. The crowd broke into chaos. Some fled blindly into the woods. Some attacked their own shadows. Some pressed their faces into the dirt, weeping for forgiveness that would never come.

Lena trembled, her throat tight, her heart pounding painfully. "What are you doing to them?" she whispered.

The Stranger turned toward her at last, and though she couldn't see his face, she felt his gaze like a cold hand pressing against her skin. "I am showing them themselves."

His words fell like stones. "The sins they named mine were theirs. The curse they preached was their fear. The evil they hunted was their reflection."

Lena swallowed hard. He was not killing them; they were killing themselves. Through denial, through guilt, through terror of truth.

Lena glanced at Father Brannigan, who clawed at the air as if strangling an invisible foe, though his hands were wrapped tightly around his own throat. He collapsed, eyes bulging.

Lena choked on a sob. "Stop," she whispered.

The Stranger lowered his hand. The fog stilled, and the shadows retreated, slipping back into the bodies that had cast them. The clearing fell silent except for the ragged sobbing of people who had survived their own reflections.

Lena stumbled toward the Stranger, tears slipping down her cheeks. "Why me?" she whispered brokenly. "Why show me all of this?"

He stepped down from the platform, approaching her with the slow, deliberate grace of something ancient and heavy with purpose. When he stopped in front of her, his voice was quiet again, gentle in a way that made her knees tremble. "Because you looked without turning away."

A long silence stretched between them.

The air hummed like something awakening.

The Stranger lowered his head, just slightly, as though acknowledging her. "You see truth."

Lena's breath hitched.

"And truth," he whispered, "sees you."

Chapter X

Morning came slowly, as if the sun itself was reluctant to shine on what the night had revealed.

The fog thinned first, unraveling thread by thread until the trees emerged like tired survivors. The lanterns, long burned to stubs, lay in the damp grass where their owners had dropped them. The elders, those still alive, sat slumped in the clearing, hollow-eyed and broken in ways that had nothing to do with bruises or wounds. No one spoke.

Not the sheriff, who kept staring at his own shaking hands. Not Mrs. Hammond, whose sobs had dried into a dull, vacant stare. Not Father Brannigan, who knelt motionless beside the old gallows, fingers still curled around a Bible that had offered him no protection.

Lena stood at the edge of the clearing, arms wrapped around herself, watching the soft gray light creep across the ruined faces of Briar's Hollow.

Lena wasn't numb. She felt everything. Every lie exposed. Every truth awakened. Every fear shattered, and beneath it all, a strange and terrifying clarity. The Stranger had not brought destruction; he had brought honesty, and honesty had undone them. A shift in the air made her turn.

The Stranger stood a short distance away, where fog still clung to the ground in thin ribbons. He watched the clearing with unreadable stillness, no satisfaction, no sorrow, no judgment. Simply present. Simply truth.

As Lena approached, the grass chilled beneath her feet, frost blooming in her footsteps.

"You're leaving," she whispered. It wasn't a question.

He turned his head slightly, an acknowledgment. Behind him, the fog began folding inward, gathering itself like a cloak being pulled across his shoulders.

"The cycle ends," he murmured. "Seven years must pass again."

Lena swallowed hard. "What happens to them now?"

The Stranger did not look at the townspeople. He did not need to. "What they saw cannot be unseen," he said. "What they are cannot be undone."

Lena felt the truth of that settle heavily in her chest. Some of the people in the clearing would rebuild themselves. Some would collapse completely. Some would flee and never return.
The Hollow would never be the same. Maybe it never should have been.

She took a slow breath. "What about me?"

For the first time, he stepped closer, not touching her, not even reaching out, but near enough that the air around her deepened, charged with cold and something else… something ancient. "You looked," he whispered. "You did not break."

Lena's throat tightened. "I don't feel unbroken."

"No one does," he said.

The fog behind him curled upward like rising smoke, wrapping around his coat. The edges of his shape blurred.

Lena took a trembling step forward. "Will I see you again? In seven years?"

His voice lowered to a hush that felt like a breath inside her ear. "If you look for me."

A shiver danced down her spine, not fear, not anticipation, but recognition.

The Stranger began to fade, not walking, not dissolving, but withdrawing, like a presence being pulled quietly out of the world. As his form thinned into mist, he spoke one last time, "Protect the truth, Lena Hart. Or this town will bury itself again."

And then, He was gone.

The fog evaporated into morning light.

The clearing exhaled.

The world resumed the slow, fragile rhythm of something that had survived its own unveiling.

Seven Years Later

The Hollow changed.

Some houses stayed empty. Some were rebuilt. Some people left, unable to bear the weight of their own reflection. Others, those who'd looked and survived, walked differently, spoke differently, carried themselves with a new, quiet humility.

Sheriff Laughton retired early. Mrs. Hammond moved in with her sister and never spoke of the Stranger again. Father Brannigan left town without a word. The elders' era ended, and Lena became what Briar's Hollow needed most, a keeper of truth.

Lena never told the whole story; some truths were not hers to share. But she said enough. Enough for people to understand that evil had never come from the woods. It had come from them.

Lena grew older, stronger, and less willing to hide from anything. But every year, when September approached, she felt the old, cold tether inside her ribs tighten just slightly.

A reminder. A promise.

When the seventh year returned, Lena, now twenty-three, walked alone to the tree line. No fear. No hesitation. No denial. Just truth.

The forest was quiet, waiting. Fog gathered at her feet, swirling softly, and from the dark between the pines, she felt him, a presence she recognized as she recognized her own shadow. Lena exhaled, steady. "I'm ready to see you again."

The fog curled upward.

The trees leaned inward.

And the Stranger stepped forward.

The Girl Who Refused to Break

Chapter 1

The people in Willow Creek had a way of settling on a story long before they bothered to learn the truth, and once they agreed, they stayed settled. It was easier that way. A town that small didn't have much appetite for revising anything, not its history, not its routines, and certainly not its opinion of a fourteen-year-old girl named Mary Ellsworth.

They called her trouble. Not in whispers, not even behind her back. Just flatly, as if it were her Christian name.

"Trouble's late again," Mrs. Henley would mutter when Mary slipped into homeroom.

"Your girl was mouthing off at the gas station again," Mr. Crane would tell her father at church.

"That one's going nowhere good," folks would say, shaking their heads like the verdict was passed and sealed.

Mary heard every word, though the adults always behaved as if she didn't. But children have better hearing than they're credited for, especially when the words are about them.

On a gray Monday morning that smelled faintly of walnut shells and engine grease, Mary trudged up the cracked sidewalk toward school. Her backpack hung off one shoulder because she'd ripped the other strap during an argument with a classmate the week before. She didn't mean to tear it; she just grabbed when they grabbed, and the fabric gave way before tempers did.

Ahead, a group of eighth-grade boys clustered around the bike rack. One of them nudged another and nodded at Mary.

"Trouble's here," he announced, as if she needed reminding.

Mary kept her gaze fixed on the ground. It wasn't worth opening her mouth. Every time she spoke, she somehow made things worse, especially when she was right.

Inside the school, the halls buzzed with their usual electricity, lockers slamming, tennis shoes squeaking, someone laughing too loudly at something that wasn't that funny. Mary slid into homeroom a heartbeat before the bell. Mrs. Henley, a thin woman with nervous hands and a clipped voice, didn't bother to say hello.

"You're late again," she said instead.

"I'm not," Mary replied.

Mrs. Henley sighed, as if the very sound of Mary's voice exhausted her. "Sit down."

Mary sat. She didn't see the point in arguing. She never won.

By mid-morning, the clouds had thickened, smearing the sky into a dull smear of powder. It looked like a day the world didn't quite feel like showing up for. Mary understood that feeling. She thought it often enough.

During the passing period before fourth hour, she saw something that turned the low hum of her day into a sharp, electric jolt.

Three lockers down, a sixth grader named Theo Hartley, small for his age, quiet as a mouse, stood with his back against the metal, his books spilled onto the floor. Two older boys were taunting him, poking him in the chest, daring him to push back. Theo didn't. He never did.

Mary didn't think. She stepped forward. "Leave him alone."

The words came out steady, low. The boys snorted.

"Oh, look, Trouble to the rescue," one said.

"Get lost," the other added.

Something inside Mary, something coiled and familiar, tightened. She could already feel the burn behind her ribs, the one that always came before she did something she'd regret later.

But Theo looked up at her with a face full of pleading, and that did it. Mary shoved one boy's hand away from Theo's chest. It wasn't even a hard shove, but the boy stumbled anyway, more from surprise than force.

And that was enough.

A teacher rounded the corner, saw the scene, and seized on the most straightforward interpretation.

"Mary Ellsworth!" he snapped. "My office. Now."

The boys scattered, leaving Theo alone to gather his books.

Mary opened her mouth to explain, but the teacher was already pointing down the hall, jaw clenched. The familiar heat rose inside her, anger, frustration, helplessness, all tangled together into something fierce and sour.

It didn't matter what she said. It never mattered.

By the time she stood in the office, staring at the speckled linoleum floor, she already knew how this story ended. She'd been here before and seen the same expression on the principal's face and heard the same disappointment in her father's voice.

The suspension slip felt heavy in her hand, as if paper could weigh more with the wrong words on it.

When she walked home that afternoon, the sky had darkened to the color of bruised fruit. Her father's truck sat in the driveway, engine off, meaning he was home early. Bad sign. Terrible sign.

Mary hesitated at the front door, but storms come whether you step inside or not.

Her father sat at the kitchen table, shoulders slumped, elbows on his knees. He looked older than forty-two, older and worn thin, like he'd been pulled in too many directions for too many years. When he lifted his eyes to hers, there was no anger in them. Somehow, that was worse.

"What happened this time?" he asked softly.

Mary held out the slip. He took it without reading her face. Suspended. Fighting. Harmful conduct.

He folded the paper once, twice, then set it carefully on the table.

"I don't know what to do with you anymore, Mary," he said.

She didn't answer. She didn't trust her voice not to shatter in the middle of a sentence. Instead, she turned and walked out the back door, feet crunching in the brittle grass as she crossed the yard toward the old walnut tree.

The tree had been there longer than she had, its trunk thick and gnarly, its branches like tired arms stretching toward the tired sky. Mary sank at its base, pulled her knees up, and pressed her forehead against them.

She wasn't crying. She refused to. But the pressure in her chest felt like something trying hard to escape.

A soft voice drifted from behind the fence. "Mary?"

She looked up. Mrs. Ellery stood there in her faded yellow sweater, hands tucked into her sleeves, face touched with the kind of gentleness that didn't demand anything.

"I just put on a pot of tea," the old woman said. "Would you sit with me a while?"

Mary hesitated, then wiped her eyes even though they were dry.

"Okay," she whispered.

Mrs. Ellery nodded and opened the gate. And for the first time that day, or maybe for the first time in a long while, Mary felt something small and fragile stir inside her.

Something like the beginning of hope.

Chapter 2

The kitchen smelled faintly of last night's coffee when Mary slipped back inside. Her father hadn't moved from the table. The suspension slip sat between them like a cracked plate no one wanted to touch. Mary hovered near the doorway, unsure whether she should stay or go. Her father rubbed his temples with both hands.

"Sit," he said finally.

She lowered herself into the chair across from him. It creaked under her weight, or maybe under the weight of everything neither of them knew how to say.

Her father's eyes were red around the edges. Not from crying, Mary had seen him cry only once, the day her mother left, but from lack of sleep and too many worries that lined up like bricks on his back.

"Mary," he began, "this can't keep happening."

"It wasn't my fault." The words came out too quickly, too sharply.

He sighed, a long, frayed thing. "It's never your fault."

"That's not what I…"

"Then what do you want me to hear?" His voice rose, not quite angry, but pleading. "Tell me how this keeps happening without you being part of it."

Mary clenched her fists in her lap. She wasn't the one who started the fight. She was never the one who started it. But once things got loud or messy, she became the easiest name to put on the line. Trouble. Disturbance. Aggression.

Labels stuck faster than the truth.

Her father rubbed his face and leaned back. "I've talked to your teachers. I've tried grounding, stricter rules, and more freedom. Nothing works. I'm… I'm at a loss, kid."

Kid. He only called her that when he felt helpless.

Mary swallowed hard. "I was helping someone."

He nodded, but there was doubt sitting behind his tired eyes. "Mary, every week it's something new. And I'm trying, I'm really trying, but I can't keep doing this."

Those last words, soft as they were, felt like a shove. She could handle yelling. Yelling slid off like rain. But defeat, his defeat, burrowed in, working its way between her ribs.

She pushed her chair back. "You don't even care what really happened."

"I care," he said quickly. "More than you know. But…"

He stopped, and that unfinished "but" was louder than anything else he could've said.

But I don't believe you.

But you never change.

But maybe you are who they say you are.

Mary felt the heat climb her throat, the kind that wasn't quite anger and wasn't quite sadness but lived somewhere miserable in between.

"I'm going outside," she muttered.

Before he could say her name, she slipped through the back door and let it close softly behind her. Not a slam, she had learned long ago that slamming meant she'd lose whatever tiny scrap of control she had left. The soft click felt more final anyway.

The walnut tree cast a long shadow across the yard, stretching wide like a slow-moving hand. Mary knelt beside the roots, the soil cool beneath her palms. The air tasted of damp earth and something metallic, as if the sky were thinking hard about rain.

Her chest tightened. The harder she tried not to break, the more the pressure grew.

She rested her forehead against the rough bark. *Why does it always go this way? Why can't anyone see what really happens? Why am I always the one they blame?*

The questions came in a flood she couldn't stop. They tangled with memories, teachers who rolled their eyes before she spoke, neighbors who crossed the street, the way her father closed his shoulders when she walked into the room on a bad day.

She always felt like she was fighting a war no one else acknowledged.

A sudden gust of wind rattled the walnut leaves, scattering a few across her shoes. Mary squeezed her eyes shut.

"I'm not bad," she whispered to herself. "I'm not."

But the words felt thin, fragile, like they had to push through too many layers of doubt to exist.

She didn't hear the gate open. She didn't hear the soft footsteps in the grass. She only felt a warm hand rest gently on her shoulder.

"Mary," Mrs. Ellery said in her soft-weathered voice, "come sit with me a while."

Even though Mary didn't understand why, the kindness in that invitation undid something inside her, something tight, something scared, something that had been bracing itself for a blow that never came.

She nodded, wiping her sleeve across her face even though there were no tears.

"Okay," she whispered.

Mrs. Ellery smiled, the kind of smile that didn't demand anything in return.

"Good," she said. "The tea's ready. And so am I."

Together, they walked back through the gate, leaving the walnut tree and the breaking point behind them. But the cracks inside Mary didn't disappear. They shifted, making room for something new she couldn't name yet.

Chapter 3

Mrs. Ellery's house sat just beyond the walnut tree, separated from Mary's yard by a fence that had leaned a little to the left ever since the storm two summers back. The house itself had once been white, but time and sun had softened it into the color of old paper. Flowers grew wild around the porch, marigolds, lavender, and a few stubborn roses that bloomed late and held on through the first frost.

It wasn't a grand place, but it looked lived-in, cared for. Loved.

Inside, the air smelled of chamomile tea and something sweet Mary couldn't quite place, maybe lemon cookies, perhaps the ghost of them.

"Sit wherever you like," Mrs. Ellery said as she moved toward the kitchen. Her steps were slow but steady, the deliberate pace of someone who had long ago learned to measure her time instead of rushing through it.

Mary chose the armchair by the window. Its fabric was worn thin in places, and the cushion sank under her weight, as if welcoming her. Sunlight filtered through the curtains, warming her knees.

A minute later, Mrs. Ellery returned with two mugs of steaming tea. She handed one to Mary, her hands surprisingly steady despite the slight tremor of age.

"Here we are," she said. "Chamomile. Good for the heart."

Mary didn't know if tea could do anything for a heart like hers, one bruised from years of misunderstanding, but she accepted the mug with both hands. The warmth seeped through her palms, calming something restless inside.

They sat quietly for a while. Mary wasn't used to silence that didn't feel judgmental or heavy. This silence felt roomy, like she could breathe in it.

Finally, Mrs. Ellery spoke. "I saw you run out earlier," she said gently. "Your father looked... overwhelmed."

Mary stared into her tea. "He thinks I'm just causing trouble."

"Do you think that?"

"No." She hesitated. "Sometimes I feel like everyone decided who I am before I even had a chance."

Mrs. Ellery nodded, not quickly, but thoughtfully. "People do that, you know. They get an idea in their head about someone, and it sticks. Even when the person keeps growing, keeps changing... folks cling to the old picture."

Mary swallowed. "Then what's the point in trying?"

"Well," Mrs. Ellery said, folding her hands over her own mug, "trying isn't something you do for other people first. You do it for yourself. The rest catches up eventually."

Mary didn't know what to say to that. No one had ever suggested she was worth trying for, not in that way.

Outside, a breeze stirred the lavender plants along the porch, filling the room with their scent. Mary took a careful sip of her tea. It was sweet, with just a hint of honey.

"You know," Mrs. Ellery added after a moment, "when I was about your age, I also got into more trouble than I intended. Not because I wanted to. Because I didn't know how else to be seen."

Mary looked up, surprised. "Really?"

"Oh yes. I was loud, angry, unpredictable. People decided I was a lost cause. My mother told me so often enough that I started to believe it." She paused, eyes softening. "But one person, one teacher, saw something else. She didn't tell me I was good. She just told me I could be."

Mary felt a slight shift inside, like something settling that had been off balance for a long time.

"What happened to her?" she asked.

Mrs. Ellery smiled faintly. "She passed many years ago, but her words remained. They helped me keep choosing, even when choosing was difficult."

They fell into silence again, but this time Mary felt the silence working on her, loosening knots, smoothing edges she didn't know were sharp.

After a while, Mrs. Ellery stood. "Would you help me with something? The roses need a little trimming. They're stubborn things, but worth the effort."

Mary blinked. She'd never been asked to help with something gentle before. People usually asked her to stop doing things, not to join them.

"Okay," she said quietly.

They stepped out onto the back porch, where the late afternoon light had softened into gold. The roses were tangled, their stems curling around each other in a maze of thorns and petals. Some blossoms were fresh; others were wilted, hanging their heads like tired dancers.

"They look like a mess," Mary said.

Mrs. Ellery laughed softly. "Everything looks like a mess before you understand it. But messes can still be tended."

She handed Mary a pair of pruning shears. "Just the dead parts," she instructed. "Let the new blooms have room."

Mary carefully clipped a brown, crinkled bloom. It fell away easily. She clipped another, then another, each cut revealing a little more space, a little more possibility.

"You have a steady hand," Mrs. Ellery observed.

Mary's chest tightened, not painfully, but in a way she couldn't name. No one had ever told her she was steady. People said she was volatile, stubborn, and dangerous when provoked. But steady? No. That was new.

By the time they finished, the rosebush looked lighter, brighter, less burdened.

"It'll grow better now," Mrs. Ellery said.

"Why?"

"Because someone cared for it." She looked at Mary meaningfully. "Everything grows better when someone cares for it."

Mary lowered her gaze, unsure whether the words were about the roses or about her.

They walked back to the porch. The sun dipped low, turning the horizon the deep red of ripe fruit. Mary had never been good with gratitude; words felt too big in her mouth, but she tried anyway.

"Thank you," she murmured.

"For what, dear?" Mrs. Ellery asked.

"For… letting me sit here."

Mrs. Ellery touched Mary's shoulder gently. "You're always welcome. Anytime."

As Mary walked home, her steps felt a little steadier. Not lighter, her life wasn't suddenly fixed, but more constant, as if she'd found something solid to stand on in the middle of all the shifting ground.

She didn't know it yet, but that quiet hour in the neighbor's house was the first crack of light in a wall she'd spent years trapped behind, and once light finds a way in, it never entirely leaves.

Chapter 4

Mary returned the following afternoon. She didn't plan to. In fact, she had told herself all morning that she wouldn't go, that visiting once had already been too much, that Mrs. Ellery had only invited her out of politeness, not out of any real desire to see her again. But when the final bell rang, and the usual tide of voices filled the hallway, Mary felt the familiar heaviness gathering in her chest.

She didn't want to go home right away. She didn't want to face her father's silence or the suspension slip still sitting on the kitchen counter like a stain no amount of scrubbing would lift. Her feet chose the direction for her.

The sun was warm on her back when she reached the leaning fence. She hesitated, studying the small house, the porch where lavender plants nodded in the breeze. She almost turned away.

The gate creaked open before she could.

"Mary," Mrs. Ellery called, her voice soft and pleased, as if she'd been expecting her. "I'm glad you came."

The simple truth in those words, *glad you came*, undid Mary all over again. She nodded mutely and stepped through the gate.

"Come along," the old woman said. "I've been hoping for a helper today."

They walked to the garden behind the house, a place bursting with color and life. Bees droned lazily over the lavender. The marigolds stood bright as tiny suns. A row of tomatoes leaned heavily on their vines, swollen and green.

"What do you need help with?" Mary asked.

"Oh, nothing dramatic. Just tying the tomato stems so they don't break under their own weight." She gave Mary a gentle smile. "We all need a bit of support sometimes."

Mary knelt beside the plants, looping twine carefully around each stem. She liked the task; it was simple, methodical, and she couldn't break anything by accident. Mrs. Ellery knelt beside her, her knees popping quietly.

"You ever garden before?" she asked.

"No," Mary said.

"Mmm. I've always liked it. Plants are patient. They don't demand anything except a little light, a little water, and someone willing to pay attention." She glanced at Mary. "Children aren't so different."

Mary tied another knot, her fingers steady. "I don't think people want to pay attention to me."

"Oh, I imagine plenty of people pay attention," Mrs. Ellery said. "They just see the parts of you that shout loudest."
Mary frowned. "Like what?"

"Your anger. Your quickness. Your sharp edges." She paused, brushing soil from her palms. "But those things grew for a reason. They're not all you are."

Mary didn't know how to answer. She kept her eyes fixed on the tomato vine.

After a quiet moment, Mrs. Ellery spoke again. "You know, I wasn't always… this." She gestured with a small laugh to the garden, the tidy rows, the peaceful air around her. "When I was young, I carried storms with me everywhere I went."

"You?" Mary looked at her in disbelief.

"Oh yes. I was furious at the world. Furious at my mother. Furious at the idea that my whole life would be decided for me because of the mistakes I made at thirteen, fourteen." Her voice softened. "When people tell you you're broken long enough, eventually you stop arguing."

Mary felt something in her chest twist. "How'd you stop believing them?"

"I met someone who didn't see just my storms," she said. "Someone who saw the quiet underneath. My teacher, Miss Rayford. She never told me I was good, just that I could be. That I could choose the kind of woman I wanted to become."

"Choose?" Mary echoed.

"It was the first time anyone had ever given me that kind of power." She brushed her fingers lightly across a blossom as if it were something sacred. "She told me a word once, *timshel*. It means 'thou mayest.' Not 'thou must,' not 'thou shalt not.' But *may*. The possibility of choosing the good. The possibility of changing your own story."

Mary sat back on her heels. "And you believed her?"

"Not at first. Belief grows slowly. But she watered that idea in me until it took root."

Mary thought about this. No one had ever offered her the idea of may. Her world had been full of musts-"you must stop causing trouble"-and nevers-"you'll never change"-and shoulds-"you should try harder."

But *may*? That was new.

They worked in silence for a while longer. Mary tied the last stem and looked down at her hands, dirt smudging the creases. For once, she didn't mind the mess.

"Mrs. Ellery?" she asked quietly.

"Yes, dear?"

"Do you… Do you think I could change, too? Like you did?"

The older woman looked at her in a long, thoughtful way, not pitying, not uncertain, but seeing.

"Mary," she said gently, "you're already changing. You came here today, didn't you? You helped with the garden. You asked a question that took courage to speak."

Mary blinked. She hadn't realized any of that mattered.

"Change doesn't come with fireworks," Mrs. Ellery continued. "It comes with choices. Small ones, made again and again."

Mary nodded slowly. She wasn't sure she understood all of it, but she felt the truth of it settle into her bones.

As they finished tying the last of the vines, the sky flushed with the pinks and oranges of early evening. Mrs. Ellery stood with a soft groan, brushing dirt from her knees.

"One more thing," she said. "Never let anyone tell you who you are, not even the loudest voices. Especially not them."

Mary felt something tighten, and then loosen, in her chest.

"Okay," she murmured.

They walked toward the house together, and the fading light wrapped around them like a warm quilt.

For the first time in a long while, Mary didn't feel like trouble following her own shadow. She felt like someone who was believed in.

And when she went to bed that night, the word, *timshel*, echoed through her thoughts like a soft lantern glow.

Thou mayest.

Maybe, just maybe, she could.

Chapter 5

By Thursday, Willow Creek Middle School looked the same as it always did, brick walls in need of paint, a flag that snapped in the wind, and a parking lot crisscrossed with chalk dust from last week's P.E. class. But something in Mary felt different, even if she kept that feeling tucked deep inside where no one else could see it.

She had returned to Mrs. Ellery's garden every afternoon that week. They didn't talk much about school, trouble, or her father. Mostly, they tended plants, pulled weeds, or sat in the shade drinking tea. The quiet gave Mary space to breathe, space she hadn't known she needed.

Even so, the halls of school still greeted her with the same looks and whispers they always did. "Trouble," someone muttered when she passed. "Watch your back," another boy joked to his friend.

Usually, Mary ignored it or let the anger rise, hardening into the armor she wore daily. But today, the words felt... smaller as though they were nothing more than pebbles tossed at the side of a barn.

During lunch, she sat alone under the bleachers at the far end of the yard. It wasn't that she had no classmates she could sit with; she'd just learned it was easier to be alone than to feel alone around others.

She pulled out her sandwich and bit into it without enthusiasm. The bread tasted dry. Her mind wandered back to the garden, to the tomato vines she'd tied, the roses she'd trimmed, and the careful, hushed conversations with Mrs. Ellery.

You may choose, the older woman had said.

Not must. Not should. May.

The word felt like a seed she carried in her pocket, waiting for the right bit of light to coax it open.

A shout jerked her from her thoughts. "Hey! Give that back!"

It came from across the yard. Mary craned her neck and spotted Theo, the same sixth grader she'd tried to defend earlier in the week. Two older boys were circling him, one gripping his backpack while the other laughed.

"Come on, twerp," the taller boy taunted. "Say please."

Theo didn't say anything. He just lunged for the backpack and missed.

Mary felt her breath tighten. Normally, she would stride over and shove someone hard enough to make them stop. But every time she stepped in with fists first, she paid the price. She could already imagine the principal's face, already imagine her father's sigh. She closed her eyes for a beat.

Thou mayest.

She stood.

Her legs felt rooted at first, as if the whole schoolyard watched her. But no one did. Not really. They'd all decided who she was; her actions didn't surprise anyone anymore.

But maybe she could surprise herself.

Mary walked toward the boys with steadiness, even though she didn't expect it. When she arrived, she didn't shove. Didn't yell. Didn't lead with the storm inside her.

"That's enough!" She yelled, scolding them.

The taller boy snorted. "What, you gonna hit us? That's all you ever do."

"No," Mary said, her voice quiet but unmistakably firm. "I'm not hitting anybody."

That confused him. It confused *her*, too.

"I'm just telling you to stop!" she said.

The boy holding the backpack blinked, thrown off balance by the lack of a fight. Theo watched her with wide eyes, his breath quick and scared.

"Why do you care?" the boy asked.

Mary grew angry. "Because it's wrong! And because he asked you to stop! Now stop being an ass and give it back to him."

The boy hesitated. Mary could see the war behind his eyes, choices scrolling past faster than he could name them. Not because he wanted to do the right thing, but because he didn't know how to respond when the script changed.

With a grunt, he tossed Theo's backpack onto the ground. The other boy muttered something under his breath before walking away.

Theo scrambled to pick up his things.

"You, okay?" Mary asked.

He nodded quickly. "Yeah. Thanks. I thought you were gonna fight them."

"So did I," she admitted.

He blinked at her, unsure if she was joking. She wasn't.

A moment later, a voice called across the yard.

"Mary, what are you yelling and cursing at?"

It was Ms. Bartlett, one of the nicer teachers, fair, observant, the kind who didn't assume before asking. She strode toward them, eyes flicking from Theo's rumpled shirt to the boys now slinking away.

"Did something happen here?" She asked

Mary braced herself. Habit. Instinct. Her shoulders tensed, waiting for the weight that always came next, but Theo stepped forward.

"They were taking my backpack," he said. "Mary told them to stop. She helped me."

Ms. Bartlett's eyes softened. "Is that what you were yelling and cursing about, Mary?"

"Yes," Mary said, her voice steady. "I didn't touch anyone."

For a moment, Ms. Bartlett looked at her, not like she was waiting to catch her in a lie, but like she was seeing her for the first time.

"Thank you, Mary, that's a start," the teacher said. "While yelling and cursing at them is better than fighting, it is still not right to curse at people."

The words struck Mary harder than any accusation ever had. Some gratitude was directed at *her*. It felt foreign, startling, like stepping into warm light after standing in shadow for too long.

"Thank you, Ms. Barlett," she whispered. Mary had thought that she had handled the situation perfectly, but obviously she hadn't done as well as she had thought. Ms. Barlett had still thanked her. That was more gratitude than any other teacher had ever shown her before.

Theo gave her a grateful smile before hurrying toward his next class. Mary walked slowly back across the yard, the air around her buzzing, her heartbeat steady in a new way.

Something inside had shifted, a small thing, perhaps, but real. A spark catches in a long, dark place.

You may choose, she heard again in her mind, and today, she had.

For the first time, Mary wondered whether that single choice could change something more than a moment. Whether it could change *her.*

Chapter 6

By the time Mary reached home, the sun had already dipped behind the hills, leaving the yard in a wash of dusty blue. The walnut tree cast a long, crooked shadow across the brittle grass. For the first time in days, Mary didn't stop beneath it. She was tired, tired in a way she couldn't name. Hope, she discovered, carried its own weight.

She'd done something good today. Something right. Someone had thanked her for it, and yet her stomach twisted as she walked toward the house.

Her father's truck sat crooked in the driveway, angled slightly toward the ditch. That wasn't like him. He parked straight, always had, always would. Whatever had happened today, it had shaken him.

Mary paused on the porch, her hand hovering over the doorknob. She imagined what she wanted to find inside, maybe her father cooking dinner, the radio humming, and her shoulders relaxed. Perhaps he'd look up when she walked in, smile a little, and ask how her day was.

But when she stepped inside, the house smelled of bitterness, of burnt coffee and stale arguments that hadn't been spoken aloud but lingered anyway. Her father stood at the counter, staring at a stack of unopened envelopes.

"Mary," he said without looking up.

Something heavy settled in her gut.

"How was work?" she asked, trying to keep her voice steady.

He didn't answer right away. He tore open an envelope with more force than necessary, read the first line, then dropped it onto the pile.

"Long," he said finally.

She nodded, not sure what else to say. "You, okay?"

He laughed, but it wasn't a pleasant sound. "No, honey. I'm not."

The word *honey* should've softened things, but it didn't. It only made her chest tighten more. He used that word when he was overwhelmed, when he didn't have space for anything else, not even her.

He rubbed his hands over his face. "I got a call from the school."

Mary froze. "About what?"

"You know what." He said.

"No," she said, trying not to sound defensive. "I mean, which part? The suspension? Or today?"

"Both," he said, voice flat.

She swallowed. "Then... did they tell you what happened today?"

He finally turned to look at her, really look at her. His eyes were rimmed with exhaustion, and something like doubt sat in the center.

"They said you were involved in another confrontation. That you were swearing at some other kids."

Her heart dipped. "Dad, I..."

"Did you start it?" He asked.

"No! I helped..."

He held up a hand. "Mary, every time you say that, things still get worse."

The words struck hard. Too hard. They knocked something loose inside her, something she'd been carefully bracing for all week.

"I did the right thing... sort of," she said, voice trembling despite her best effort to hold it steady. "A teacher saw it, and she thanked me."

Her father's jaw tightened, not in anger, but in disbelief. "Mary... I'm tired. I'm so tired. You say these things, and I want to believe you. I really do. But I don't know how anymore."

The tremble in her chest grew sharper, darker. "So, you think I'm lying," she said quietly.

"I think," he began, then stopped, searching for words that wouldn't hurt her but finding none, "I think this isn't getting better. And I don't know what else to do."

Something snapped, not loudly, not visibly, but inwardly. That small spark of hope she'd carried since the garden sputtered. All at once, the warmth of Ms. Bartlett's praise, Theo's grateful eyes, and Mrs. Ellery's quiet wisdom felt faint and far away.

"You didn't even ask me," Mary whispered. "Again."

"Mary..."

"No! You didn't ask what *really* happened. You just assumed." Mary yelled.

Her volume startled him. She rarely raised her voice at home. But she couldn't stop the surge, the storm she'd been working so hard to quiet.

"You think I can't change," she said. "Everyone thinks that."

"That's not…"

"Yes, it is." Her voice cracked. "Why should I even try if no one sees it?"

Her father pressed his palm to his forehead, a gesture of defeat. The sight of it hurt more than his words.

"Mary, please," he said softly. "I've got enough going on. I can't handle this tonight."

He didn't shout. He didn't punish her. But the quiet dismissal carried a sharper edge than any anger could. Because it told her she didn't matter. Not enough. Not now. And that cut deeper than any punishment.

She turned away before he could see the expression twisting her face. Her feet moved without thought, down the hall, past the living room, past the photographs of better years, until she reached her bedroom.

She closed the door gently, careful not to make a sound. Then, when she was alone, she pressed her back against the door and slid to the floor.

The storm she had held back all week roared through her, silent but fierce. She dug her palms into her eyes, but tears came anyway, hot, uninvited, unstoppable.

"I tried," she whispered to the empty room. "I tried."

The words didn't comfort her. They didn't lessen the hurt. They only echoed back at her, fragile and raw.

And for the first time since stepping into Mrs. Ellery's garden, Mary wondered if she'd been foolish to believe she could outrun the shadows people threw on her.

Hope, she realized, it wasn't a warm and steady flame; it flickered, and it faltered.

Tonight, it nearly went out.

Chapter 7

Mary didn't go to the garden the next day.

The shame was too heavy, clinging to her like damp clothing. She moved through school in a blurry haze, head low, shoulders tight. Theo waved at her once from across the hall, tentative and hopeful, but she pretended not to see him. She didn't feel like someone worth being grateful for. She didn't feel like the girl who had made a brave choice yesterday.

She felt like the girl her father saw, too much trouble, too many mistakes, too much of everything except what she should be.

When the final bell rang, she walked home slowly, dragging her feet through the dust along the shoulder of the road. Her house came into view, small and tired under the afternoon sun. The walnut tree loomed over the yard like an old sentinel, its branches reaching toward her.

Mary didn't go to it. She didn't even look toward the leaning fence.

Instead, she slipped inside the house, shut her bedroom door, and curled up on her bed. She stared at the ceiling until the shadows stretched long across her room.

She didn't notice the knock at the front door. Or the soft murmur of voices. Or the gentle footsteps that approached her room, but she heard the quiet knock on her door.

"Mary?" Mrs. Ellery called softly. "It's me."

Mary sat up, startled. She wiped her face quickly, even though her tears had dried hours ago. She hesitated, then whispered, "Come in."

The door opened slowly, as if the older woman were giving Mary time to change her mind. Mrs. Ellery stepped inside, her yellow sweater wrapped loosely around her shoulders. She glanced around the room, neat, spare, with a few fading posters on the wall, and her eyes settled gently on Mary.

"Oh, child," she said softly. "I wondered where you'd gone."

Mary looked down at her hands. "I didn't want to bother you."

"You don't bother me," Mrs. Ellery said. "Not ever."

The certainty in her voice pried something open inside Mary, something she'd been pressing shut.

"I messed everything up," Mary whispered. "I thought… I thought I was changing. But then my dad…" Her voice broke. "I tried so hard, and he didn't even believe me."

Mrs. Ellery nodded, her expression full of quiet understanding. "People don't see change right away. Especially when they've grown used to expecting the worst, sometimes it takes time for their eyes to adjust."

"But what if they never do?" Mary asked. "What if no matter what I do, I'm still… me?"

"Ah," Mrs. Ellery said, pulling a chair beside the bed and lowering herself into it. "That's the part Miss Rayford never told me outright. The part I had to learn the hard way."

Mary looked up.

"Changing isn't about making others believe in you," the old woman continued. "It's about choosing to believe in yourself again and again, even on the days you fail. Especially on those days."

Mary shook her head. "I don't know how."

Mrs. Ellery reached into her sweater pocket and pulled out a small, worn book. Its cover was faded blue, the edges frayed. She handed it to Mary with care.

"I want you to have this," she said.

Mary turned it over in her hands. It wasn't a big book, more like a journal or a pocket diary. On the inside cover, written in looping, elegant handwriting, was a single word:

TIMSHEL

Mary's breath hitched. "This was yours?"

"It was Miss Rayford's first," Mrs. Ellery said. "She gave it to me when I was just about your age. I carried it everywhere. Some days, it reminded me I had a choice. Other days I forgot. Some days I threw it across the room."

She chuckled softly. "Change is messy work."

Mary traced the letters with her thumb. The word felt heavier than the little book should have allowed, but it was a good weight—a grounding one.

"I want to tell you something I've never told anyone," Mrs. Ellery said, her voice lowering. "I didn't change overnight. In fact, I made more mistakes after meeting Miss Rayford than before. I hurt people. I hurt myself. I failed, again and again."

Mary swallowed. "But you turned out... good."

"Good?" Mrs. Ellery smiled sadly. "Oh, child. I spent years believing I was broken beyond repair. I lost friendships. I lost jobs. I walked away from people before they could walk away from me. But every time I thought I'd ruined everything... I chose to try again."

She reached out and took Mary's hand.

"Change isn't a clean line. It's a long, winding road. And sometimes you step backward. That doesn't erase the steps forward."

Mary's throat tightened.

"I wanted to come by earlier," Mrs. Ellery added. "But I waited because I didn't want you to feel forced. I wanted you to know I'm here because *I care,* not because you owe me anything."

Tears welled in Mary's eyes, not from sadness, but from the unfamiliar experience of being treated gently.

"Why?" she whispered. "Why do you care about me?"

Mrs. Ellery brushed a strand of hair behind Mary's ear. "Because someone once cared for me when I didn't think I deserved it. And because I see the goodness fighting to grow in you. Even when you can't see it yourself."

Mary opened the little book again, staring at the single word on the inside cover.

Timshel.

Thou mayest.

"Do you really think I can change?" she asked.

Mrs. Ellery squeezed her hand. "I think you already have. Today wasn't a step backward, Mary. It was simply a hard day on a long road. But you're walking it."

A long silence settled between them, not heavy, but full, like the pause between one breath and the next.

Finally, Mary whispered, "Will you help me? Keep helping me?"

"Always," Mrs. Ellery said. "As long as you choose to keep trying."

Mary nodded, clutching the little book to her chest. The ache inside her didn't disappear, but it softened, as if someone had placed a warm hand over it.

She wasn't healed.

She wasn't transformed.

But she wasn't alone anymore either.

And sometimes, that was where change truly began.

Chapter 8

Monday arrived cold and restless, the way autumn sometimes announced itself in Willow Creek, without warning, without gentleness. Mary walked to school clutching the small blue book in her backpack, feeling its weight press between her notebooks like a secret she wasn't ready to share.

She hadn't told her father about her talk with Mrs. Ellery. She hadn't told him about the book. She kept both close, as a flicker cupped in her hands, afraid a single breath from the wrong direction might blow it out.

At school, the usual hum filled the halls: lockers slamming, morning announcements crackling, groups of students forming their little islands. Mary passed through the noise as if moving underwater. She nodded at Theo when she saw him, and he gave her a small, grateful smile that warmed a corner of her heart.

It was almost enough to steady her.

Almost.

The bell rang for the third period, and Mary joined the flow of students heading toward the science wing. She reached her classroom door when a sharp shout broke across the corridor.

"Give it back!"

Theo's voice. High, frightened, unmistakable.

Mary spun around.

Two older, bigger boys crowded him near the drinking fountain. One held Theo's sketchbook high above his head, flipping through it with a mocking laugh. The other blocked Theo's path each time he stepped forward, jabbing him in the shoulder hard enough to make him stumble.

"Look at these dumb drawings," the taller boy jeered. "What are these supposed to be? Cats? Clouds? You draw like a little kid."

"They're not dumb!" Theo snapped, and his face flushed. The boys only laughed harder.

Mary's pulse quickened. Anger surged, old, familiar, hot. The instinct to shove, to strike, to force the world into fairness rose like a tidal wave.

She saw it happening before she moved: her fist connecting, someone falling, teachers rushing in, faces turning cold, her father's shoulders sinking under a whole new disappointment.

Every path she had walked before led straight to that moment, but another path, small, fragile, newly formed, ran alongside the old one.

Thou mayest.

Mary stepped forward. "Stop," she said, her voice low but steady.

The boys turned, surprised, flickering in their eyes. "Oh, great," the shorter one scoffed. "Trouble's here. What are you gonna do this time, Mary? Swing first or yell first?"

"Neither," she said.

They weren't prepared for that.

"I'm asking you to give him back his sketchbook."

"Why should we?" the taller boy demanded.

Mary paused. This was the crossroad, where the old Mary would explode, and where the new one had a chance to breathe.

"Because it's his," she said. "Because he asked you to stop. And because you know it's wrong."

The taller boy opened his mouth, then shut it again. Not because her words overwhelmed him, but because her *stillness* did. She wasn't shaking. She wasn't yelling. She wasn't threatening.

She was standing there, choosing. A few students gathered nearby. Not a crowd, but enough to shift the balance. Enough to make the boys hesitate.

"Come on," the shorter boy muttered. "Let's go."

The taller one stayed a bit longer, his fingers tight around the sketchbook. Mary held his gaze, not challenging, not pleading, just steady.

A moment passed. Then, with a sharp exhale, he dropped the sketchbook at Theo's feet.

"Whatever," he muttered, pushing past his friend and stalking down the hall.

Theo scrambled to pick it up, checking the pages with trembling hands.

Mary let out a slow breath.

That's when the teacher rounded the corner.

"Is everything all right here?" Ms. Bartlett asked, eyes flicking from Theo to Mary to the retreating boys.

Theo looked up, chest rising and falling, nervous energy buzzing through him. He opened his mouth to speak, but this time, Mary gently touched his arm.

"It's okay," she said. "I've got it."

She turned to Ms. Bartlett. "Those boys took Theo's sketchbook. I asked them to stop and return it. They did. It's handled."

Ms. Bartlett scrutinized them both.

"Thank you for telling me," she said. "And for stepping in the way you did."

Her eyes held no suspicion. Just trust.

Mary nodded. "I didn't want anyone to get hurt."

Something in Ms. Bartlett's expression softened, recognition, maybe, or pride. "You made the right choice."

The right choice.

The words didn't echo like praise. They settled, warm and sure, somewhere deep inside her where doubt had lived for so long. After class, Theo caught up to her. "Thank you," he said quietly. "I, I think you're courageous."

Mary managed to smile. "I'm not brave. I just…" She paused, searching for the truth. "I just didn't want things to go the way they always do."

Theo nodded as if he understood, but as Mary walked down the hall, she realized something important:

She *was* brave. Not because she'd stopped the fight. Not because the teacher saw her goodness. But because she'd faced down the storm inside her, the one that had controlled her for years, and chosen a different path.

And when she reached her locker, she slipped the little blue book from her backpack and ran her thumb over the word inside.

TIMSHEL.

Thou mayest.

Today, she had.

Chapter 9

After school, Mary walked home under a sky soft with thin clouds. The air carried the first bite of autumn, cool and crisp, brushing against her cheeks as if to remind her she was awake, fully, newly awake in a way she hadn't been before.

She passed beneath the walnut tree, its branches swaying lightly overhead. The shadow it cast was long, dark, and familiar, but it no longer felt like something reaching to pull her under. It felt like a boundary she had finally learned how to step beyond.

She didn't go inside the house right away. Her father's truck was parked neatly today, straight and thoughtful, but she wasn't ready to step into that space of uncertainty just yet.

Instead, she walked the few steps to the leaning fence and tapped the post lightly. The gate creaked open before she touched it.

"I saw you coming," Mrs. Ellery said, already stepping out onto the porch with a smile that warmed the entire yard. "I was hoping you'd stop by."

Mary felt that strange, fluttering warmth again, gratitude, maybe, or the first fragile threads of belonging weaving themselves around her.

"I wanted to," she said.

"Well then," Mrs. Ellery replied, "that's enough."

They settled on the porch steps, the old wood sighing beneath them. The lavender rustled in the breeze, and the marigolds glowed like little fires against the fading day.

For a while, they didn't talk. They existed side by side, letting the quiet settle comfortably between them. The quiet that didn't press, didn't demand, just held.

Finally, Mrs. Ellery spoke.

"You seem lighter today."

Mary nodded. "A little. Something happened at school."

"Oh?"

"I… made a choice." Mary's fingers brushed the edge of her backpack where the small blue book rested safely inside. "And not the kind of choice people expect me to make."

Mrs. Ellery's eyes shone with quiet pride. "Tell me."

Mary did so slowly and carefully, but with growing confidence. She told her about Theo, about the boys, about her steady voice that surprised even her. She told her about Ms. Bartlett's words and how they had landed gently instead of heavily.

When she finished, Mrs. Ellery rested her hand over Mary's.

"And how did it feel?" she asked.

Mary thought about it. Really thought.

"It felt like… like I finally listened to myself instead of the noise around me," she said softly. "Like I wasn't trapped by what everyone else thinks I am."

Mrs. Ellery nodded as though she had been waiting for Mary to understand this very thing. "Growth is quiet, child. It doesn't shout. It whispers. And you heard it today."

Mary's chest swelled, warm, full, calm.

"I don't think I'm fixed," she said. "I don't think everything is suddenly going to be easy."

"My dear," Mrs. Ellery laughed gently, "nothing worth building is easy. And you are worth building."

The words sank into Mary like water into thirsty soil.

"What if I mess up again?" she asked.

"Oh, you will," Mrs. Ellery said without hesitation. "We all do. But you'll choose again. And again. That's how change takes root. Not in perfection, but persistence."

Mary leaned her shoulder softly against the older woman. It felt natural, like leaning into a safe harbor after a long journey.

As the sky dimmed to a dusky violet, Mary stood to go. "I should talk to my dad," she said, though her voice trembled slightly at the edges. "I don't want to hide from him."

"That's brave," Mrs. Ellery replied. "Go gently. And remember, he's human, too. He's learning how to walk his own road."

Mary nodded, grateful for the reminder. Her father's mistakes didn't erase his love. His weariness didn't erase his hope for her. They were both learning how to see one another again.

She started toward the fence, then paused and turned back.

"Thank you," she said. "For everything."

Mrs. Ellery smiled, a soft, knowing smile that crinkled the corners of her eyes. "You came to me, Mary. I just opened the gate."

Mary stepped through the gate and crossed the yard. The walnut tree towered behind her, but it no longer felt like a shadow she hid beneath. It felt like a landmark she was walking past on her way forward.

When she reached the back door, she took a breath, deep, steady, hers.

Inside, her father sat at the table, his posture weary but softer than it had been days ago. He looked up when she entered, and something unspoken passed between them, an opening, a hesitant peace.

"Hey, kid," he said quietly. "Can we talk?"

Mary nodded and took a seat. She didn't know what tomorrow would look like. She didn't know how many steps backward or forward lay ahead. But she knew this:

She would take those steps.

She would choose again and again, and she would not break.

As she slipped the little blue book from her backpack and laid it gently on the table beside her, the word on the inside cover glowed faintly in the warm kitchen light.

TIMSHEL.

Thou mayest.

And for the first time in her life, Mary believed she honestly might.

Author's Note

The Girl Who Would Not Break was born from my love of *John Steinbeck's East of Eden*, a novel that taught me about choice, the weight of our pasts, and the quiet, stubborn hope carried in the word *timshel*.

Steinbeck wrote that "thou mayest" is the most important word in the world, because it reminds us that we are not trapped by where we came from or by the names others give us. We may choose to step forward. We may decide to become something better than our circumstances, our mistakes, or our fears. That idea has stayed with me for years.

This story is my small attempt to honor that truth. Mary is not Cal Trask, and Mrs. Ellery is not Lee; their world is not Steinbeck's Salinas Valley. Yet their journey echoes the same quiet battle between who we are told we must be and who we *may* become. Every step Mary takes, forward and backward, is a reminder that growth is never a clean line. Change is messy, halting, fragile. But it is *possible*.

I wanted to write a story where the miracle wasn't a dramatic transformation, but simply a girl learning that she is allowed to try again. A girl who realizes she is not broken beyond repair. A girl who discovers that sometimes the lifeline comes not from grand gestures, but from a neighbor with a warm cup of tea and a steady presence.

If this story leaves anything with you, I hope it's this: You are not what others say you are. You are what you choose, one small act at a time. Timshel. Thou mayest.

Thank you for reading.

—Brett C. Persson

Bench 42

Chapter I

The city park woke gently, as if reluctant to disturb the quiet that had settled overnight. The first threads of morning sunlight slipped through the canopy of maple branches, lighting the drifting leaves like tiny embers falling from the sky. A thin veil of dew shimmered on the grass, and the air held the clean, incredible scent that only existed in the earliest hours, before footsteps, voices, and the day's obligations began to reshape the world.

Bench 42 sat beneath the old maple as if it had always been there, its wooden slats worn smooth by years of weather and weary bodies seeking rest. The brass plaque, simple, unadorned, slightly tarnished, caught a brief flash of sunlight before the tree's shadow reclaimed it. Most people passed it without thinking, but to Tom, this bench was a landmark in the geography of his life.

He appeared on the winding path with his familiar, measured pace. Even from a distance, it was clear that he walked not with urgency but with purpose, the kind born from routine, or need, or something more profound that kept pulling him back. His left leg dragged slightly, a reminder of a surgery long healed but never fully forgiven. Still, he moved steadily, one hand nestling the strap of his worn leather satchel against his side as though guarding something fragile inside.

Reaching the bench, Tom paused. He didn't sit immediately. He stood with his hand resting lightly on the top slat, his fingers brushing the wood in a tender, absent-minded stroke. It had become part greeting, part grounding, an unspoken acknowledgment of the place he returned to again.

Finally, he lowered himself onto the left side of the bench. He always sat there. Habit, maybe. Or memory.

He unscrewed the lid of his thermos, letting the faint steam rise into the cool air. The smell of coffee, strong, dark, probably brewed too early, folded into the morning. Tom took a sip, winced slightly at the bitterness, then set the thermos beside him with a small sigh.

From the satchel, he pulled a stack of envelopes bound with twine. He held them carefully, almost reverently, as if they were made of something that might crumble beneath rough handling. Some envelopes were crisp; others looked softened by time, their edges feathered and fragile.

He sat with them in his lap for a long moment before doing anything else.

The park around him slowly began to stir. A dog barked in the distance. A cyclist passed on the far path, tires humming against the pavement. Somewhere high above, a bird called out, a single, lilting note that echoed faintly before fading.

Tom heard none of it the way others would. His attention was fixed on the envelopes and the weight they carried. His mornings had a rhythm now: arrive just after sunrise, sit beneath the maple, and let the world shrink until only the bench, the letters, and the quiet mattered.

Tom slipped the twine loose, but he didn't open a letter yet. Instead, he exhaled softly and gazed at the space beside him, the right side of the bench, where someone else had once sat.

The sunlight pressed warmly against his face. The breeze lifted a few strands of his thinning silver hair. And in that moment, before the first envelope was opened, before memory could do what it always did, Tom whispered something into the quiet morning that only the trees and the passing wind could hear.

"Good morning," he murmured.

Then he reached for the first letter.

Chapter II

Tom chose the first envelope, the way a person decides which memory to touch, carefully, almost shyly. It was the one least weathered by time, its paper still firm, its edges still neat. The handwriting on the front, though his own, looked steadier than it did now. He traced a finger along the ink, remembering the day he wrote it, recalling how the words had felt easier then.

He unfolded the letter, letting the paper rest lightly between his fingers. The breeze tugged at one corner, playful, as if inviting the memory out into the morning. Tom cleared his throat and began reading quietly, more to himself than to the world.

"Dear Elaine,

You wouldn't believe how cold the coffee is at that new café on Elm. Thought I'd give it a try yesterday. Mistake. Nearly froze my dentures off."

He let out a soft huff of amusement. The sound surprised him a little, as though laughter was a visitor he hadn't expected. He continued.

"I can still hear you telling me, 'Tom, don't be cheap, get the latte.' And I can hear myself telling you, 'It's dollar fifty more.' You always rolled your eyes at that.

And somehow, somehow, you always won."

Tom lowered the letter for a moment, his smile lingering but faint.

Tom could see the memory as clearly as if it were happening on the path in front of him: Elaine standing in line ahead of him at the coffee counter, her coat still damp from that morning's rain, shaking out her auburn curls with mock impatience as she turned to say, "Honestly, Tom, for a man who spends thirty bucks a month on crossword puzzle books, you sure get riled up about coffee prices."

She had said it loud enough for the barista to hear, too, and the young woman had snorted as she foamed the milk for Elaine's latte. Tom had pretended to be embarrassed, but he wasn't. He had loved the way Elaine's humor filled a room, even ones he thought were too small for laughter.

He could still picture her leaning over the small, round café table, hands curled around the warm cup, steam fogging her glasses as she repeated, with exaggerated patience, "Just try it, Tom. You might even like fancy milk."

He hadn't liked the milk. But he loved watching her enjoy hers.

Tom blinked away the image and lifted the letter again. The paper rustled gently, catching the morning light.

He continued reading, though he already knew the words by heart.

"You always had a way of making the simplest things feel like… more. Coffee. Sunday afternoons. Grocery runs. Even arguments over coupons. Everything was brighter with you in it."

He paused again, chest tightening with the soft ache of a grief that had grown familiar, less a wound now, more a bruise he had learned to live around.

A jogger passed on the trail, shoes tapping rhythmically against the pavement. The sound faded quickly, swallowed by the quiet. Tom folded the letter carefully along its original crease and placed it on the bench beside him, smoothing the surface with his palm.

"This was always your favorite kind of morning," he murmured to the empty right side of the bench. "Cool air. Quiet. Just enough wind to keep the leaves dancing."

The maple obliged his sentiment, releasing a handful of amber leaves that spiraled gently toward the ground.

Tom watched them fall and let himself imagine her sitting there again, elbow resting on the back of the bench, foot bouncing lightly, humming some old tune she loved and never quite remembered the words to. She would have nudged him and teased him for drinking the same plain coffee every day. She would have asked if he brought enough cream packets this time. She would have leaned against him when the breeze grew too cool.

The memory settled over him like a warm blanket and a slightly heavy one. After a moment, he reached out and touched the first letter again, fingertips lingering on the folded paper. Then he drew in a slow, steady breath.

One memory down. The easier one. The others would not be so gentle, but he was here. He had come to read them all.

Chapter III

Tom's hand hovered over the remaining envelopes, hesitating for the first time that morning. The lightness he'd felt with the first letter had already begun to fade, like a sunbeam slipping behind a cloud. The second envelope lay beneath the first, darker in color, its edges softened by years of being held too tightly and too often.

He drew in a breath and picked it up.

This one felt heavier. Paper shouldn't have weight, he often thought, yet grief could make anything unbearably dense.

He slid a thumb along the seal, opened it, and unfolded the letter. The handwriting was shaky here, uneven strokes that betrayed the emotional state he'd been in when he wrote it. As he began to read, his voice sank lower, the way a person lowers their voice when speaking a truth that they wish weren't real.

"Dear   Elaine,
I had the dream again last night, the one where I'm driving, and you're beside me, smiling like nothing in the world could ever go wrong."

Tom paused. His jaw tightened. The dream had come more often lately. Sometimes he wished his mind would stop resurrecting that day; other times he feared the day he wouldn't dream of her at all.

He continued.

"Everything feels normal for a moment. Your hair is tucked behind your ear the way you always did, without thinking. You're telling me something about dinner plans, something small, something ordinary, and then the sound comes."

Tom swallowed. His throat was suddenly dry.

"I can never stop it. I can never slow down enough. I can never turn the wheel in time, but this time… This time, you spoke before the crash. You said, 'It wasn't your fault, Tom.'"

He stopped reading. The breeze brushed against the page, lifting the corner gently, as if urging him to keep going.
But Tom closed his eyes.

Out of all the memories he carried, this was the one he wished he could rewrite. Not erase, no. Erasing would dishonor her. But if he could shift one moment, change one decision, maybe she would still be sitting here beside him, telling him to quit brooding and drink his coffee while it was hot.

The accident itself wasn't complicated, a slick road after a long day. A driver is coming around a blind curve too fast, a fraction of a second where the world pivoted. People spoke afterward using words like *unavoidable*, tragic, and *fate*.

But Tom didn't believe in fate; he believed in choices. He opened his eyes and forced himself to continue reading.
"The police report said the other driver lost control. They said I did everything right.
But I remember how tired I was, Elaine.
I remember you telling me that morning to let you drive.
And I remember brushing you off.
'It's just ten minutes,' I said. Ten minutes."
His voice cracked, just slightly, just enough.

He lowered the letter to his lap, hands trembling now, and stared at the ground. A yellow leaf landed beside his shoe, curling at the edges, delicate and brittle. He watched it for a long moment before speaking aloud, not reading this part but letting it spill out in the raw honesty the letter only hinted at.

"I should've listened to you," he whispered. "God knows, you were always the wiser one."

He pinched the bridge of his nose, feeling the familiar pressure build behind his eyes.

She had survived the initial impact. He had held her hand on the ride to the hospital. She had told him she was okay, even when the monitors suggested otherwise. And he, believing her, believing in her stubborn strength, had smiled and told her she would be home in a day or two.

He never forgave himself for believing that. Drawing a steady breath, he lifted the letter again. He read the closing lines quietly.

"*I know what everyone says. I know what the doctors said, the police said, and what your sister said. But none of them were behind the wheel. None of them ignored your offer, and I can't stop thinking that if I had just handed you the keys… you'd still be here.*"

He folded the letter with slow, deliberate movements, as though the act itself was fragile and sacred. He didn't place this letter beside the first; instead, he kept it in his hands, thumb running along the crease again and again, as a man smoothing out a scar he wished would disappear.

The park was busier now, but the noise felt far away, muted, distant, as if Tom sat inside a bubble the world couldn't quite penetrate. A cyclist rolled by. A dog barked somewhere beyond the oak grove. None of it registered.

When he finally spoke, his voice was barely louder than the shifting leaves.

"I'm sorry, Elaine," he whispered. "I'm so damn sorry."

The wind stirred, brushing past his cheek like a comforting hand. Or at least, he allowed himself to imagine it that way.

He laid the letter on the bench, this one gently, almost apologetically, and rested his palm over it for a long, quiet moment.

The hardest part was still ahead. The last letter waited in the stack. The one he'd avoided writing for years. The one he had written only when he knew he couldn't keep standing still.

Chapter IV

Tom stared at the remaining envelope for a long time before he touched it. Unlike the others, this one looked untouched by time, crisp and clean, almost out of place among the softly worn stack. It was the only one he hadn't reread since writing it. The only one he folded carefully and hid at the bottom of the bundle, as if afraid the words inside might spill out and force him to confront them again.

He brushed his palm over it. The paper was smooth, firmer than the others. Newer. More final.

He felt his breath catch. This letter wasn't about a memory. This one was about the future, and that, somehow, was the hardest part.

The breeze quieted around him, the maple branches barely shifting. Morning light spread slowly across the park, warming the ground and creeping toward the bench as though waiting politely to join him.

Finally, Tom opened the envelope. The first line alone made his chest tighten.

"Dear   Elaine,
This will be my last letter."

He stopped. His vision blurred for a second, not with tears, though they were there, pressed at the edges, but with the weight of what it meant to write such a sentence, let alone read it aloud. He forced himself to go on.

"Not because I've run out of things to say, but because I finally need to say the one thing I've been avoiding."

Tom looked up briefly, as if expecting her to be there, sitting with her legs crossed, leaning toward him the way she used to when something serious was coming. She always had this way of listening, with her whole face, whole body, softening the harshest truths simply by receiving them with love.

He wished he could borrow that calm now. He swallowed and read the following lines quietly.

"*I don't know who I am without you.*

I keep waking up waiting to hear you in the kitchen, humming off-key.

I keep reaching for your hand in the evenings out of habit.

Every day feels like I'm walking through a house after the furniture's been moved, familiar, but wrong."

A tear slipped down his cheek. He didn't brush it away. The letter continued, and with each line, Tom felt himself confronting truths he had long skirted around but never stepped into fully.

"*I thought grief would be loud, dramatic... something I'd feel crashing through every day like a storm. But instead, it's quiet. Quiet, and constant, and everywhere.*

I see you in strangers' faces. I hear you in distant laughter. I feel you in moments when I reach for someone who isn't there."

He tightened his grip on the paper.

Bench 42 had become a refuge for him, but also a place where time stopped. Where he allowed himself to stay motionless, anchored to a world that no longer existed except in memory, he came here because it hurt to stay away and because he feared what it would mean if he stopped coming.

Without the ritual, without the letters... what was left?

"*I'm afraid, Elaine.*

Afraid that moving forward means leaving you behind.

Afraid that if I stop hurting, it means I've stopped loving.

Afraid that this, sitting at this bench, writing to a woman who can't write back, is the only thing I have left of us."

Tom's breath shook. The admission was like stepping into cold water, sharp, jarring, breathtaking.

He looked around the park and at their bench again. The bench felt different now. Not cruel or lonely, but heavy with the truth that maybe he had been clinging to the pain because it was the only part of her he felt he had left.

He forced himself to read the final paragraph.

"But I know you wouldn't want this for me.

You wouldn't want me trapped in the worst moment of our lives together.

So today, I'm doing something I never thought I could do.

I'm not saying goodbye to you, never to you.

I'm saying goodbye to the grief.

To the guilt. To the weight I've been carrying like a punishment.

I have to try living again.

Even if I fail. Even if it hurts."

The letter ended there. No sign-off. No "love always." Just the truth, laid bare.

Tom folded the paper slowly, carefully, pressing the crease with trembling fingers. When he finished, he didn't put it beside the other letters. He held it in his lap, staring at it like something precious and dangerous at the same time.

The park around him had fully awakened now, children's laughter drifting from the playground, a dog sprinting after a ball, a couple strolling hand in hand along the path. Life is moving, gently but undeniably forward.

Tom took a deep breath. The kind that starts somewhere deep in the ribs and rises all the way to the eyes.

"God, Elaine…" he whispered, voice cracking. "I hope this doesn't disappoint you."

He closed his eyes for a moment, letting the sunlight settle on his face, letting the sounds of the park fill the spaces grief had occupied for so long. When he opened them again, his gaze lowered to the ground beneath the bench.

He knew what he needed to do next. What this letter was meant for, and for the first time in a long while, he felt, not ready, but willing.

Chapter V

For a long moment, Tom didn't move. The final letter rested in his hands, folded into a neat, slender shape that somehow felt far too small for the truth it carried. The park moved around him, unaware of the seismic shift happening on an old wooden bench beneath a maple tree.

He looked at the space to his right again, but this time not with the hollow ache of longing. There was something gentler in his expression now, something that softened the lines around his eyes. Bench 42.

Other people passed it without noticing. To them, it was just another place to rest, to tie a shoelace, to check a text message while jogging. But for Tom and Elaine, this bench had been a chapter marker in the long book of their life together.

He brushed his hand across the slats, feeling the grooves worn by weather, by time, by countless mornings exactly like this one.

He remembered the first day they found it. They hadn't planned to stop. They'd been walking through the park on a warm afternoon in late spring, holding ice cream cones that melted faster than they could eat them. Elaine had laughed as strawberry dripped onto her wrist, and Tom, flustered, had insisted on cleaning it with the edge of his napkin. She'd pulled her hand away and teased him, *"Let it be. You're too serious sometimes, Tom."*

She dragged him toward the bench, the one positioned beneath the sprawling maple that offered just enough shade to cool their ice cream but not so much they couldn't feel the sunshine. They had sat there for the first time with sticky hands, sun-warm shoulders, and the kind of laughter that came without restraint.

They returned to the bench on their anniversaries, on days they needed a quiet moment, on evenings when life felt like too much or too little. They made plans there, small ones, like dinner for the week, and larger ones, like the trip to Oregon they never got to take. It wasn't a bench. Not really. It was an anchor.

He remembered one frigid morning, years ago, when Elaine had pressed her gloved hand against the plaque and declared, "This is our seat in the universe, Tom. Our little patch of permanence." He'd rolled his eyes, smiling, but the sentiment stuck.
She always had a way of making simple places feel sacred.

When the accident happened, Tom had avoided the park for months. He couldn't bear the thought of being there without her next to him, the reminder of what the world had taken. But grief had a way of circling back to the places where love was once alive, and eventually he found himself walking the familiar path again.
The bench had been waiting.

He hadn't realized until then how much it held, echoes of laughter, fragments of conversation, the warmth of her hand slipping into his. A thousand small memories that softened the unbearable truth of her absence. In time, Bench 42 became the only place he could talk to her without feeling foolish.
The only place where his grief didn't feel out of place.

He ran his fingers along the plaque now, feeling the cool metal against his skin. Sunlight flickered through the leaves, dappling the wood with shifting patches of light.

"Do you remember," he murmured, "how you said this place belonged to us?" His voice softened. "You were right. You were always right."

He leaned forward, letting his gaze fall to the shadow beneath the bench. That small, quiet space felt oddly fitting, sheltered, private, a place where something could rest safely out of sight but never forgotten.

Tom held the final letter in both hands. It wasn't just a goodbye to grief. It wasn't even really a goodbye. It was a turning point.

The bench had carried their past for years. Now it would take this moment too, the moment he chose not to let loss be the only story he had.

He inhaled deeply, then, slowly, carefully, he slid from the bench and knelt beside it. His knees protested, but he didn't care. He reached under the slats and placed the folded letter gently against the wood, as if returning something borrowed.

Then he reached into his jacket pocket and pulled out a small, pressed flower, one Elaine had once tucked into his wallet during a picnic, and joked, "Now you'll always have something pretty with you." He'd kept it ever since.

He laid the flower beside the letter, the pale petals glowing softly in the filtered sunlight. The gesture wasn't final. It wasn't closure. It was something quieter, something truer: a promise to let love remain, but not let sorrow be its only expression.

Tom exhaled, a long, trembling breath that felt almost like release. The bench would now hold the letter, just as it had held their memories, just as it had held him through the worst of it.

He rested his hand on the wood one last time before standing. What came next wasn't certain. But for the first time in a very long while, he wasn't afraid of the uncertainty.

Chapter VI

Tom rose slowly from the ground, steadying himself with one hand on the bench. His knees ached, and his back reminded him of the years he'd carried, but the familiar discomfort grounded him. He wasn't rushing anything, not today. Not with this moment.

The sunlight had crept farther across the park, warming the grass and drawing faint glimmers from the dew. The world had fully awakened around him now: children shrieking with laughter near the pond, a dog tugging its owner toward an enthusiastic squirrel, the rhythmic squeak of a stroller wheel that needed oil. Ordinary life. The kind he used to take for granted.

He turned slightly, looking down at the shadow beneath Bench 42, where he had placed the final letter and the pressed flower. They were hidden out of sight, but he knew they were there, kept, sheltered, becoming part of the place that had held so much of their story.

For a moment, he felt the urge to sit back down. To stay. To hold onto the ritual a little longer, because stepping away felt like stepping into a world where he no longer knew the shape of things. The bench had become a boundary line between who he was with Elaine and who he had been stumbling around without her.
But today, that line felt thinner. Not erased. Not healed. Just... thinner.

Tom let his eyes drift to the space beside him, the right side of the bench where Elaine used to sit. He didn't imagine her there; he was long past pretending. But he did feel something quieter. Not present, exactly. Not absence, either.
Something in between.

A soft ache that no longer hollowed him out but still anchored him to the truth that she mattered. That she always would.

He swallowed against the tightening in his throat and whispered, "I'm still going to miss you." The words didn't sound broken. They didn't collapse under their own weight the way they once had. They were simply honest.

The breeze answered by nudging a handful of fallen leaves across the path, brushing them gently against his shoes before carrying them onward. He watched them go and wondered, for the first time, if grief moved like that, restless, always in motion, shifting shape without warning, but never entirely disappearing.

He turned away from the bench, slow and uncertain. The path stretched ahead of him in the dappled sunlight, curved slightly to the left, the way the park always had, a familiar walk. But today, it felt different, not easier, not harder. Just different.

He took a step. It wasn't brave or bold. It wasn't decisive. It was small, quiet, and real. His foot met the path. Then he took another step.

Behind him, Bench 42 remained nestled under the maple, watching over the memory he had left beneath it. The bench didn't feel abandoned. It felt entrusted.

Tom paused a few feet down the path and looked back over his shoulder, not longing, not regretful, but with a soft, almost sad affection. The kind you feel when leaving somewhere that shaped you, even if it hurt.

"Goodbye for now," he murmured.

Not goodbye forever. Not that, I'll never come back. It is just for now.

Then he turned again and continued walking, slow but steady, into a world that was still unfamiliar without her shape beside him.

Somewhere between the shadows and the sunlight, between memory and movement, between holding on and letting go, Tom realized something quietly devastating and quietly comforting:

You don't stop loving someone when they're gone. You learn to carry that love differently. The path curved ahead. He followed it.

Embers Before the Storm

Chapter I

The city of Galadine did not sleep; it waited.

Stone buildings leaned toward one another along the narrow streets as if sharing secrets. Lantern light flickered against damp walls, stretching shadows into long, nervous shapes that trembled with every gust of wind. Somewhere far off, a bell rang once and then fell silent, leaving the night thicker than before.

People moved quickly here. Heads stayed down. Hands stayed close to knives. At the edge of the market square, Olan stood. He was hard to miss. Broad-shouldered and thick through the chest, he looked carved rather than born, arms corded with muscle, hands scarred and calloused from years of work meant to break other men. His chain mail was worn but clean, hanging heavy against his frame, and a longsword rested at his side like an extension of his body rather than a threat he needed to advertise. His brown hair was pulled back into a practical tie at the back of his neck, revealing a stern but not cruel face. His eyes moved slowly, carefully, as if he were constantly measuring the world for danger rather than looking for it.

He did not belong to the city's shadows, and the shadows knew it. A few steps behind him, half-hidden beneath the archway of a crumbling stone building, stood Derick. Where Olan was solid, Derick was sharp. He wore a dark cloak that blended easily into the night, its edges dusted with road grime and old frost. Beneath it, lighter armor hugged his lean frame, designed for movement rather than endurance. His light brown hair fell just past his ears, untidy and unconcerned, and a faint scar cut through his right brow, which continued down past his eye to his right cheek, pale against his skin, as if it had never fully healed. His green eyes were alert, almost bright in the low light, tracking every shift in the square. A compact crossbow rested across his back, blackened wood polished smoothly by frequent use.

Derick watched people the way a hunter watches prey, not with hatred, but with certainty. Across the square, the door to a tavern creaked open. Warm light spilled out, accompanied by the low hum of voices and the smell of ale and smoke. Framed in the doorway was Bellox.

Bellox the dwarf was thick through the torso, built like a block of iron wrapped in layered wool and leather. His beard, dark and braided close, was threaded with silver rings that caught light when he moved. A heavy apron covered his broad chest, stained from years of work behind a bar that had seen more blood than laughter. His eyes were sharp and intelligent beneath heavy brows, constantly shifting between the street and the room behind him. A battle axe hung on the wall just inside the doorway, placed there not as decoration but as a promise.

Bellox rested one hand on the doorframe and nodded once, slow, deliberate, toward the square. He had seen something he did not like. From the opposite end of the street came the soft sound of boots against stone.

Christiana emerged from the shadows without haste, her presence calm, the air around her strained by contrast. She wore a long, travel-worn cloak, the color of ash, clasped at the neck with a simple silver pin. Strands of dark hair escaped her hood, framing a face marked not by age, but by resolve. Her eyes were steady, clear, and unsettlingly focused, as though she were listening to something more profound than the city's noise. A leather-bound satchel hung at her side, no visible weapon. No fear.

Christina stopped when she reached the edge of the square, her gaze lifting first to Olan, then drifting briefly to the shadows where Derick stood, before settling on Bellox's open door.

For a moment, no one spoke. The city held its breath. Though none of them said it aloud, each of them felt the same truth settle quietly into place: Whatever was coming had already begun.

Chapter II

Olan shifted his weight, and the chain mail settled against his shoulders with a dull metallic whisper. He had learned long ago how to stand without looking like he was waiting for trouble, though trouble always seemed to find him anyway.

A merchant cart rolled into the square from the eastern road; its wheels caked with dried mud and salt. Two guards walked beside it, both young, both tense. Olan recognized the look, men trying to appear braver than they felt. He stepped forward before either of them could speak.

"This is far enough," Olan said, his voice low and even.

The merchant glanced up at him, eyes widening just slightly. Olan saw the quick calculation pass across the man's face, size, armor, sword, before relief followed. "We were told someone would meet us," the merchant said. "Someone reliable."

Olan nodded once. Reliable. That word followed him everywhere, though he had never chosen it for himself. He walked alongside the cart as it crossed the square, his pace unhurried, his eyes scanning rooftops, doorways, and alleys. He noticed the way people edged away as he passed, how conversations died down, how even the shadows seemed to pull back. It wasn't fear exactly, more like respect earned through reputation rather than intention. Olan didn't enjoy it, but he had earned it.

At the edge of the square, one of the guards stumbled, nearly dropping his spear. Olan caught the shaft before it hit the ground and handed it back without comment. The young man flushed with embarrassment.

"Keep your grip steady," Olan said quietly. "If you're nervous, breathe slower. Fear makes hands shake."

The guard nodded, grateful, though Olan could tell the advice would only help so much. The guard was just too inexperienced to use the advice properly.

As the cart slowed near Bellox's tavern, Olan felt it, a subtle shift in the air, like a tightening string. His hand moved instinctively closer to his sword, though he did not draw it. He turned his head just enough to catch a glimpse of movement near the alley to the south. A pair of figures lingered there longer than necessary, pretending to argue while watching the cart too closely.

Olan frowned. "Stay close," he told the merchant. "And don't stop unless I tell you to."

The merchant swallowed and nodded. For a moment, nothing happened. Then a stone clattered across the square. Olan reacted without thought. He stepped between the cart and the alley, shoulders squaring, stance widening. His presence alone was enough to make one of the figures hesitate. The other took a step back, muttered something Olan couldn't hear, and the pair disappeared into the darkness.

The tension drained slowly, like blood from a wound. Olan exhaled and lowered his hand. He hated moments like that, not because of the danger, but because he never knew if he had done the right thing. Had they truly meant harm? Had he prevented violence, or merely delayed it? His strength solved immediate problems, but it never answered the questions that followed.

When the cart reached the tavern, Bellox was already waiting. "Inside," the dwarf said, his voice calm but firm. "Now." The merchant didn't need to be told twice.

As Olan watched them disappear through the door, he felt the familiar weight settle in his chest. He was good at protecting others. Good at standing in the way of blades and fists meant for someone else. But once the danger passed, once the choices became less clear, he found himself adrift.

From the corner of his vision, he sensed Derick watching him, measuring, judging, already planning the next move. Olan did not look back. He rested his hand on the pommel of his sword and stared into the darkened streets beyond the square, wondering, quietly, uneasily, how long strength alone would be enough.

Chapter III

Derick had seen the ambush forming long before the stone hit the ground.

From his place beneath the broken archway, he watched the square as a pattern rather than a place. People moved in rhythms: entry, pause, exit. Tonight, two of those rhythms were wrong. A man who lingered too long near the south alley. Another person who crossed the square twice without buying anything or even looking at anything in the market. Small things. The kind Olan noticed only when they grew loud.

Derick noticed them while they were still quiet. He shifted his weight, the leather of his armor barely whispering beneath his cloak. One hand rested near the strap of his crossbow, not because he intended to use it, but because he liked knowing it was there. Weapons were tools, and so were people.

When Olan stepped in front of the cart, Derick allowed himself a faint, humorless smile. Predictable. Strong. Honest. Exactly what the city would try to exploit.

Derick moved. He slipped from the archway and into the narrow side street without drawing a glance. The city had learned not to look too closely at men like him. He moved quickly, silently, cutting around the square until he reached the mouth of the alley Olan had been watching.

The two men were still there. Derick approached them from behind, his steps measured, his presence unannounced. He stopped just close enough for them to sense him before they heard him.

"Wrong night," he said quietly.

Both men spun around. One reached for a knife, but Derick was faster. He didn't draw his sword. He didn't need to. A short, brutal motion, his elbow crashing into one man's throat, crushing his windpipe, and a twist of the man's wrist sent the knife skittering across stone. The second man froze, eyes wide, breath coming fast.

Derick quickly pulled a throwing knife from his belt and sent it soaring towards the man, finding a home deep in the man's neck. Blood sprayed from his neck, and the man fell to the ground.

Derick watched the life ebb from his body, both men dispatched quietly in just a few seconds. Unlike his brother, Derick never had any regrets about killing; it was a necessity, and he did it well. He adjusted his cloak and returned to the square as if nothing had happened.

Olan was still standing guard, unaware of how close the violence had come. Derick paused just long enough to study his brother, how he stood openly beneath the lantern light, how the weight of responsibility bent him slightly forward, as though he were carrying more than just his armor.

Derick felt the familiar tightening in his chest. Not guilt. Not regret. Resolve.

Someone had to see what Olan could not. Someone had to act without asking whether it felt right. The world did not reward hesitation, and Derick had learned long ago that mercy, when misplaced, only created more graves.

As Bellox ushered the merchant inside, Derick melted back into the shadows, scanning the rooftops, the windows, the distant movement at the far end of the street.

This city wasn't finished with them. Derick reached up and brushed his fingers briefly against the scar on the right side of his face, a habit he had never quite broken. The cut from that magical blade had left a tingling sensation along the scar that never seemed to fade or fully heal. Whatever was coming next, he would meet it the same way he always did. Quietly, efficiently, and without asking for permission or forgiveness.

Chapter IV

Bellox closed the tavern door himself. Slow and deliberate, the heavy wood settled into place with a final thud that seemed to quiet the entire room. There were only a few patrons left in the tavern, and the people who needed to be there. The patrons knew Bellox and knew if he was locking the place down, something was happening. They weren't concerned with Bellox and Olan both there. The patrons in the tavern knew them both well.

Bellox was not tall, but he was solid in a way that made the space around him feel smaller. His thick arms bore old scars, pale lines cutting through skin darkened by years of heat and labor. His beard hung heavy and well-kept, braided close with silver rings marking favors owed and debts paid. His clothes, layers of wool, leather, and an apron, were practical, stained, and honest. Nothing about him invited challenge.

Bellox was an old warrior who had retired to own a tavern, and his eyes did not miss much. Years of battles and adventures had raised his awareness, and that had never faded. He scanned the room, counted heads, noted hands, and measured the silence. When he was satisfied, he motioned the merchant and his guards toward the back without a word. Only then did he turn his attention to Olan.

"You're late," Bellox said.

Olan stiffened. "The road was..."

"I know," Bellox interrupted gently. "I heard." Bellox stepped closer, lowering his voice. "And you shouldn't have been followed."

Olan frowned. "We weren't."

Bellox's gaze flicked toward the ceiling, then toward the shuttered windows. "You were."

Bellox turned away before Olan could respond and reached behind the bar, lifting a trapdoor with one thick hand. The hinges barely creaked, oiled and maintained with care. Bellox gestured downward.

"Bring them," he said. "Quietly."

As Olan helped guide the shaken merchant below, Bellox moved through the tavern with practiced ease. He checked the door to the kitchen, tapped twice on a support beam near the back wall, and set a mug upside down on the bar, signals, all of them. Conversations resumed in low tones, the tension thinning but never fully fading.

Bellox leaned back against the counter and folded his arms. Only then did he address the empty space near the doorway. "You can come out now, Derick."

Derick emerged from the shadows without surprise. "You're sharper than you look, old timer," he said.

Bellox snorted. "I've buried men sharper than you."

They regarded each other for a moment, one built for endurance, the other for precision. Bellox's eyes lingered on Derick's cloak, his stance, the faint tension in his shoulders.

"You've been busy tonight," Bellox said.

Derick nodded, "Four on the road, two in the market."

"That kind of attention," Bellox continued, "comes from people who don't forget, and people who don't forget usually don't forgive."

Bellox glanced toward the stairs that led down into the cellar. "You brought trouble with you. Again."

Derick's jaw tightened, but his voice remained calm. "It would've come whether I was here or not, now there are just a half dozen less of them."

Bellox studied him for a long moment, then sighed. "That may be true," he said. "Which makes it worse." He reached up and took one of the silver rings from his beard, turning it thoughtfully between his fingers. "You boys are standing on old ground. Dangerous ground. The kind soaked so deep with blood it never really dries."

Olan returned from the cellar, wiping his hands on his cloak. "They're safe," he said. "For now."

Bellox nodded. "Good."

Bellox looked between the two brothers, his expression unreadable. "Finish your business quickly. The city's changing, and when it does, the ones who survive won't be the strongest or the fastest."

His eyes settled on Derick. "I fear there is something large brewing; I can feel it in the air. It's coming not now, but soon."

Olan approached Bellox, "What do you think it is, old friend?"

Bellox stroked his beard, "I am not sure yet, but it is an evil we haven't seen since before you both were born."

Chapter V

The knock came once. Soft. Measured. Bellox stiffened.

He did not move at first. Instead, his eyes went to the door, then to Derick, then briefly to Olan. The tavern had gone quiet again, the kind of calm that pressed against the ears.

Bellox crossed the room as the door began to open to greet her. She was the only one he had ever met who knocked on the door of an open tavern. A long-ago personal superstition she had never let go of.

"Evening, boys," the voice of a woman that was calm and unhurried. "It feels wrong not to knock."

Christiana stepped inside, bringing the night with her. She moved with quiet confidence, her long ash-colored cloak dusted with road grit and damp from the cold air. The hood fell back as she crossed the threshold, revealing dark hair pulled loosely at the nape of her neck and a face marked not by softness, but by endurance. It was a beauty, as few other women had. There was no fear in her expression, only resolve shaped by long experience.

Her eyes were steady, searching, and when they met Olan's, she paused. "You're the one holding the line," she said.

Olan blinked, unsure how to respond. "I, what?"

She gave him a faint, tired smile. "You don't know it yet. That's all right."

Christian's gaze then shifted to Derick, and the smile vanished. "You," she said quietly, "are the reason I'm here."

Derick did not flinch. "People say a lot of things when they're frightened."

Christiana removed her satchel and set it carefully on the table, as though its contents were fragile or dangerous. "People say less when they're dead," she replied. "And more of them are dying than you think, and you know me well enough to know I'm not frightened."

Bellox closed the door and returned to the bar, his usual confidence dimmed. "You shouldn't be walking the streets alone anymore," he said. "Not tonight."

"I wasn't alone," Christiana said. "I was watched."

Derick's eyes narrowed. "By whom?"

Christina shook her head. "By something patient."

Silence followed that. Even the tavern seemed to lean closer. Christiana turned back to Olan. "You protect people because you believe strength should be used that way," she said. "And you," she added, facing Derick again, "use it because you believe mercy is a luxury, and sinful."

She met Bellox's gaze last. "And you know better than to believe either of you is wrong."

Bellox exhaled slowly. "Then say it, girl," he said. "Whatever it is you came here to say."

Christiana opened her satchel and removed a small, weathered object wrapped in cloth. She did not unwrap it. She rested her hand on it. "The city is stirring," she said. "Old names are being spoken again. Old loyalties tested. Something wounded is waking, and it remembers all of you, all of us."

Olan felt a chill run through him that had nothing to do with the night air. "I don't know what you think we're part of," he said, "but we didn't choose it."

Christiana's voice softened. "No, Olan," she said. "You didn't." She looked at each of them in turn. "That's what concerns me."

Chapter VI

The tavern felt smaller now.

Bellox moved first, setting three mugs on the table and pouring without asking. The ale sloshed thick and dark, foam barely rising. No one reached for it.

Christiana remained standing, one hand resting lightly on the wrapped object in her satchel. Olan stood near the table, shoulders squared but uncertain. Derick leaned against the wall, arms crossed, eyes sharp and unreadable.

Bellox gave Christina a warm embrace. "I've missed you, and we will catch up later, but you came with warnings," Bellox let her go. "You came knowing who'd be here. That means you didn't come to ask."

Christiana nodded. "No."

Derick's mouth curved slightly. "Then say what you mean before someone mistakes this for a sermon."

Christina's eyes didn't leave Derick's. "You're already being hunted."

Olan turned sharply. "Who are you and who is hunting us?"

Christiana hesitated, not long, but long enough to matter. "Derick never told you about me. Why am I not surprised?" Christina shook her head as she turned to Olan, "Not guards, not thieves, at least not yet. That would be easier."

"That's not an answer," Derick said.

"It's the only honest one I have," she replied. "What's moving doesn't wear colors or banners. It uses people, animals, brutality, and fear."

Bellox swore softly and reached for his mug, draining it in one pull. "I told you," He muttered. "I told you the ground was wrong, that something was coming."

Olan shook his head. "This doesn't make sense. We escorted a merchant. That's all. No relics. No messages. No…" He stopped, looking at Christiana's satchel. "That thing isn't ours."

"No," she said gently. "But you're close enough to it that it noticed."

Derick straightened. "You're speaking in circles."

"I'm speaking carefully," Christiana said. "Because once I say it plainly, there's no stepping back."
The silence stretched.

"Say it already. I know you wouldn't be here if it weren't important," Bellox growled.

Christiana drew a slow breath. "Something old is trying to reclaim what it lost: power, influence, memory. It remembers the names of those who once stood in its way, and the name of their descendants."

Olan felt his stomach drop. "We didn't stand in anyone's way."

She looked at him with something like sorrow. "Your blood did."

Derick's eyes flicked to Olan, just once. "You should've led with that."

"Would it have changed anything?" she asked.

"No," Derick said. "But it would've been honest."

Christina's eyes shot daggers at Derick, "Really, Derick, you want to talk about honesty? You of all people? That seems just a bit hypocritical!"

Bellox slammed his mug down. "Enough. This isn't a debate. This is a crossroads." Bellox glanced between Derick and Christina, "You two need to bury it, and bury it now."

Bellox pointed at Olan. "You want to protect people. That makes you visible." Then he pointed at Derick. "You tend to control and change outcomes, and that makes you dangerous."

Finally, he looked at Christiana. "And you want to stop something you barely understand. That makes you desperate."

Christiana didn't argue. "Yes."

Olan ran a hand through his hair. "So what are you saying? That we run? Hide? Pretend none of this is happening?"

Derick answered before she could. "We don't run blind."

Christiana's eyes met his. "And we don't strike first without knowing what we're striking."

Bellox stepped between them, voice low but absolute. "Then here's the truth none of you want."
They all looked at him.

"The city already chose," Bellox said. "Word's moving. Eyes are watching. Whether you stay or flee, something's coming. The only choice left is how you meet it. This is only the beginning, a prelude to something much bigger that is coming."

Olan swallowed. "We can't let innocent people get caught in this."

Derick pushed off the wall. "We also can't risk our lives because we hesitated."

Christiana closed her eyes briefly, then opened them. "We can't act out of fear or ignorance."

For a moment, the four of them stood locked in opposition, strength, shadow, knowledge, faith, each pulling toward a different future.

Then Bellox nodded once. "Good," he said. "That means none of you is lying."

Outside, a distant horn sounded, faint, but unmistakable. No one moved.

Lines had been drawn.

Chapter VII

Dawn came slowly to Galadine, as if the city itself were reluctant to see what daylight might reveal.

A pale gray light crept over the rooftops, washing the streets clean of shadow without truly warming them. The fog that clung to the lower roads thinned, unraveling into the morning air, and with it went the illusion that the night's tension had passed.

Bellox stood at the tavern door, watching the city wake. He had removed his apron and donned a heavier coat, leather layered over wool, the familiar weight of his battle axe secured across his back. He locked the door from outside, sliding the bar into place with a finality that made the decision real.

Inside, the tavern would wait until one day he returned.

Olan adjusted the straps of his armor in the open street, the metal catching the early light. He looked tired, more tired than a single night should allow, but there was something steadier in his posture now. His sword rested at his side, not as a symbol of violence, but of responsibility. He glanced toward the market square, imagining the people who would pass through it in a few hours, unaware of how close the city was to breaking.

"I don't like leaving," Olan said quietly.

"It won't be forever," Bellox replied. "You'll come back. Cities always need men like you."

Derick stood a short distance away, checking the tension on his crossbow string. His cloak hung loose around his shoulders, its dark fabric already blending with the thinning shadows. His eyes never stopped moving, windows, rooftops, alleys, mapping escape routes and threats alike.

"This is only a beginning," Derick said. "Whatever's stirring won't move openly yet."

Christiana knelt near the edge of the street; her cloak pooled around her as she pressed her palm briefly to the stone beneath her. She whispered something too soft to hear, words shaped by faith, but sharpened by realism. When she rose, her expression was calm, though the weight behind her eyes had not lessened.

"It's listening now," Christina said. "Not to us, but to what we do next."

Bellox looked between them, then nodded toward the northern road, where the city walls thinned and the land beyond opened into uncertain country. "Then we don't give it silence," he said. "We give it movement."

They gathered without ceremony and headed to the stable to retrieve their horses. Olan walking in front, broad and visible, a shield without needing to say so. Derick drifted to the rear, already fading into the margins, watching the city recede behind them. Bellox walked at the center, steady and unhurried, every step measured by experience. Christiana followed closely, her satchel secured at her side, her gaze fixed ahead rather than behind.

As they rode past beyond the last stone marker of Galadine, Olan paused and looked back once more. The city stood quiet under the morning light, unchanged to anyone who didn't know where to look.

"Whatever's coming," Olan said, "it won't find us standing still."

Christiana inclined her head. "No, it won't."

They turned north together, four paths drawn into one, carrying questions they could no longer set down, and a future that had already begun to move toward them.

Behind them, Galadine exhaled.

Ahead, the world waited.

Between the Knock and the Silence

I open the door and see the police standing on my porch.

There are two of them. They are close enough that I can smell the outside on their clothes. One is older, with lines in his face. The other looks younger, like he hasn't been doing this job very long.

They are both wearing dark uniforms.

For a second, I think they might be here for someone else. A neighbor. A mistake. I looked past them, down the street, half expecting them to turn and say sorry and walk away.

They don't.

The older one looks at me and says my name.

He doesn't ask. He already knows.

"Yes," I say, even though my voice sounds strange to my ears.

The younger one shifts his weight. I noticed his hands. They are empty, but they are tight, like he is holding something invisible. The older one keeps his hands still.

"We need to speak with you," the older officer says.

Right away, my mind starts filling in gaps. It runs ahead of him, trying to finish the story before he does. My heart begins to beat faster. I feel it in my throat.

I think of my wife.

Then I think of my daughter.

I don't know why my brain goes there so fast. I tell myself to stop. This could be about anything. A traffic question. A noise complaint. Something small that I'm turning into something big.

"Can we come inside?" he asks.

I hesitate. I don't mean to. My body doesn't move right away. I stand there, holding the door, feeling the weight of the moment pressing against me.

If they stay outside, maybe this stays outside too.

I step back and let them in.

They walk past me, careful not to brush against anything. I watch them cross the doorway, and something inside me tightens. The house feels different with them in it. Smaller. Less safe.

I close the door behind them.

The lock's click sounds too loud.

I know then that whatever they came to say is already here.

We stand in the living room. No one sits. Sitting feels wrong now, like it would mean staying too long.

The older officer takes a breath. I see his chest rise and fall. It feels like he is bracing himself, not me. That makes my hands go cold.

"I'm very sorry," he says.

Those words come first.

They always do.

I stopped hearing clearly after that. My mind locks onto them like they are a warning sign. People only say they're sorry when something is already broken.

"There was an accident," he says next.

The word accident hit me harder than I expected. It sounds small. Clean. It is trying to soften something sharp. I wait for the rest of the sentence to fix it.

He says my wife's name.

I don't remember telling him her name, but he knows it anyway.

He says my daughter's name after that.

That's when my ears start ringing.

The room tilts slightly, as the floor has shifted. I focus on a picture on the wall to keep myself upright. It's one my daughter drew with crayons, the lines uneven, the colors too bright. I think about how proud she was when she gave it to me.

The officer keeps talking.

I hear words, but they don't line up right. Fatal. Scene. Immediate. I recognize them, but they don't belong to my life. They feel like words meant for someone else.

"They didn't suffer," he says.

I don't know why he thinks that helps.

My mouth opens, but nothing comes out. My tongue feels thick. Heavy. I swallow and taste metal.

I want to ask him to repeat himself. I want to tell him he's wrong. I want to point out that my wife hates driving in the rain, that my daughter always falls asleep in the car, and that they were probably talking about something small and normal.

This can't be how it ends.

But the officer's face doesn't change. He doesn't look confused. He looks sure. Sad, but sure.

That certainty is what breaks through me.

My knees feel weak. I sit down without deciding to. The soft couch catches me, but I don't feel it. My hands are shaking now. I stop trying to hide it.

"They're gone," the officer says.

Gone.

Not dead, not killed.

Gone.

The word floats in the air between us.

I think of the empty chairs at the table.

I think of the lights they forgot to turn off.

I think of the sound of my daughter's feet running down the hallway.

All of it is gone.

The officer says something else, but it doesn't matter. The words have already landed. They are inside me now, heavy and sharp, and there is no place to put them down.

Once the words are said, everything else rushes in.

My brain doesn't move in a straight line anymore. It jumps. It stumbles. One thought crashes into the next before I can stop it.

I see my wife standing in the kitchen, one hand on her hip, reading a recipe on her phone. She always double-checks things, even meals she's cooked a hundred times. She used to say she liked knowing she hadn't missed anything.

I see my daughter at the table, swinging her legs because they haven't reached the floor yet. She hums when she's happy. Not a song. Just a sound, like she's filling the space around her.

I smell coffee.

I hear the sink running.

I hear laughter.

It all feels too real, like it's happening now. My chest tightens because for a moment, I almost believe it is.

I remember the last time they left the house together. My wife was looking for her keys. My daughter was already wearing her shoes, tapping her foot as if she were in a hurry to grow up. I told them to be careful. I always say that. The words feel useless now.

Did I say I love you?

I think I did. I would remember if I hadn't. But doubt creeps in anyway. It always does.

My mind goes looking for a last moment. A last text. A last smile. Something I can hold onto and prove they were real, that this life wasn't just taken out from under me.

I remember my daughter waving from the car window once, her face pressed against the glass, leaving a smudge I never cleaned. I remember my wife rolling her eyes at that and smiling at me over the car roof.

Small things.

Stupid things.

Everything now.

The memories don't ask permission. They come fast and hard, filling every space. I feel them in my throat, in my hands, behind my eyes. I don't cry. Not yet. My body hasn't caught up to my mind.

I wonder if they were scared.

That thought hits like a punch.

I try to push it away, but it stays. I picture my wife gripping the wheel. I picture my daughter reaching for her. I hate myself for thinking about it. I hate that I can't stop.

"They didn't suffer," the officer said.

I cling to those words even though I don't trust them. I repeat them in my head, hoping they will settle something inside me. They don't.

I think of all the days ahead that now look different. School mornings. Birthdays. Holidays. I see empty spaces where people should be.

The future I was sure of only hours ago is gone, replaced by a blank I don't know how to step into.

The memories keep coming.

And I don't know how to make them stop.

After the memories come the questions.

They don't ask politely. They push and claw and refuse to leave me alone.

What if I had driven them myself?

I had the time. I could have gone with them. I think about how I stayed home instead, how I chose the quiet of the house over the noise of the road. That choice feels heavy now, like it mattered more than it should have.

What if they had left five minutes later?

What if I had asked them to stop somewhere first? What if I had called right before they left and distracted them just enough to change something?

I know none of this makes sense. I know accidents don't work that way. But my mind doesn't care about logic right now. It just wants someone to blame.

And it chooses me.

I think about every small moment I didn't give enough attention to. Every time I was tired. Every time I was short with them for no good reason. Those moments line up in my head like evidence.

I should have been better.

I should have been there more.

I should have protected them.

A husband is supposed to keep his family safe. A father is supposed to be stronger than this. I don't know where I was when it mattered most.

I'm still standing here; they are not.

That feels wrong in a way I can't explain.

I imagine the world continuing without them. Cars passing. People laughing. Dinner is being cooked in other houses. It makes me angry. The world should have stopped. It should have noticed.

I wonder if loving them should have been enough. I wonder if I missed some sign, some warning that today was dangerous. I replay the morning again, searching for clues that were never there.

I hate myself for every normal thought I had before the knock at the door.

I think about the future and feel sick. How am I supposed to carry this? How am I supposed to live a life they don't get to have?

The guilt settles in my chest, heavy and tight.

And no matter how hard I try, I can't find a place to put it down.

The officer starts asking questions.

His voice sounds calm, like he is trying not to scare me. He asks if there is anyone he can call for me. Family. A friend. Someone who can come over.

I don't know how to answer. I can think of names, but none of them feel real enough to say out loud. Saying a name would mean explaining what happened, and I don't think I can do that yet.

I shake my head.

He asks if I understand what he's told me.

I want to say no. I want to tell him this doesn't make sense, that he must be wrong. But my head nods again, the same way it has all afternoon. My body keeps agreeing to things my mind hasn't caught up to.

He hands me a card with his name on it. The letters blur together. I hold it anyway, like it's something solid I can hang onto.

The younger officer looks around the room. His eyes stop on the drawing on the wall. He looks away quickly. I wonder how many houses like mine he's been in. I wonder if he will go home at night and hold his own family tighter.

They tell me what will happen next. About paperwork. About arrangements. About things that sound far away and unreal. I don't remember most of it.

When they finally leave, the house feels too quiet.

The door closes behind them, and the sound echoes longer than it should. I stand there for a moment, staring at the empty space where they were.

Nothing else happens.

No loud noise.

No collapse.

No release.

Just silence.

I walk through the house slowly. I touch the back of the chair. I run my hand along the counter.

I stop outside my daughter's room but don't go in.

The life I had this morning is gone.

The one I have now hasn't started yet.

I stand there, caught between the two, and take a breath that feels too big for my chest.

This is what remains.

And I don't know how to live with it yet.

I stand in the middle of the house and listen.

There is no sound of a car in the driveway.

No footsteps in the hallway.

No voices calling my name.

I tell myself to move. To do something useful. To call someone. To sit down. To cry. None of those things happen. My body feels locked in place, like it doesn't know which version of me it belongs to anymore.

This house still looks the same. The walls didn't shift. The pictures didn't fall. Everything is where it was this morning.

I am the only thing that has changed.

I think about how people say life goes on. That time keeps moving. I believe them, because I have no choice. But right now, time feels like something I am being pushed into, whether I'm ready or not.

I don't know what tomorrow looks like. I don't know how to wake up in a world where my wife and daughter don't.

All I know is that I am still here.

Breathing.

Standing.

Carrying the weight of what has been taken.

This is not strength.

This is not hope.

This is just the beginning of learning how to survive what I never wanted to lose.

This is my Hell.

11/14/2011

God grant me the
serenity to accept the
things I cannot change;
Courage to change the
things I can;
And wisdom to know the difference.